# UNFORGIVABLE

# LIES

# D. Harvey Rawlings

Book Design by D. Harvey Rawlings

Contact the Author
Like Me on Facebook
D. Harvey Rawlings Page
www.dharveyrawlings.com

Thanks:

To my son…you are a great guy…

Thanks to all the readers that have supported me throughout the years with your reviews, time and presence…

Hope you will enjoy this sequel. I didn't think that I had another story to tell with these characters; but your feedback inspired me.


To my loving grandmother,
                    Elizabeth…I hope I make you proud.


              D.

# CHAPTER ONE

In the late hours of the night, Dr. Paul Monarch sat at his desk. He sat, happily reviewing the latest feedback from his team's discovery. They are about to make the company he works for; Cultrax Pharmaceutical Laboratories a lot of money. Plus elevate their names above the food chain in the medical community. He is elated. The team has worked hard. They have created two new diabetes drugs that will revolutionize a new approach to the chronic illness. It's now in its final stages of solidified tests and ready for trails. He ran the prosperous department and a team of experts. Only, poor Craig McNair should be here to enjoy the spoils as well. He was as much a part of this as any of them. He shouldn't have been, caught in this nasty business of someone attempting to steal their work. He didn't deserve to lose his life.

The police changed their minds about his death. It was determined that it was murder not due to Craig just dying of a random heart attack. It made sense because Craig McNair was only thirty-five years old. He was an avid swimmer and he ran in the Chicago Marathon the last seven years. Even though it's possible it was highly unlikely with his health that he would have a heart attack.

His murder was part of a killing spree that involved Mona. It's a dirty shame.

Speaking of Mona, she should be at work for this to help him march in this new drug. After all, it has been almost three months and Cultrax has been honoring their agreement; about clearing her name. It's true that she has gone through some ordeal and that the accusations just made a bad situation even worst.

Overall, he knows that she is just punishing Cultrax for their rush to judge her. She definitely knows how to bleed a situation.

He has worked with her for several years now on their team at Cultrax and knew her even before that. He knew her when she was a raw, bull-headed, brash, enterprising person, fresh out of college. Before, she was up to doing anything that would advance her career.

That is why he didn't step up to help her during the inquiry. He wanted to protect his own future even if she didn't care anything about hers. He felt that if she took a chance on doing something criminal he couldn't support that.

He isn't obligated to her anymore in that regard. What they did together in the past was permanently, severed then. They *all* had agreed to that.

It was a new day. There was no agreement to, ever encounter each other again. However, somehow he ended up working with Mona once more, at this prestigious company. It is too good of an opportunity to pass up so he stayed on. He just simply remained cautious of her; watching her closely.

However, he has come to trust her; but he didn't at first. She had to prove herself to him and she did. Therefore, when this arrest thing happened, he couldn't let her careless behavior; which he thought was happening all over again at the time; destroy his future with this company.

He is a middle-aged, forty-five year old man. He wanted to make sure that he has a safe, honest, financial cushion for the long life ahead.

Overall, it turned out that she was perfectly innocent.

Mona Daniels, I am so proud of you, he thought. Now he gladly works alongside of her, without the fear of the past ever coming up, again. She is his valued friend. She is perfectly, legal and so is he.

However, there is always the possibility of the opposite, isn't there? The threat of the desire to return to the safe familiar path of the past even those that would do you harm. No one should be hunted and haunted by their past. However, time is a constant memory of how flawed humans really are.

The door to his office opened and a man entered. The doctor looked up to see who came in. He surprised the doctor only because it's late. All of the staff except a few has since gone home; for the three-day weekend, Cultrax has promised all the workers. It's an evening custodian worker. He forgot that they were, spread out all over the office areas doing their usual nightly cleaning. He resumed looking down on his work not acknowledging the worker.

"Sorry to bother you doctor. I didn't see the lights on." The man said as he walked into the office, boldly.

"That's alright, you can empty the trash, but I don't need any other cleaning done tonight. I'll be working late into the morning. Please hurry up." The doctor said never looking up from his papers.

"Well, I see that you have been raise correctly to at least say please."

"What did you say?" the doctor said looking up from his desk to address the stranger.

"I said that you have good manners. It's good to see that in someone as high up in the corporate world as you."

"Humph." The doctor retorted.

"Well I know you haven't always been this pristine. The blood on your hands is thick."

"I beg your pardon."

"You know those forgotten times."

"Can you just do your work, I'm busy?"

"I know Paul, no one has talked like this to you in a long time and I clearly see that you are upset about my intrusion."

"Mr. Ah....?"

"Final."

"Mr. Final kindly do not be so causal with me. Gather this trash and get the hell out of my office, before I get you thrown out and fired." He said angrily.

"I knew I would get to hear that side of you again, before it was all over. I remember it very well; those sorts of words very well, that arrogant tone. All the big medical, boisterous words, I would hear you say over the phone. All of the threats."

"I don't know what you are talking about, I don't know you."

"I know. I don't think that I rate high enough on your food chain to be, remembered offhand. I'm just someone from your past."

"Who are you?"

"Just someone who knows who you really are and what you've done."

"What do you think you know? I haven't done anything. Are you some kind of nut?"

"Wow, you surely have a guilty conscience, doctor. No I'm just like you pretend to be now; a concern citizen that needs to, deal with scum like you and your group."

"I don't have the slightest idea what this is all about. If this is some sort of way you think you can extort monies from me; let me assure you that I will not be blackmailed."

"Who said anything about blackmail?"

"Obviously I'm on the right track. What do you want?"

"My life back, the life that, you and those others took from me, with your schemes."

"What others? Who are you?"

"I'm sorry, I haven't been around much lately, but I have been close. Do you remember Lennox Laboratories in Detroit, Dr. Monarch?"

The doctor looked at him closely. Once his mind registered the memory he responded as if he seen a ghost. It's the last one. The one who determined it was time to stop or else they all would suffer. What did he want, money? The doctor knew that he would pay anything to keep the past a secret, but how much does he want?

"Look, I really didn't have anything to do with what happened to you. I was not involved up to that time. You can ask any of them."

"You knew. You were the one who cleared the way. You assured me that it would work; that you knew your business very well."

The doctor decided it would do him no good to argue with this man, because he did play a part. He was as deeply involved as the other. He participated enough and now he has to pay the money.

"So how much money do you want? I know it's about money. It's always about the money. I don't have much but it can give you a brand new start in another city, say Washington D.C."

"That would make you happy wouldn't it; for me to just disappear? Now you have the money and prestige to make my dreams come true don't you. Funny, how life changes and the dirty deeds that we do goes unpunished. Well, that is God's will isn't it to forgive and forget. In most cases that would be the best thing to do; but I don't live by that rule not anymore. I serve another god."

"It'll take me a few days but I'm sure that I can get the money to you. How much do you want?" Dr. Monarch asked him almost begging him for an answer.

His fear very obvious to Mr. Final.

"I don't want your blood money."

"Why, then what is this all about?" Dr. Monarch demanded, hearing the nervousness in his own voice.

"Well, the prize always goes to the first. Well you're not technically the first." The man said retrieving latex gloves from his chest pocket then putting them on.

"You need to leave now sir. This is ridiculous."

The doctor picked up the phone determined to call security.

"Since you insist on being rude...I wanted to talk more."

The man moved toward Dr. Monarch, behind his desk, swiftly. The doctor just had enough time to stand up as the man drove into him. His body smashing hard into the doctor and the doctor fell back into the credenza behind him. He tried to stand upright but Mr. Final did some quick moves. It wasn't until the knife went in a third time that the doctor even realized that he's been, stabbed and bleeding profusely.

"No prize for you..."

The doctor started to collapse to the floor grabbing his stomach and staring helplessly into the face of Mr. Final. He hit the floor with a thump onto his stomach. Mr. Final wiped the blood off his knife on the white sleeve of the doctor's lab coat. He walked around to the front of the desk and took a black marker that sat on it into his hand. He walked back around the desk and turned Dr. Monarch over onto his back. The blood poured steadily from the specific way that the wound was, opened from the knife. It saturated the white shirt and lab coat that the doctor wore. He knew exactly where to stab him and he congratulated himself because the doctor was dead for sure. With the marker Mr. Final, wrote one word on the forehead of the dead man.

He grabbed a note pad and began to scribble words on the paper. When he finished, he tossed the note pad back on the desk.

Pulling the latex gloves off, he wrung his hands as if they were being washed in a sink.

He grinned to himself as he walked out of the office door.

He spoke in a low whisper to the doctor.

"I guess you really did get the big prize after all. Don't worry Doc you won't be alone. You'll have plenty of company real soon." He said with a laugh.

He began to walk out of Dr. Monarch's office. He stopped at the trashcan and tossed the latex gloves into it.

****

Later he sat at the desk where he lived, holding the picture of his daughter, in her usual pose and her happy face. It has been a long time since he last heard the laughter that followed from that smile. His world was everything that it should have been when he was with her mother and her. He deserved it. He was very happy and they were happy with him. Now, however they were all apart, everything is gone.

It's late and he just, got home an half of hour ago. He was drunk already from celebrating. He got up and stumbled around his apartment. He's alone now and drinking is his only release, the only release from the pain. It all happened as if it occurred in quick stages. First, they were happy and then they came, then the sadness, then the end. However, not quite the end, he will make sure of that. Not the end until he's finished.

On the desk where he kept all of anything he has to remind him of his research, he slowly scanned everything. He liked to keep these things now because this is how he dealt with his pain and especially how he now planned his days.

As he sat down at the desk again, he picked up the latest evening edition of the newspaper and started to flip through it. The room barely illuminated with light. He liked it dark. This is how he kept the darkness in his heart. He would just be in the dark, waiting; waiting for the day he could unleash what he is building up.

With tears in his eyes, he felt the sting of it all as he read the latest headlines.

The police decided to reopen a string of strange, unusual heart attack deaths in Chicago. They are allegedly, related to the attempted murders at a local cable station a few months ago by attempted murderer, Kimberly Stanford.

It seems that there is extenuating evidence. It caused the coroner to decide that the deaths weren't natural or in one case drug related. This came about from a tip from someone very close to the case. The informant told the police of his theory and the inquiry expanded from there.

That's exactly what he wanted to do. Why couldn't he have this same attention? He thought about how it would be poetic justice if he could get the police to have a looked into his, theories. He is after all a victim of unnatural circumstances as well. What, did he have to be some radio personality?

He told a few of his peers of the situation and carefully did not disclose any incriminating information. They told him that he didn't have enough evidence; but he was sure he did. He had the cause, the effect and the guilty parties. Sure, the evidence was concrete but because it was complicated; he couldn't use the direct information he had. They even tried to blame him because of his background. They felt that he should have known better and that it could cost him his career. He couldn't risk the exposure because he needed to make money and his freedom to continue what he set out to do. Too much will be lost if he's connected in all of this. She would be lost. Still the evidence is there. It's there for someone to focus on and to retrieve it. He's even willing to submit a body for autopsy.

He has to stop them. He will stop them.

The doctors at Lennox Laboratories were all in it together. It's simple of course. The sicker patients are, the more they could pump their drugs in them; the more money is, made. It's all about money. It all made sense. It is a source of income with all the trimmings.

First, they make them sick with their untested miracle medicines or new and different, evasive treatments. Then the doctors come with their diagnosis months later about the new drugs, which eventually cause something terminal. He paid the price for their greed.

He has to stop them, true, but first he has an old score to settle with the woman who took his daughter away from him. She was a swindler then and she's still a fraud. She is an insult to the medical community.

There's no reason for her to have done his family the injustice that she did. He believed in her and believed that she could set his family back on track. Not only did she do their dirty work but also it all interfered in his marriage.

Now all of it is gone, he thought as he poured another drink from the glass that sat empty on his desk. He never even bothers to wash out the glass because he knew he would be using it repeatedly. He isn't drinking to get up the nerve to do what he is going to do; it is to ease the pain of not having his beautiful daughter around.

He continued to skim through the Chicago Post, newspaper and he saw the other article. A well-known VPO, Mona Daniels, of Cultrax Pharmaceutical Laboratories has been, vindicated. She was, accused of selling trade secrets.

He slammed his fist on the desk. How could everyone else get all of this assistance, this vindication, even those who don't deserve it? Why wasn't he important? He is innocent. He had been important before; he had the life that he's been reading about lately. Now all he has is despair and all his plans are out the window. This is his last chance to be relevant in his life. He is going to live again.

He got up from the desk, staggering; he almost fell to the floor. His head barely missed the end of the desk. How quick it would've been over and he would be relieved of this burden. Maybe the fortunes were trying to prove a point to him. That he should keep his mind clear if he wanted to accomplish anything that he is setting out to do. He'll have to keep his mind straight.

So tomorrow, because he needed that drink tonight he will start his first day of sobriety. He has to clean himself up for what he has planned because he has convinced many people, of many things.

First off, he will resume what he had with her. They were something together, then, well what little time they were together. She left him alone without taking responsibility for what happened between them; just blaming him. It's her fault as well as his but he needed to hear that she is sorry that their plans went astray.

No one should have to pay for his mistaken choices. He made that one mistake and he lost her. She left him and reverted into her own world. He was the one that couldn't stop. He needed something from that time to be whole again.

To imagine what it did to her; he couldn't. He has to make amends. She's in the place that she's in because of him. He is so, wrapped in guilt it's almost breath stifling he never did anything to help her.

He went to the other room next to his bedroom. This is his room of darkness; he calls it this in his mind. This is where he sits and thinks of the many ways he is going to enact his vengeance; like tonight.

He pondered long and hard almost causing his head to ache in the thought process of it all. For sure, he knew when he does get the opportunity to implement the act; he would savor it like a thirsting man walking through the hot dessert. It will be painfully, nice and slow.

****

He couldn't believe his luck as he heavily browse through the Chicago newspaper. One of many newspapers cluttering the coffee table that stood in front of him. The newspapers are from the different cities and counties that surrounded the Great Lakes. During his downtime, this is what he does; peruse the newspaper for targets.

He laid back on the couch feeling like this is the end, only because he has no more options. He would have to give up his mildly better comforts to return to the gridlock of the rat race. He couldn't do it, he wouldn't do it and now he won't have to do it. Now in the twenty-fifth hour he has been, redeemed.

The place he is staying at is a step down from the highly rated places he has stayed at before; but he couldn't help that. It's been more than a year since his woman friend and he has scored something that even paid out as much as their works; did in the past years. He is excited because he found her. He simply picked up the section of the paper called Recap and Resolve and there she was.

This section highlighted the conclusion to some high profile cases adjacent to the Great Lakes. How fortunate it is to have stumbled on this story. Routinely, he would essentially recover papers from different cities; within and surrounding the Great Lakes. This is to ensure that he is well verse on all his prospects.

Today low and behold there she is, bright and shining, almost screaming to be, seen.

She was their greatest achievement and she made them a lot of money. She was their perfect addition to their group, with savvy and smarts. Then when things got too heavy, they all quit and she disappeared. Just fell off the map.

They weren't looking for her anymore, anyway, because she didn't want to be, found. There were too many side projects for them to do after Lennox and she wasn't, needed. Besides, there's a lot of miles between Chicago and Detroit. Enough distance between the old partners to keep them out of each other's way. They did worked well together though, he must admit and the money was exquisite.

She was always the determined one, the one to get it done. A spitfire she was. There's no denying that and it paid off. However, she broke the pact. She became too personal. They could no longer control her and that's why it ended. However, they never really had control of her. She was always willing to get what she wanted no matter what the cost. She would sell her soul if she had to. A very ruthless woman.

They all agreed then that they would keep, each other's dirty deeds a secret. They also, decided that once any of them would be successful the others would be, contacted to share the wealth.

She's on top of the world now and she isn't sharing. Now that isn't nice. He got up from the couch he was sitting on. He walked over to the phone by the window and picked it up.

He dialed a number and waited for a response.

"Hello?" the female voice asked.

"Have you seen the paper lately?"

"Yes the business section; the only thing I'm interested in." She joked. "There's nothing for us."

"Our girl made the Chicago paper."

"Really, Mona, what did she do, die?"

"No of course not, that would be good news but I think you'll like the alternative better."

"Well, did she murder somebody or what? What's going on?"

"It seems as though she's hit the big time and forgot to call us in on it."

"Well that's not fair. She knows the rules. I take it we will be leaving to visit Chicago in the next twenty-four hours?"

"Just as soon as I can get us some train tickets; and find out where our partner is. She is supposed to be working at this pharmaceutical company called Cultrax. Should be easy to find out more from there; don't forget to pack light."

"Mona Daniels, we're coming for you." She laughed as she hung up the phone.

# CHAPTER
## TWO

In the late, midnight hour Kimberly Stanford pleased with herself continued to; exit Chicago Mental Hospital. She made her way to the parking lot, to her car. She parked far away from the hospital, instead of in the garage. She didn't want many of the staff to notice that she was actually there. She is being overly cautious she reasoned. She has a reason to be there. They thought she was there to care for her pathetic patient; but she was there to silence her. She could not allow her cousin to regain her senses. If she did, it would be all over. All her hard work to start anew ended.

All her hard work up in smoke.

Immediately, like switching on a light switch, she became enraged. Her mind began to flood with the thoughts of what her cousin told her. It was something that meant that she outwitted her. All these years of planning slowly; stealing her identity to be her and now this. A simple note may stop her from achieving and continuing her ultimate goals.

What did she give to Michael Montgomery that will expose her to him? She told her that she gave him something that he would be opening soon. She walked hastily to her car, faster and faster. The success of all her other accomplishments could not cool her; building enragement over the betrayal of that stupid bitch.

"Dr. Edwards?" A man called out to her.

She didn't respond. He called to her again. When she did not answer, he ran up on her and then he grabbed her shoulder. He startled Kimberly until she realized who grabbed her. It's one of the Mental Hospital's doctors, Dr. Morris Murphy. He caught her off guard.

Is he stopping her because he knows that she has left her cousin, the real Dr. Edward to die inside the mental hospital? It will only turn out to be very bad for him if he is because she will not hesitate to kill him to protect her secrets. Besides, the traitorous bitch had it coming to her anyway. It's all for her good, she is no use to Kimberly anymore. She would have just been in the way. She was so weak.

Now is the time to recover from these mistakes and continue in her guise as Janice Edwards, Doctor of Psychiatry. Those who have hurt her will still have to pay and anyone else that stands in her way. She isn't going to stop and she isn't going to be, stopped.

"Yes." She said evenly as she turned to face him, trying not to seem distracted.

Dr. Murphy is much like those men that she despised, the lecherous ones. She wanted to stab him in his neck with a needle like the one she just recently, violently used on Janice over a half hour ago.

What did he want? They were just talking earlier before she left out. There's nothing else to say. She is not going to date him, as he once suggested. He would be best to stay clear from her.

"Just a few minutes after you left, the nurse found Kimberly unconscious and not breathing, but…" He said in a panic pausing.

The doctor was out of breath. It's clear that he has been running after her for some time.

"What!? Oh my God, she's dead?" Kimberly tried to sound horrified and not amused. "I tried to help her. The poor woman didn't have a chance at all. She…."

"No, no that's not it at all. I mean, she's not dead. The nurse was able to revive her and she's on life support. They're about to run test to find out what actually happened. I just thought you might want to know what happened. Are you alright?"

Kimberly looked at Dr. Murphy in bewilderment. She's sure he wouldn't be able to read her expressions and felt that it was safe to be enraged in her mind.

She wanted to scream.

How could this be, it was the right dosage? She's been careful to give her just the right amounts over the last few months. This ensured when the day came to give her the big dosage it would be over quick. What went wrong, it was foolproof?

"Did you notice anything?"

"No I didn't."

"Did she seem ill I mean?"

"No, she didn't," Kimberly responded frustrated.

"You were monitoring her carefully, right?"

"Excuse me?"

"Janice you know what I mean. I know it has to be, kept between you two. However, you were never, really known lately for your anonymity regarding your patients. Did you see or hear anything that may shed some light on this?"

She couldn't hold back any longer. He is after all insulting her competency as a psychiatrist and that cannot happen. She will never let anyone disrespect her or her position as a psychiatrist. She's every right to be a psychiatrist just like Janice. It wasn't her fault that she had to leave school because of what Sebastian Black, had done to her. He ruined her life and insured that she would never be able to return to Michael.

"How dare you, question me like I'm some two-bit, charlatan." Her voice sounded icy. "I think that I am competent enough to do something, had I seen something."

She began breathing deeply, her breast heaving noticeably, to Dr. Murphy. She seemed upset to him, very much so. She shocked him but he also became intrigued and aroused. Could she be that sensitive? Things like this happened to these types of patients all the time; no one's blaming her.

This is a side of Janice Edwards that, he has never seen. She seemed sinister and confrontational. She seemed as if she should be a patient inside the mental hospital herself or else she is a real cold-bitch like they say. However, she is sexy he thought as he couldn't keep from staring at her breast.

"Janice I'm sorry." He said to her gently trying to salvage his chances to be with her. "I'm not questioning you. I guess I'm just baffled. This is the most action this quiet old place has gotten in a long time. It's all a buzz inside and you're about to be right there in the middle of it. There will be a lot of inquiry and well I want to help. Know that I will be there for you if you want."

He's so a-typical of a disgusting, perverted, man, she thought. She knew what he was alluding to and she didn't like it. These are the types of men who; have caused all this pain within her. The ones that like to use her and discard her like trash. She will play his game, however. Play it well, then one day she and one of the other doctors will be discussing his death.

"I know I'm going to need it." She said faintly. "This woman has caused me so many problems. I should have never took her on as a patient when she came begging me for help. Walk with me please, back to the emergency room."

"Okay and maybe later we can have an early morning meal once this business is settled."

She nodded.

She will have to go along with him because it's good for her to have an ally at this hospital. However, when he outlives his usefulness, outlive being the operative word that will be the good part.

****

Early in the morning, Kimberly stood over Janice. She laid in the private room the hospital staff put her in after their successful attempt to keep her alive. The barrage of questions seemed non-stop as she fielded answers for the many inquiries. She was finally able to rid herself of them when dawn broke.

Kimberly watched Janice angrily. She lay motionless; deep in the coma that, Janice unintentionally induced her in; instead of killing her.

She was supposed to die.

What could have gone wrong?

There were enough drugs in her system to choke a horse and remain undetected. She was careful to make sure that the hospital staff gave her medications that she wanted her to have. Somebody is going to be, fired for this accident. After the blame is pointed in another direction once again, Kimberly will be free to do what she plans to do. However, she will have to be patient and wait.

If anything, she admires Janice's resilience. She's incredibly strong. She's always been like that even when they were kids. She's the strong one because she didn't live the life that Kimberly lived. She lived the happy life that Kimberly was never, allowed to live. It's because her bitch of a mother allowed her lascivious father to wreak havoc over her life. Her mother only thought about herself and her status in life. As long as her father provided the luxuries of riches for her, it seemed as if her mother gave him free rein to do whatever he wanted to Kimberly.

She will have to give the old girl a visit soon; the last visit. Kimberly's new timetable is going as planned. She isn't going let Janice's stubbornness to die interfere and interrupt her schedule.

Speaking of schedules, she has to get to her parents to put an end to this. They are the last on the list. The last two to finally relieve her of the pain that all started with them. Their deaths will bring her so much pleasure. Now that her father is out of jail, serving what they found out was multiple counts of assaults on minors; she can really move on the two of them.

Her mother is still living a lavish lifestyle with her stepfather. He doesn't know of her evil deeds.

Her stepfather will at least live. He is one of a few people who tried to make her miserable life worth living. He is the only good that came out of all this. She is sorry that he will have to mourn for his bitch of a wife.

Her mother and father will indeed pay. They will have to wait their turns however, at least until she's dealt with Janice, Sebastian and the rest.

What could have gone wrong, she thought returning to the conundrum? She was careful to iron out the details as she has always done. When she entered the hospital a few days ago after being away for a while, she resumed her plans.

She always insured that she was present before the medicine was, dispensed. She would replace one of the vials with one that contained her special blend. She made sure all along, since Janice was brought to Chicago Mental; that she would be kept heavily sedated. She wanted her that way so she could continue to operate unhampered with the threat of exposure. It allowed her time to take care of all the other goals that she needed to take care of; like come up with another foolproof plan. Janice botched the original one. She didn't want her coming out of her drugged-induced delirium.

For the last few days, she has been introducing elements of barbiturates and paralytics into her system. When the time came, she gave her the final combination of the potassium solution. It was supposed to be like an execution and she was supposed to be done with her.

What went wrong?

Her irritation mounted so much that she thought about just taking the heavy ceramic statue that; stood in the corner of the room and bashing Janice's head in just to be, done with it.

****

Later, that night Mona Daniels sat waiting in her car outside the second Precinct Police station. This has been her routine for months earlier. The first time she came here was months before, because of her fight with Abigail Black. She swore she would never come here again. However, this is now her home away from home.

It has been since she has taken some more time off from work. The accusations from Cultrax defeated her. One thing to be, accused of something that you are doing criminal but to be, accused unjustly is another. Maybe some years ago there were reasons to lock her up, but not lately.

Her crimes of the past are all, forgotten now. There's never any need to consider the past again.

She's glad that the time has moved on almost three months since Cultrax cleared her from the accusations they placed on her. They were kind enough after all to do a public apology by placing news clipping in the paper, periodically since. It's the least that they could do after that public humiliation. After all that has happened, she's thankful that she has escaped it all with her life.

Since then she has moved on in the relationship department as well. She's been enjoying some time with Detective Stephen Dunn of the Ninth Precinct.

He's one of the detectives that helped process out her case. He handled all the police fieldwork. He was so wonderful to her. He'd come to her condo to interview her and bring her up-to-date news on the case.

She never once had to go down to the police station. She didn't like to deal too much with the police except that one time when the female detective called. She asked her the same things she told Stephen for his report, which she felt, was counterproductive. It was really, weird because the detective made it seem as though she didn't know him. He later cleared it up that she was newly, transferred there and not familiar with all the members of the force. She mistakenly honed in on his case.

Mona knew that it's too early from her time with that conniving Jackson Crane but; Stephen seemed so strong with his gruff exterior. Also, she felt safe with him. He seemed familiar to her somehow. The two of the seemed like two kindred spirits. She discovered his strength made her believe that he's familiar to her. He's everything that Jackson wasn't, wrapped up in mystery. Most importantly, he is hers and hers alone. She knew it and it has to be true. Somehow she is changed from all of the past months traumas.

To think that Jackson and Kimberly planned to make her the scapegoat for multiple murders. Kimberly's notes reveal that. The police would have been looking for her as a fugitive. No one would have known that she'd been, killed with the others.

Their plan was almost foolproof, except for the meltdown that Kimberly had. That allowed Natalie time to get to the cable station to save them. How fortunate that Janice Edwards and Natalie were talking like girlfriends do; and coincidently started talking about the exact same person.

It really could have turned out differently and although she isn't a saint, she suddenly felt how precious life is. She found that you have to live life to its potential or you may end up gone before ever really, finding real love.

She was never in love with Jackson she knew that. In her mind, he was nothing more than a plaything because, he was married well, whatever Kimberly and he were. He would have never come to be hers, because he was using her.

News of his murder didn't really bother her, because she never really knew him. She wished she had known the other hidden parts, though. The parts like he was using her for her position at the pharmaceutical company and that he never did care for her. It was so funny that he didn't have the balls to be upfront with her. He didn't know her or what she had been before in her life. Not that she would have joined him against Cultrax; but there are other things.

He did pull the wall over her eyes she has to admit that. He was a pro. This couldn't have been the first time he's done this; and she thought she was the slick one. How easy it was for him to play the role of the devoted lover so willingly to leave his frigid, loveless, wife to be with her. He acted just as he was all the others that took their chances from their wives and children to be with her. They would sacrifice everything. She knew them well. Her past is flooded with those types of men.

Mona wrapped the opened sweater she wore around her tighter; as if to gain comfort from it. It is in the late summertime but the night air somehow seemed like it had a bone chill in it. Or it could be an omen. It's most likely from all that she has gone through recently.

She thought she would be tougher by now with all that she has done to get where she is today. It all seemed another lifetime away her antics; some of which she wished she somehow could redeem herself from.

Stephen had better be the one or…or what? What will she do? Nothing, she will be disappointed like she has been before with other guys. Nothing will be, done. That is the problem. Maybe it's time that she changed her life to prevent these ridiculous men from ruining her life.

Dealing with these men in her life, she's feels like she's been prey. Even now, she feels like prey. This was not how she was years ago. Before, she was the one that was heartless and was considered ice cold and unattached. Even in her work as an intern, she had been considered cold and calculating in front and behind the scenes.

She was treacherous then but she's changed all that.

Back then, that was the only way she knew how to survive. Fighting fire with fire was the only way to deal with corporate men that were always ready to lay her down or walk all over her. Could Jackson and Kimberly's murderous plans have been fate finally paying her back for her reckless behavior? Well if so, she has a trick or two left up her sleeve to prevent fate from making her its plaything or its victim again.

She mused over the idea of returning to being, who and how she was many years ago. Her mind drilled deep in those thoughts. Then she saw Stephen walking up the block.

He did what he always seemed to do every time she saw him. He subconsciously twisted that odd ring he wore on his right hand. It appeared to be a part of him. It looked like an old family heirloom that may have been, passed down generations. He sure was preoccupied by it.

He told her to meet him in front of the station and he would come right out. He always says that. Then he comes trotting up the street out of nowhere, probably from the police parking lot, around back. He would tell her that it is quicker to exit the precinct than to go through the station. He didn't like being, stopped by his co-workers.

She wished he would admit that he's just anxious to see her. She felt the same way. Seeing him seemed to ease her thoughts.

"Hey pretty lady," He said to her through her window. "I've decided to leave my car on the police lot and ride with you, wherever you want to go, it's the start of the weekend."

He smiled at Mona with so much intensity that she actually swooned. His rugged, temperament threw off all of the alpha-female, blocks she's been putting up. What finesse that he could do that? She didn't know what to make of him. However, she knew she has to go for the gusto because this one is worth keeping.

****

A few days later, Monday morning, at Chicago's number one radio station WXBB 95.8, Sebastian Black, Radio Personality and his radio team are about to begin his return segment.

It took him a little more time than he predicted to recover from the bullet, Kimberly Stanford shot in his leg. That was the night that they were just celebrating the news that Michael's cable show; *Life Talk with Deena Williams* was, picked up nationally. He almost met his end when she did that, but now he's back with a vengeance. Especially with these two on his, radio team. They've been on a mission while he was recuperating to try to replace him by stealing his show. They didn't think he knew what they were doing but he has eyes everywhere.

"Good morning, 95.8 listeners. It's Mr. Sebastian on the Mr. Sebastian, Morning Lover's show," he said glancing at the other two across from him. "I am back and to all of my Chicago friends who flooded the hospital with flowers and gifts I thank you. I hope you don't mind, but I gave them away to some of the elderly and kids while I was at the hospital. I knew they needed them, more than me. Oh, let me say hey to my morning crew, Hot Cinnamon aka Ms. Veronica Lane, sexy, great to see you baby and DJ Lenny Martin, always my dude."

"Welcome back, Sebastian…we missed you while you were gone. We were thinking about you and trying to keep Chicago busy till you came back." Veronica said enthusiastically although, she stared at him expressionless.

"You were missed dude." DJ Lenny added, sounding too much like a rehearsed line.

"Yes, well it's good to be back in the Chicago location and with our fans all over the states who; have been supporting 95.8 while I was down for the count. They kept moving with us, even with the many guest DJs. But the master is back, willing and ready, with a vengeance…"

**** 

Four hours later in Sebastian's, private office, he sat there with his station manager, Raina Webster.

"I don't care what you do, make up an excuse or not. Nobody that works for me is gonna be that disrespectful."

"Sebastian, think about it. You publically turned her into some sort of groupie chick, Hot Cinnamon. The whole morning segment was demeaning to her. That's not her name; quite naturally she's going to be a little upset."

"I did her a favor. The top twenty songs that is on our playlist brings youth. I made her hip and besides, I've given her nicknames before…"

"And they were tasteful. She's trying to make a name for herself as well. Her name is Veronica Lane. You couldn't just say V or VL or V. La?"

"Seriously, I'm having this conversation with you because this slut wants me, the Morning Lover to respect her on the radio. Broads don't listen to me because they think that I'm the perfect gentleman. They like the mystery about me and the sexiness. And the guys well you know they like what I say. I'm saying things they can't say. These sidekicks are going overboard and it's going to start with her; she's the hell out of here. Don't make me go cliché on you and threaten to take myself somewhere else. *I* boost ratings. What does Hot Lane do? Fire her ass."

"Sebastian, please. Please be reasonable, I've always been able to talk to you about…"

"Well until you've been shot in the leg and your life is threaten; then you can't know how it is to run out of patience and I'm there. Fire the trash now or else."

**\*\*\*\***

"…and I was thinking to myself that you could actually help me get pass this and I could be with my husband again. Right now, he's living in a condo near the other woman, the friend and I'm not comfortable with that. I still love him." Abigail Black said to the woman who sat dutifully behind her desk listening to her talk.

She listened to Abigail intensely.

"So this other woman, is she aware of you? Does she know that you know her?

"Well yes. She has always been around since I've known him. She is supposed to be a close friend of his but I've never trusted her and I believe they are having sex. I finally got the confirmation a few months ago. That's when I left him and filed for divorce."

"Abigail…"

"Dr. Tanner, I really like to be called Ambrosia like I said earlier…"

"Well Ambrosia, okay and remember you can call me Olivia. I know the need for an alias sometimes."

Abigail nodded her head in agreement. It felt strange sitting in this office of, Marriage Counselor, Dr. Olivia Tanner. She's been here for two hours and it's now noon.

She didn't think of herself as weak. She surely thought that she was, done being married to Sebastian Black. He has hurt her beyond, belief and she just knew it was over. He is nothing but a filthy rapist and sadist.

Just when she was going to move on from him and his philandering ways, she found this business card. It was on the front counter of the newly renovated Craft Store; she works at with Sonja Montgomery. It was just lying there almost begging to be, found. The card had Dr. Tanner's name on it.

It brought her clear across town from the store and her home, but she didn't mind. Even the office being high up twenty stories brought on a feeling that it's meant for her to attempt this undertaking. That she should work on rekindling her, fail marriage. It's as if you are rising to the sky. This one lonely card could be her salvation because what will she do without Sebastian Black in her life. After all the two of them were together for so long, she couldn't think of being anywhere else. It's worth a try to Abigail because she missed Sebastian more than she dared to admit.

She knew that Sonja didn't leave the card for her. She knew that Sebastian has never been her favorite. Those two literally despised each other. So here, she is talking to this psychiatrist hoping she could tell her what to do.

"So Ambrosia, what is the game plan?" Dr. Tanner said to her, while flipping through the file in front of her.

"I don't know. I thought you would tell me?"

The doctor took a deep breath and then spoke.

"You came here for some reason. Remember you said you wanted to get back with your husband. Well what is the game plan about the other woman? Will you continue to live in fear that she will always have access to him or do you want to do something about her?"

Abigail looked at her with surprise. Is she suggesting to her that she should do bodily harm to Mona Daniels; and be done with her?

The doctor noticed the confusion in Abigail's expression. She knew she had to get to her quick because she didn't want any hiccups in getting to the goal.

"I only meant...well let's do this. You ask your husband if he will come to our counseling sessions. When that happens, I will have an opportunity to build your relationship together with the two of you from within. Do you think that you will be able to do that?"

"I'm not sure...I am not sure of anything these days. I know that I have a lot to overlook and I am willing. I will surely try to get Sebastian comes to these meetings with me."

"I think that would be best. It will give us an opportunity to relive the past and bury it for the last time. We will be able to move on from it all."

****

Veronica Lane sat in her small cubicle office crying very hard tears. What just happened she thought? Everything was fine until Sebastian return to work. DJ Lenny and she were about to take over the morning show with his name as the banner. It would have went that way for a little while until their new segment grew in strength; then the name would have been changed. Now their plans were, halted and the cynical ego was back.

She simply went to the station manager and asked her to ask Sebastian if he wouldn't debase her on the radio; that's all. She has been very loyal to him these past years and he has always treated her like trash. What is his problem? Could he be that backwards or is it that who he really is? So this is it, out the window without as much as a goodbye. She couldn't believe it.

Sebastian Black is a complete monster.

It's bad enough that she has to work under these conditions in this broom closet of an office space. He gets a suite and the rest of the program crew gets whatever he wanted to give. He is a tyrant. However, she isn't going to take it anymore.

She dried her tears with her hands.

She got up from her desk and left her office. She went down the hall to the other side of the space where Sebastian's office is. She knocked heavily on his door.

"Come in…Veronica."

He surprised her by calling out her name. How could he have known she was coming there to see him?

She walked inside.

"Sebastian, I want to talk to you. I just got finished meeting with Raina and she told me that I'm, fired. I know it's from what I said to her about you this morning. Why?"

"You don't seem to know who holds the keys to your future, do you. You don't get to choose what I say on the air, on my show bitch. I don't have to answer to you or any other tart with a tight, tee-shirt, in hot panties; trying to tell my station manager how to manage my successful show."

"I wasn't doing that. I just thought that…well I don't want to be, called Hot Cinnamon and all those other names. Those names catch on to public and stick. I am a serious radio anchor and a mother. We are fine with our current names," she stopped as she looked at his expression before continuing. "It's not a big deal. I need to work and I'm sorry if you thought that I overstepped my barriers but I was just asking for respect. I need this job."

Sebastian suddenly realized she is right where he wants her, like ripen fruit. He looked at Veronica as though she is prey. His leer is enough of a snarl to frighten any back street prostitute.

"Well if you do, then show me just how much…"

# CHAPTER
## THREE

Dr. Gellar Austin sat nervously at his office desk, holding the phone handset to his face. He dialed the number and something in his gut told him that it's a wrong move, but he couldn't help it. He is really, desperate. His career could use the boost that this edge will give him. The money from referrals alone would put him back in the red.

He has had a clean run here at Chicago Memorial; but it is time to move a little further faster. He is facing his second divorce and this one plans to drain him dry. The times have changed from the quick money he used to make years ago. He actually found himself drained financially. So, if he could secure a solid position within this hospital he should be able to avoid bankruptcy and live a little.

"Hello, Dr. Bower…sir this is Dr. Gellar Austin, OBYN."

"Yes, Dr. Austin?"

"You may have be aware of it or not but I'm your wife's doctor. I have some certain information that I don't think you're aware of."

"Okay…"

"Before we go on, I want to be sure that we are clear what needs to happen here. Integrity for my patients is something that I strive for but I'm not getting any younger sir. I need to know that once you are the new Chief of Staff that, I will have your backing."

"I'm not sure what you mean. What makes you think you can even speak to me in this manner or even that I won't turn you in for being this bold to approach me? So I suggest you cease with the cloak and dagger approach and get to the point of your call."

"Your wife is pregnant."

Christopher paused before he responded to Dr. Austin. He made sure that he didn't display any feelings to Dr. Austin.

How in the hell could she be pregnant?

He really didn't want the children that he has now; but it made sense in his scheme of things. A loving, married, father of two.

"Dr. Austin, I may be able to help you after all. All you have to do is one thing for me and I will ensure you that you will be my right hand from then on. Something just between the two of us and I want it done immediately."

"That would be?"

"Listen very carefully and make sure it is done this way…"

He spoke slowly and compellingly into the phone to Dr. Austin as he hashed out a very detailed plan. Minutes passed as Dr. Austin listened intently to the details, his face suddenly going blank from assault of information.

"…What? I can't do that." He said shockingly.

"Yes you can my fellow board member." Christopher taunted him calmly.

Dr. Austin let the words work themselves into his mind. He saw the doors to his career finally open up wide for him and he just couldn't resist the temptations.

"I will do it."

Christopher smiled. He is very full of himself right now. See the power that he possesses. No secrets could elude him at Chicago Memorial. How dare Natalie do this to him and his career? She was, told to be discreet. Now she is having a baby. No one knew his secret, not even her. It would be an embarrassment to him if it got out. He has to do what he has to and when he becomes Chief of Staff, she will thank him for this decision.

It is down to the wire now. The Chief of Staff position is, guaranteed to be his. Two doctors that were competing against him have already excused themselves from the position. That just leaves him and his old nemesis Dr. Bradley Warfield. They have been rivals here at Chicago Memorial for more than five years. All the hospital staff nervously calls him, Dr. War because they fear him. He's nothing to fear.

However, I will be, thought Christopher.

**** 

Dr. Austin breathed heavily, as he hung up the phone. This is it he thought, the flagship. Although he is no stranger to the illegal side of life, he's glad that he was able to strike this deal with Dr. Bower.

He is notorious for his aggressiveness.

Something made him jump on this news quickly. It would pay Dr. Austin to find out what. He will make sure that he finds out the answer.

This is it, he's sold his soul to the devil again for personal gain and he hoped he won't regret it. It's time to get to work.

He reached for the speaker button on his desk phone.

"Sabrina, bring me the sonograms belonging to Mariam Marcum, now."

****

Thank God for mothers, Michael Montgomery thought as he drove away from his mother's house. His daughter, Tiffany is going to stay there for a while. She's always there when he needed her. She never asked questions. She took care of her granddaughter well especially now that things weren't going on that well with his wife, Sonja. It has been a few days since his world with Sonja came to a head. She was upset and he couldn't reason with her.

The night that Natalie came to his house, he was real, glad that she didn't want to come in. He didn't know if he could deal with telling Sonja about the baby but he knows he will eventually have to.

It's hard dealing with this thing that Natalie and he has gotten themselves in; especially with both of them being, married. He didn't know that it would be this different from their time together years ago; but it was. There were other things to consider that he didn't take in consideration at first. Well he didn't know that months ago Natalie would come back to his life. He was, caught off guard and he was flooded with so much pent up feelings that he made some desperate and permanent moves. Moves that maybe he would have waited on if he had the chance to do it all over again. Overall, he knows that he will always want to be with Natalie; that will never change. He won't let Sonja stand in his way.

He has made up in his mind that he is going to leave her. It's no turning back now. All that is, left to do is to tell her. She's going to have to hear it, anyway. With the baby coming, she will have to know now. He doesn't want Sonja thinking that he's leaving her because Natalie is pregnant. He's leaving her because he really doesn't love her anymore. Then again, what difference does it really make?

He already knows that no matter how peaceful and quiet he would want to make the divorce it will not be. Sonja will be incredibly difficult but he will handle it. To be with Natalie again he would do it.

Earlier he was on his way to meet Natalie. They decided that they would meet for a late lunch to discuss what is going to happen between them. There is much to do to readjust his life.

He wanted to the opportunity to look for an apartment. Some place where he could sort his feelings out; but really there is nothing to sort out; he has made up his mind.

Why Sonja, how did he end of with Sonja? He always thought that Natalie had that question in the back of her mind to ask him. He wanted to be prepared to give her an answer if he could. At first, he tried to convince her and himself that he didn't know why he married Sonja. He is lying of course because he knew why.

He wanted to hurt Natalie, like he was hurt by her.

There it's out in the open in the forefront of his mind. He wanted to hurt her. He admitted it to himself. He was different when she left. He was angry with her and Sonja was available. Moreover, she was willing for whatever reason she had to collaborate with him in his stupid decision.

He could never tell Natalie this. He wouldn't risk destroying what they have rebuilt over these last few months. He was stupid in those days. Now he made sure that when he made any decisions he keeps Natalie first. She isn't first before his daughter but definitely before everyone else.

Michael took time to stop off by the house; he wanted to change his clothes. He went in through the garage and into the kitchen. Unconsciously he grabbed the mail that Sonja obviously placed on the baker's rack. He noticed the previous mail from the last few days there and the envelope that he never really thought about until now.

The one that revealed Janice Edwards and Kimberly are related. It is something that requires him to stop by Janice's office and speak with her about one day. He is still curious as to what set Kimberly off. Since he knows now that she is a patient of Janice how does having the same last names factor into it. Michael felt that he should get, to the bottom of it if only just to cure his own curiosity.

He decided to brush it aside for now until his talk with Natalie. That is what's important right now, he thought as he exited the house.

****

Mona just got out of bed. She had a wonderful weekend with Stephen. She thought she could really get into this leave of absence deal. Maybe she will get Cultrax to foot another three months before she goes back to work. So this is what those with so much money feel when they don't have to leave their beds, to work?

Her phone rang beside her bed and she just stared at it. She didn't know if she wanted to interrupt her leisure time to answer it. She looked at the caller id to check on who it is. Once she reached over and picked the cordless phone from the base, she saw that it was her assistant, Jill from work. She answered it.

She spoke quickly before Jill could.

"Hi Jill, no I'm not coming back for a while so don't ask."

"Ms. Daniels, Mona, Dr. Monarch is dead, he's been murdered. The police…"

Once Jill went into the details of the crime scene, Mona's mind drew a blank. After she hung up the phone from Jill, she noticed that she was shaking. She didn't know what was going on. Paul Monarch is dead, murdered. First Craig and now Paul; two, key members of her Cultrax team. The team that has developed the newest diabetes drug and she is the only head left. Nothing is making sense and she may be at the center of it.

Jill said that Paul was, stabbed three times in the stomach. She overheard the police say that it looked like the killer really hated him. That is only because the killer twisted the knife while it was; still embedded in him. She also said that the word 'killer' was, written in black marker on his forehead and on a note pad; it read 'I am coming'.

That was strange. What is the killer trying to say? Is he describing his name or is he calling Paul a killer. The other phrase 'I am coming' didn't make sense either.

Once again, a psycho is loose and on some tandem. Is Chicago the only place that breeds this kind of thing? She just survived a maniac that held on to issues since they were in college and she creatively put it all together. They would've all been killed that night if it weren't for Natalie.

Well it looks like Mona will be off for some more time to deal with this tragedy. She thought to herself a little too callously.

At any rate, it did scare Mona to her core. She knew of Paul's past and there's a possibility that he may have still been active. It's a new world that they live in. If he did reestablish his activities, he may have crossed over someone else's territory. Their business was not only profitable it was competitive.

She didn't think that he was doing anything other than his work at Cultrax. They agreed when they found that they would be working together that the past is the past. That remained true because neither of them discussed anything about those years ago. It was a time years ago when she was fresh out of college and looking to make her mark on the world. They were not, caught and that was it; they were safe.

However, the fact is that Paul Monarch has been murdered and that is something that is too real.

**** 

Michael walked into La Maria restaurant feeling as if he has come home. It's weird he thought that this place seemed timeless. It meant so much to, Natalie and he at a time. It's a good choice to meet her here amongst their memories. She loved him all this time. They never got their chance and now they have a baby on the way, he is sure of it. However, it is going to be a grueling eight months to wait.

He know it was a possibility that the baby could be her husband's child. He wasn't that naïve to think that Natalie wouldn't sleep with him to keep up pretense. It's a possibility he has to accept.

He saw her in their usual section of the restaurant.

That sight of her helped him focus on some other thoughts.

Natalie looked up and saw Michael heading towards her. He seemed happy to her even though they were in the middle of this chaos; or is it chaos? They have a baby on the way she and the love of her life: how cool is that? She should be happy but all she does is worry; well not today. Today she is going to relish in the arms of her lover and they're going to celebrate the birth of their child be damn the fates.

"Miss Vincent, I swear you get more and more beautiful the more I see you and now you have a glow." He said with passion.

She noticed that he never uses her married name when he speaks to her. She could tell he still didn't want to face that she married someone else. It didn't matter anymore because he won't have to; she wasn't going to be Mrs. Christopher Bower for long.

"I'm already in love with you Mr. Montgomery; you don't need to lay it on so thick. Have a seat."

Before he sat down, he went over to her. He passionately kissed her so deeply that the woman sitting at the table next to them with her husband, smiled brightly.

He felt as if he would never leave this moment. He felt it, their connection, like years before; like months before.

Like before, when he told her in that hotel room at the Montague Hotel that he wanted her to leave. He lied. He was being stubborn because he was not getting the answers he wanted. He simply wanted to return to her life and to the love that made him feel like he was a superman. A true love can make someone feel like that.

He wanted to know the answer to what has been bothering him all this time since he first lost Natalie. He wanted God to answer, this, one question that he has to, desperately know. What would've happened to this world if the two of them had gotten together in their love, Armageddon? Why is the love of his life not his, not fully?

He bowed his head to the silence when he sat down. Well, that is two questions.

Although he has a love for Natalie, this is against everything that was righteous. God would never stand behind their relationship to be brutality honest.

Michael shook the thought from his mind. He didn't want to know that. He didn't want to admit that so he returned to his fantasy.

"You know that you're making me the happiest man on the planet right now?" He said to break up his thoughts.

"In this state of things, we risk a lot."

"Seriously Natalie, you think this is a risk?" Michael said seeming not agitated, but defeated. "Those two don't care about us. We're like trophies to them, that they bring out only when they want the world to see that they have achieved some sort of social normalcy."

"I know I'm not sure why I said that. I'm happy that we're back together; at least even if it's like this."

She isn't sure that they were; she just played the cue from him. He sure kissed her as if he is back with her. She's already felt how it would be if Michael and she were not together and she did not like that. Now, she is willing to do whatever it takes to ensure that he stays hers. After all, she's the one that started all this that day months ago in this very same restaurant.

Michael had gone on with his life and was making the most of it. She entered back into his heart and it is no way she is going to leave him behind, not this time.

"We have to stay together this time, no matter what. It's time we go straight-ahead and not turn back." Michael said determined to get Natalie to agree.

"I do want to be with you and I've realize that yes I will leave Christopher."

Michael couldn't believe his ears. When he looked back on the last months, they spent together; he wished he had approached her years ago before it became a mess. Why didn't he tell her eight years ago that he was still in love with her? Was it his pride?

Maybe it was because it all happened too fast. One minute they were broken up and in the next, he was lying in bed with Sonja. He was numb and if it hadn't been Sonja, it would've been some other woman. He was lost and he lost who he was. He was off and didn't have the strength to face Natalie to, even fight for her, to get her back. However, he did want her back that has never changed. He just let her slip through his fingers like sand.

He never had that chance to process all that came at him in those days.

He heard that she was dating some doctor in under graduate school and that it was getting heavy. It further weakens him, made him feel inadequate and he just gave up. He had nothing he thought but his love to give her; and that wasn't good enough for him. He had to do something, anything to regain his strength, so he connected with Sonja.

He was emotionally gone and Sonja took advantage of that. When Natalie left him, she took every bit of his soul with her and it took a lot of bargaining with the fates to get it back. He only got enough back to realize he is alive and he longed for her always.

It isn't, settled now either, but he could exist now in this newly created parallel world. The one that has been, created because he chose to move left, when he should have moved right.

At any rate, he is happy now that she wants to be with him. That she still loves him. However, he has the strangest feelings that something else is coming and so he couldn't rest that easy.

"And I want to be with you baby."

Not really, willing to dwell on the subject any longer so that Natalie would change her mind, Michael decided to change the subject.

"Well, I have somewhat of a mystery, I would like for you to help me solve. I received this envelope a few days ago as a matter of fact that night when you told me you were pregnant. I was so distracted with what went on with us that I put it to the side. It came through the mail without a return address. There were two birth certificates and one marriage license, inside."

"Hmm, it does sound like a mystery; a very scary one. 'Mystery of the Mistaken Post Office Delivery'," she joked and laughed.

"Wait for it. The first birth certificate has the name Kimberly Prentiss. Does that mean anything?"

"What?"

"Wait there's more. The second birth certificate has the name Kimberly Stanford and the marriage license has Kimberly Stanford and Everett Edwards, ta-da."

Looking at Michael, Natalie's, smile left her face. As she thought about what he just said, the names he called; it all involved Janice. Janice's maiden name is Prentiss. That makes Kimberly and her related.

"I can't believe that she did not tell me that she is related to Kimberly. I mean not before when we didn't know that we were talking about the same person but after when Kimberly was, caught. Why didn't she tell me that she's, related to her? She purposely hid that from me, but why?"

Michael shook his head. He couldn't answer that question for her. He noticed by the looks of Natalie, that this funny, harmless, little mystery has just become serious. He thought he was telling her a meaningless bit of hospital chatter, someone's idea of a joke. However, now he realizes that this related to the attempt on their lives three months ago.

"Michael, Janice purposely deceived me; by not telling me that she is related to Kimberly. I just can't get past that. It makes me believe that she had something to do with Kimberly's meltdown."

"Well that would fall into what, Kimberly said, that night at the cable station, at the party; she said that she didn't want her to leave witnesses. Natalie how long have you known, Janice?"

"I've known Janice a long time, almost six or more years. Kimberly said that?"

"Yes."

"So she purposely sent me to the party knowing that I would end up walking into a scene of multiple murders?"

"Why would you say that?"

Natalie pondered his question. Why did she say that? They were only talking that night by chance; or were they? It was Janice's insistence to bring up the sessions with Kimberly to her every chance she got. That much is true. It just didn't make sense.

Maybe she was too embarrassed to say that she is, related to her. There were just too many questions and too many of those had additional questions attached to them.

There were many little things here and there, but she heard them. She heard Janice speak the words.

The only way to get to, the bottom of all of this is to confront Janice and ask her straight out.

"I have to say it. When I look back on it, she all but told me where to find Kimberly. I thought it was just dumb luck but it may not have been. It may have been a well-drawn out plan. Too many unanswered questions. One right off is that Janice's maiden name is Prentiss. You never knew Kimberly as Prentiss and neither did I. Now there's a possibility that they were married to the same man, because Janice's, husband's name was Everett Prentiss. Come to, think of it, now looking back, from the police mug shot that hit the internet lately; you can see the resemblance of those two. Then when she spoke about Everett, she didn't even mention that he was once married to Kimberly. I just don't get it."

"Yeah I'm beginning to get the picture and beginning to see the confusion. Every time you go down a path, it leads to more questions and the previous ones aren't, answered. We have got to, talk to Janice face to face. We have to…"

Natalie's cellphone rang and she retrieved it from her purse to answer it.

"Hello."

"Good afternoon Natalie, this is Dr. Austin."

"Hi, Dr. Austin, I've been waiting for your call."

"Well I wanted to know if you could come by my office today. I have something I want to show and to do some additional test." He said to her nervously.

He didn't intend on sounding this way but he couldn't help it. He has always been like this and because of the pressures he's been under lately, the tension within him has been heavy. It did however fit into his plans.

"Is there something wrong?" Natalie said being cautious.

Good, yes-yes, he thought.

"I want to do some further test first before we talk more in-depth. Let's say in an hour around 2 o'clock?"

"Okay. I'll be there." She said while staring intensely in Michael's eyes.

She didn't want to alarm him by making any sudden gestures or faces. Dr. Austin wasn't clear on what he wanted and it didn't mean that it was anything bad. It would be best to wait and see.

****

That day at Cultrax, two people walk in calmly pass the security officer and down the hallway of individual offices. They pretended that they were pharmaceutical sales associates and surprisingly they were able to just waltz pass security due to its heighten threat level.

Wasn't there just a murder here four days ago? Isn't Chicago in the middle of a high crimes spree? Well if not it's about to again.

Once they were, guided to where Mona's office location is; they went in her section to meet with her.

"Good afternoon, may I help the two of you?" Jill, Mona's assistant asked, politely.

"Yes, I'm Diana Martin and this is Kurt Brenner. We have an appointment with Ms. Daniels, is she available? I know we're early." Diana said evenly.

"I'm sorry I thought I contacted all of the upcoming appointments that I scheduled for Ms. Daniels. She's is not in. She will be away from work for maybe another month, maybe three now because of our crisis. I could reschedule the appointment for you if you would like?"

"Um, no, we'll reschedule when we are ready for her."

The two left the office in silence. Once they got outside in the courtyard entrance, they spoke.

"What do we do now, Kurt?"

"We pay our partner a visit at her home. I have the address."

# CHAPTER
## FOUR

Chicago Memorial Hospital is busy and bustling as usual. This hospital in spite of its location on the upper north side of town still seemed to gather a lot of attention in regards to emergencies. Natalie didn't think that it should be a ghost town; but there were an especially large amount of gunshot victims and critical injuries from multiple car crashes here. It's a little past the middle of the weekday, not a Saturday night. It just didn't fit.

She made her way through the emergency room without being, asked too many questions. She is a pediatrician after all and she saw many kids that needed her. She took this time off from her office so that she could get things cleared up with Michael; and figure out what she could do with her kids for the rest of the summer.

Dr. Austin was waiting for her as she entered his office. The solemn look on his face unnerved Natalie.

"Natalie, come in." He said.

Natalie followed the doctor into his office and sat down near his desk. Dr. Austin had her file folder out and some sonogram pictures lying on top.

"Well Gellar, what is going on?" She said brave but nervously.

"I want you to look at these and you tell me." He replied pointing to the sonograms.

Natalie studied the pictures and instantly her tears began to flow. How could this be happening? She isn't experiencing any pain. However, here it is on the sonogram, these dark patches.

"What does this mean Gellar?" She asked trying to be calm.

"I'm not sure and I want to before I say anything more. As you can see there seems to be a shadow alongside this area of the uterus. Has there been any bleeding? Have you noticed anything?"

"No, I feel fine. I haven't noticed anything and no pain."

"I don't know why you don't. So okay, it may have just begun. I'll give you an iron vitamin and an estrogen shot that should help reinforced the uterus walls. Since you are not experiencing any pain you should be all right. I want to do more pictures."

The doctor asked his assistant Sabrina to come in and she brought in the sonogram machine with her. They started to prepare for the scans. Sabrina saw a file sitting on the desk area. She picked it up to move it and it caught her eye.

"Doctor, I'm sorry did you still need Mrs. Marcum's sonogram pictures."

The doctor instantly and abruptly snatched the file from her hands.

"These are not Miriam Marcum's pictures, their Dr. Bower's. Just get the scans ready." He said dryly and sharply.

Sabrina looked at Dr. Austin, obviously bothered that he would embarrass her in this manner and in front of another doctor. She will have to speak to him about this. This is not the first time that he has let his frustration cause him to lash out at her. Those pictures do belong to Miriam Marcum's file and for whatever reasons he is acting as if they do not.

His behavior to her has always been disrespectful and she has her own reasons for staying in his employ. This however is the last straw.

To Natalie, Dr. Austin seemed agitated but she just passed it off. She knows in her own practice the need to have competent staff around her is necessary. Mixing up sonogram pictures and patient files could cause many problems for a doctor. He or she need to have the correct information.

****

When Natalie left the doctor's office, she seemed at ease. Once they were able to see another set of sonograms of the baby, it showed that everything is normal. He gave her the estrogen shot for nothing. He assured her that the estrogen shot would help her.

She didn't see the reason why Dr. Austin would suggest giving it to her; but she respected his knowledge.

Putting that on the back burner she decided that now is as good as any time to confront Janice about her recent discovery that she is, related to Kimberly.

She proceeded to Janice's office. She arrived a moment later and went in the office. Dr. Edward's receptionist, Vicki sat at her desk. She announced Natalie's presence. Seconds later Kimberly opened the door and then she waved her in. Apparently, she is not with any clients.

Once inside Janice's office, Natalie sat down and neither of the women exchanged any words, just yet. Could it be that, Janice knew somehow why Natalie came to see her unexpected; and is anticipating an encounter?

"Natalie, hi, I didn't know you were coming in today." She said surprisingly and pleasantly.

Kimberly looked at Natalie. It's clear that she has something on her mind and found it difficult to talk about it. She hoped it's some juicy gossip because she could surely use something funny to occupy her mind. It is stressful, this thing with Janice. She was, almost caught.

"I wasn't, but I had something to do." She replied.

As she took a breath, Natalie pondered whether she should even confront Janice about the lack of information she was, given by her. She didn't know whether if she is ready to face the truth or not.

"Janice I have to talk to you about something."

"About what, you sound so serious?"

"Something serious and I'm going to be honest with you and I want you to be honest with me."

Kimberly didn't want to betray herself by lashing out at Natalie. She's not ready for any more inquiries about anything and she felt one is heading her way now.

"Yes Natalie," she said obviously annoyed.

"Well I want you to know that I find this very difficult to speak to you about. I'm not sure what's going on but I need an answer. Why didn't you tell me you are related to Kimberly?"

The room immediately grew an eerie silence as Kimberly got out of her seat. She approached Natalie and instantly grabbed her head with both hands. Natalie went flying backwards in her chair as Kimberly tackled her toward the floor. Once they landed to the floor, Kimberly aggressively banged her head hard on the floor. From behind her back, Kimberly produced a gold statue and she started to hit her with it.

Natalie tried to fight her off, but she jumped on her. She bled from the minor strikes Kimberly was throwing. She slowly began losing conscious until she passed out.

Kimberly got up from atop Natalie wiping the blood from her face. With the blood that soaked on her hands, she lapped at it as if she is a ferocious lioness celebrating her kill. She simply stood up and went back behind her desk and sat down calmly.

"Janice, did you hear me. Why didn't you tell me about Kimberly?" Natalie asked, sitting calmly in her chair.

Kimberly shook her head as if to awaken herself from a dream. It slowly came into focus that she had another one of her delusions; the kind that Janice claimed she was having. It was the medicine that she was giving Janice; but these she is having were not medically, induced. They were increasing by the day as the stress of everything that's occurring around her is closing in. Now Natalie has found out her secret and she didn't know what to do. She's not yet ready to kill her. It would have been easier on Natalie if she had just waited her turn.

"I just can't." Kimberly begged as she answered the thoughts in her mind. Realizing what she said she began to cry attempting to sound sincere. "I just couldn't, I'm so embarrassed that my cousin is this disturb. I thought I could control her."

She's her cousin, Natalie thought in disbelief.

"But you sent me to the cable station that night. I could have been, killed or at the least walked into murder. I ended up being, shot. You never told me that she is your cousin. You acted like she was just your patient."

It's not as bad as she thought at first. Natalie has the right to question her actions, as her friend. She however did not have the right as a friend to know everything. She decided that she is going to toy with her some more to figure out what else she knows.

"What am I to do, my career? I tried to talk to you to reveal a little at a time. At first, I thought you were talking about your friend's wife. After you told me that I felt it would open too many doors. Too many that were already opened by compromising my patient's confidentially. My cousin I mean. I guess I was just looking out for myself."

"It turned out to be her. Didn't she say anything to you that led you to believe that she was coming after us?"

"No, Natalie, I can't…"

*That witch*, she heard her own voice say in her head. *I am going to kill her, I will.*

"Can't what Janice? I was almost killed by that bullet and you saw me the very, next day; and didn't say anything about it to me. Try putting yourself in my shoes. What could make you be so careless and unprofessional?" Natalie yelled at her out of frustration.

*Selfish, self-righteous, adulterous, BITCH! I will kill, I will kill you; I will kill you.* Her thoughts screamed as they exploded inside her mind.

"No! You will not talk to me like this Natalie. Get out of my office, now!" Kimberly blurted her words out.

She clutched her fist so hard that she felt a few nails dig deep into the palm of her hands. This stopped her from reacting physically.

Natalie drew back from her realizing that she angered her, severely. She could feel her stomach erupting as she listened to the icy, cold way that she responded. To anger her wasn't Natalie's mission and perhaps she was a little harsh in her approach to this subject. As she thought about it, she would be embarrassed too if it was her relative that is less than desirable. She feels embarrassed to be married to Christopher.

Lately the two of them have not been exchanging any words. It has been a cold war going on at her house. Just like Michael, she left her daughters in the care of her mother. It is until she can figure out what it is she is going to do. It was easy to adjust to that since they have been with her mother since the shooting.

There would be no way that Christopher would have taken care of them and she didn't want him to.

Focusing back on Janice, she just got up out of her chair and walked towards the door. She turned back around to see Janice staring at her as if she could slit her throat.

"We'll talk about this later, Janice." That is all that Natalie felt safe to say as she exited the office.

Once Natalie left her office, Kimberly exhaled. She almost lost her cool where she would've exposed herself by killing Natalie. How did she find out about her connection to Janice? She covered her tracks carefully, she thought.

Janice, her mind spoke to her.

That is it. Janice. She told Kimberly that she sent Michael a letter. The information could have been from that. Is Natalie toying with her? She has to find out how much is, known. Should she be packing her things to flee?

It's all Janice's fault. She couldn't follow simple directions. She was to shoot all of them at the party, Sebastian, Mona, Sonja and Abigail. Not Michael, she was only supposed to place him in a deep sleep. She had planned something special for just for him.

Once Jackson came into the picture with the idea to frame Mona for selling company secrets it made the plan even more exciting. He was going to help move Mona's body from the cable station. She would be, blamed for the murders. She had that frame all worked out that people would think that Mona fled to Puerto Rico; after selling company secrets to a rival company. The murders would have been the icing on the cake.

It was the greatest plan, but around her were nothing but incompetent fools. Now her plans were ruin because of her stupid cousin once again. However, she always has a contingency plan.

Natalie surely will go to the police, she thought or would she? Actually, the only person she will go to right now is Michael. He will want to pick up where she left off and come see Kimberly. On that day, she will be ready.

****

Natalie held herself together long enough to get down to her office. She wasn't feeling well in her stomach as it began to burn even more. The tension she felt while talking to Janice was enough to cause anyone undue stress.

She sat behind her desk in her office at Chicago Memorial to try to calm down; but it wasn't working. Her stomach began to burn even more and now she's in pain.

She attempted to get up from her desk but that is when the pain hit her intensely and she fell to the floor crumpling over with the pain. She felt herself begin pass out and that frighten her.

It is still early afternoon. She's sure that Dr. Austin is still in his office so she got herself off, of the floor and made her way to her desk.

She hit the speaker button and then dialed the doctor's office number. Instantly a sharp, pain, wrenching, attack on her stomach occurred and she fell to the floor behind her desk as the line connected.

"Hello, Dr. Bower," Sabrina said.

Natalie didn't answer.

"Dr. Bower, hello are you there…Dr. Austin, Dr. Austin…I think there's something wrong at Dr. Bower's office. She called and then there was no one on the line…"

****

About an hour later, Sonja Montgomery and Abigail Black were working at Sonja's Favorite Crafts; Sonja's arts and craft business. This is the place she spent her days lately.

After the previous fire that literally destroyed it, Sonja started to spend more of her days at the store. She needed a retreat to plot her strategy and she couldn't do that with Michael around.

He doesn't think she knows about the baby but she does. Knowing is half the battle. Michael and Natalie will rue the day that they did this to her.

She looked over at Abigail and thought how stupid it is for Abigail to see a marriage counselor. All of the trouble that rapist has caused her and she's literally crawling back to him. Abigail thinks Sonja is in the dark about her sessions. She saw that card on the front counter. Sonja thought about throwing it out but forgotten about it. She thought Abigail left it for her.

"Do you still really want to be with Sebastian, Ambrosia?" Sonja asked her, standing behind the counter.

"It's a thought. I miss him."

Abigail didn't want to tell Sonja about her initial consultation with Dr. Tanner. She didn't want the disapproval she will surely get from Sonja. Sebastian and she have gone through so much together that she really didn't know anything else. As much as she didn't want to admit it to Sonja, Sebastian will never go away from her heart.

"I mean after all that we heard that night. Most likely he will go to jail for those crimes." Sonja said flatly.

"There aren't any charges. Kimberly didn't say anything and now she's in a nut bin. No one's coming out of the woodwork for him and he's willing to get help." Abigail responded annoyingly.

Part of the healing will be to acknowledge that he has a problem with women. That surely will be something to watch and will probably be their last session with Dr. Tanner. However, it will prove, hopefully to Sebastian that Abigail is here to stay.

"What about you? Are you going to make up with Michael? After all it was just one little indiscretion; Michael is a good guy."

"You really think so Ambrosia?"

"I do."

"Then you get back with him." She said belittling and writing what Ambrosia said off as nonsense.

"It's so typical of you to blow this off Sonja. You would rather stew in your own stubbornness than admit that you really want him back."

"I already did that and he spat in my face. He chose Natalie Vincent Bower. There's something serious going on with those two. They're planning something. I know it."

How could he think that he would be able to get another woman pregnant and just cast her to the side?

Natalie will pay a hell of a price for messing with her husband. The quicker that she talks to Natalie's husband again, the quicker he will put a stop to her affair with Michael. He will insist they raise that bastard child as his to save face at Chicago Memorial and Natalie will, be trapped with him; until death do they part.

That will give Sonja time to work on Michael and he will stay with her. She has manipulated him before and it's worked very well a little girl and a marriage. He will love her again or else.

"Ambrosia, I have too much to worry about these days. Especially since the store took such a loss from the fire. I don't have time to run after Michael. I guarantee one way or another he will be mine." She said without even realizing how threatening it sounded.

****

Mona sat at the little table on her balcony. She hasn't did much since she heard about Paul Monarch.

What was he doing at work when the rest of the staff went home? Didn't he know that the city has become dangerous to be out late at night?

She reminded herself that she at once thought about leaving Chicago, because it isn't safe anymore. All of this death and it was not just death; it's murder. When Craig was murdered, Michael suspected it was Kimberly and that's who it turned out to be.

Craig was a member of her research lab team and now Dr. Monarch. Could this revolve around her again? Did the killer think that she was working with Monarch that night?

Her thoughts were broken with the sound of her doorbell. Is it Stephen, she wondered because he's due to be off from work by now? He said he might drop by to see her later. She got up to answer the door.

She opened the door without looking through the peephole.

"Mona, baby how are you?"

Instantly Mona recognized Kurt and Diana. She immediately reacted by attempting to slam the door in their faces.

Kurt stuck his foot out hard bracing it against the heavy door, stopping it from closing.

"Ouch Mona, is that some way to treat your family, that hurt?" He said mocking her.

"What the hell are you doing here Kurt and bringing that trash with you? Are you kidding me?"

"Bananas in a bunch, Mona. We're just one big bunch of bananas." Diana said.

"You two are definitely not welcome here. You know the deal. Remember?" Mona hissed at them.

"We know that you have gotten really high on the hog there, pretty little liar and didn't call; and you didn't write." Kurt said mockingly to Mona, pushing pass her into her condo home.

Diana followed in behind him, laughing loudly.

Mona slammed the door shut and turned to address the two seemingly, unwanted visitors.

"You two can't be here, I'm through you know that right. I've been through for a long while." She said trying to block them from entering all the way into her condo from the entrance hall.

"No seriously?" Diana joked. "Well, so are we. We want a job at your company. You're a big time CEO right?"

"All of the companies to work at with your backgrounds and you come to me for help, that's priceless? You two wrote the book."

"Don't try that with us Mona. The buttering up treatment used to work back in the day when people actually trusted what you said. Now that we know who and what you are and that you can pull strings; we really need to get a job." Kurt interjected.

"That's a big no. I don't recommend criminals." Mona said smugly.

"Now isn't that priceless. How soon do we forget?" Diana said to her slyly. "Everyone needs redemption; you of all people should appreciate that. I see this is going take a little persuasion. Do you have you have something to drink?"

In that instant Mona's cellphone rang. She didn't recognize the number right off but then realized it as a number from Chicago Memorial.

"Hello."

"Miss Daniels, this is Kelly, Dr. Bowers' assistant. Dr. Bowers collapsed in her office a little while ago. I thought I should call you to let you know." The assistant said calmly.

"Is she alright?" Mona replied not wanting to give into panic. Natalie told her that she is pregnant.

"She's alive if that's what you mean? They took her to the emergency room so they could see to her. She was unconscious when they found her."

"Okay I'm on my way. Thank you for calling me Kelly."

She hung up the line.

Diana and Kurt were staring at her. Presumably wanting to continue with the discussion that they were having; but Mona is not going to continue. Her best friend is in a serious state and she's going there to see what.

"We're done, I have an appointment. Don't call me, I'll call you or better yet go back to Detroit and drop dead."

"Whew, you are a pistol these days. Almost like a desert eagle, pew-pew." He made the sound and pointed his finger in the shape of a gun. "Don't worry about it we'll be contacting you again to discuss this further." Kurt said.

Diana was about to say something as they were preparing to leave.

Mona grabbed her keys and her purse. She all but pushed them out of the door with her. She has to get to Natalie and the first person she has to call is Michael.

# CHAPTER
## FIVE

Dr. Austin paced his office floor. If it wasn't against the rules, he would light up a cigarette; right here on the spot. A cigarette would calm him down and ease the tension he feels now. He's on the edge, but also really elated. It worked, the plan worked. Now he can enter into some real money. Dr. Bower is going to take care of him but he wondered why he wanted him to go this far. To him it was a bit, extreme but he guessed he has his reasons. He made his involvement in this as smooth as silk like he used to be several years ago.

Those were the glory days when there were thousands of dollars to be, made weekly. That's how he was able to pay alimony and child support to his ex-wife. At the same time, he also married his then fiancée who is now also his ex-wife.

Nothing was out of his reach then and he wants that life again.

His phone rang and he pushed the speakerphone.

"Doctor Austin?" Sabrina's voice came over the speakerphone.

"Yes, what is it?" He said to her flatly as if she is disturbing a critical operation.

"I am leaving now. I'll transfer the calls to the service."

The doctor said nothing as he bolted out of his chair, went to his door, opened it and walked out in outer office.

"By the way, Sabrina," He said pointing his fingers at her. "You made this office look bad today with that poor display of incompetence."

Sabrina still sat in her chair as she looked up at the doctor. He is insane she thought and way out of line.

"I don't know what you mean."

"You let one of my colleagues see that my office is unorganized and the joke is it's due to you. Those sonogram pictures were not of Miriam Marcum's baby, they were Dr. Bower's pictures. Don't ever embarrass me like that again or you're fired. Do you hear me?"

She couldn't believe what she was hearing. The doctor has been rude to her before but this is to the extreme. It's almost as if he wanted to strike her. Sabrina just sat in her chair and nodded to him, teary eyed. This is more than she could take. Then she got up quickly from her chair and darted out the door, into the hallway.

Dr. Austin seeing that he has made his point and shaking his head he walked back into his office. Good riddance he thought. He felt relieved a little from the tension he had been experiencing. Once he walked through the door to his office, he pushed the door hard with his backhand. It slammed shut only to open again slightly. The sheer force of the slam was with so much force that the door didn't get to connect with the door strike. The doctor didn't notice as he sat down at his desk and picked up the phone receiver.

Entering back in the outer office Sabrina walked in. She was clearly, shaken still from Dr. Austin sudden verbal assault. She decided she is going home without this on her mind; she is going to confront the doctor. She walked to the door about to knock and she heard the doctor talking on the phone.

"I just wanted you to know how things went…yes sure, I made sure that she would think it just happened, just like you said to…Dr. Bower, I know your wife and she trusts me, she won't question a thing. She won't question the loss of her baby. She won't know that I aborted her baby for you…"

Sabrina backed away from the door in revulsion. Why did he do it and for her husband? How could he abort Dr. Bower's baby? What kind of doctor does this she thought? He won't get away with it.

****

Michael held Natalie as tight as he could possibly because he is hurting too. Why did this happen he thought to himself? They were going to be so happy together and now…

In the emergency room, Dr. Austin told her that he didn't understand how something like this could happen. There was a little to be concern about but it didn't appear to be serious. There is nothing that, he could do but run test to see what did happened, is what he told Natalie.

Natalie hadn't said a word since they brought her to the hospital room from emergency. She just cried silently to herself cradled in Michael's arms as Mona looked on.

Natalie instructed Dr. Austin not to call Christopher as he insisted he should to do. Mona assured Dr. Austin that it is the right thing to do to give her time to deal with the pain on her own. Of course, that isn't the truth but it has to serve its purpose to give Michael and Natalie a chance to grieve over the loss of their baby.

Michael is being very strong and Mona could see that he is torn up inside. She felt his loss deeply.

He closed his eyes and a tear fell from his eyes down his face. It just isn't fair. What is fate doing to them? Toying with them and making them believe that they have a chance. It's unfair. This whole thing is unfair. He loves Natalie so much that it hurts. She is hurting now and he can't do anything to right this wrong.

Mona watched helplessly while Michael cried with Natalie uncontrollably. She didn't mean to be here to witness this. This is their private time that, they surely needed. So, she simply slid out of the door of Natalie's room and stood guard so they could have their moment.

"I just keep hurting you Michael." Natalie said to him as he still held her close.

They weren't concern that at any minute Christopher could come barging through the door. Natalie and Michael were so far gone in their grief that they didn't care.

"No I don't think that. It not you, this is just one more thing that whatever force is moving against us is doing," He said as he turned her face towards his. "But I won't stop. I won't give up being with you because I know how much I love you. I swear it."

****

It broke Mona's heart to hear his declaration and his pain. Michael truly loves Natalie and he would never want her to feel hurt. Mona closed the door completely this time.

Walking down the corridor from the room Mona felt that she could at least breathe, now. She is only going to take a break and be right back. It is incredible all the tragedies that they have been through lately. JC's death, the attempts on their lives and now the baby; what could be next?

She thought about her life. How she was able to change her circumstances from the life she chose years ago to how she is today. Today she is a respectable VPO, at one of the most prestige pharmaceutical companies in Chicago. She is a woman who is now in real love and looking forward to getting married herself one day soon. That's how Stephen makes her feel. It's very different from her life before when all she cared about was money and sexual satisfaction.

During those days, she would do anything and practically everything that would turn a buck and advance her career. When she started working at Lennox Laboratories, it was the first time she saw a clear path to her future. Although it was illegal, it was a clear path.

However, that could possibly be looked, at in a different light. Many things occurred in those days that she wasn't proud of and if she had the chance to go back she wouldn't do as much. The fortunate thing is that nobody was, caught. They all decided especially in the end that it would be wise to quit and went their separate ways.

Actually, one of the doctors thought that way and they all just follow his lead. He always acted as the leader and even still today.

"Mona, how is my patient?" Dr. Austin asked her, interrupting her thoughts and surprising her.

"She's upset Gellar. My friend is sitting with her now while I took a break." She said to him wishing she could get back to the two of them to warn them that he is coming.

"I was meaning to talk to you when I saw you a few days ago. How have you been?" He asked lowering his voice.

They were feet away from the nurse's station but he still didn't want to be overheard.

"I've been good. Did you want to walk back to Natalie's room?" Mona said annoyingly and dryly.

Why are these people trying to come back in her life? They agreed no contact.

"Not right this moment, let's talk for a few minutes. I heard what happened to Monarch. He was on your team at Cultrax right?"

That is the last straw.

"Gellar, do you remember the phrase 'no contact'?" Mona said coldly.

"That was a long time ago. Nobody remembers us and no harm has been, done. I just thought I would see how you were doing. I thought it would be okay for you and Monarch seemed to not have maintained that agreement. What's the problem, it's just us?"

"Paul Monarch was my friend. He didn't try to throw me underneath the bus when things looked like they were going to get heavy. Not like the rest of your friends and you."

"Hey relax. I wasn't with them on that setup. That was Diana and Kurt. No one trusted those two anyway. Can we forget about all that like we said we would do?"

Mona thought about it for a bit before she spoke. Lately it has been chaotic around her. She felt herself being on guard now about everyone and everything. She has to get herself together or she'll snap.

"I guess. The last few months have been out of control. Plus the fact that Kurt and Diana are now here in Chicago; breathing down my throat."

She wanted to tell him that, to work a theory that she has been brewing in her mind. She finds it strange that everyone that worked at Lennox with her; is now together in Chicago. This seemed like more than happenstance and it appeared to be, orchestrated with her at the center.

There is no going back to that life of crime again. She will be damned if she will allow them to blackmail her into doing anything like that again.

"Really, what's their problem? Of all of us, those two chose to continue their little illegal 'get rich quick' schemes. It's any wonder that they haven't spent any time in prison. My advice to you is to stay clear of them because those two are unscrupulous. They will no quicker have you under their control than it take to have a heart attack."

"I agree. Thanks for the advice. Let me check on Natalie to see if she is ready to see you." She said walking ahead of him.

She didn't want him to walk in and see Michael holding Natalie.

"You did say that your friend is in there with her; a guy right?" He asked curiously.

"Yes, she was in the bathroom when I left and he was supposed to come get me when she came out. So, she must be still in there. I'll check, give me a minute." Mona said to him as she was going into the room. "Hey you two Gellar is ready to come in."

Michael and Natalie broke their embrace and she attempted to get herself together. He just simply stood a little to the side of the hospital bed until he realized that he hovered over her. He backed away slightly.

When it became clear, Mona motioned Dr. Austin in.

"Natalie again I am so sorry." He said as he looked at Michael and wondered about his presence here.

Something in the air just seemed odd to him right now. It hit Gellar all of a sudden. Mona is acting as if she is cover, not upset about the past. Yes, he walked in and there's this staged scene like two little teenagers caught doing something they weren't supposed to be doing.

This is even deeper than he thought. Dr. Bower was too insistent in aborting this child and now he knows why. It may not have been his. He smirked to himself not really listening to Natalie babbling on about her pain.

He's fallen into a goldmine.

Christopher Bower is more treacherous and heartless than Gellar imagined.

He will move heaven and earth not to let this information hit the hospital like a storm, he is sure of it.

He is going to go far.

****

"Are you sure you heard this correctly, Sabrina?" Dr. Bradley Warfield asked her.

"He said exactly that, he did as Dr. Bower said and aborted his wife's baby. He said she will never know the truth." Sabrina said visible shaking.

"Dr. Austin is a slimy bastard but he would never go as far as to physically harm an animal least of all a child. He is an OBYN after all."

He wanted to make sure that he sounded convincing to Sabrina. He knows what she's saying is true because he knows Gellar Austin all too well. He knows that he would do anything for the right price. That's why he's steered clear of him for all these years. Their bad dealings in the past have made sure that he will never trust him.

"I know what I heard. This man kill Dr. Bower's baby and we have to do something about it."

She became hysterical with fright.

"You need to calm down. What we need is proof. We need to have proof before we can take this to the board. We still have an obligation to the hospital to make sure that this thing if it is true; not reflect on the hospital negatively."

"I have proof there was another sonogram that he used. That's the reason why he had me pull that specific file. That woman lost her baby from medical complications. However, Dr. Bower didn't have those symptoms. He gave her some shot during the examination. What kind I'm not sure. Her blood was drawn in ICU."

"Okay that's good. I need to get that before Dr. Austin has a chance to get a hold of it. With that, we can go to the hospital board and we can figure out what to do next. We are going to give that son of a bitch what he deserves." Dr. Warfield said as he looked away from her and smiled.

This is playing right into his hands. This is just what he needed to boost his position in running for the Chief of

Staff position and enact his revenge. Well Christopher guess this is endgame.

Now there's one more thing to add to the coup de grâce.

****

The next day running through the halls of Chicago Memorial, Dr. Christopher Bower went. He moved faster than anyone has seen him move in all the time that he has been at this hospital. Some know where he is going but others did not. The news only just seemingly has been told to him even though, he orchestrated it all.

Staff is all about. Some were crying because of how he looked so despaired. Some were just in shock for the emotions that they've never seen. Christopher made his performance epic.

To him this is just what he needed to ensure that he's, chosen as COS. What could be so alluring than the grief of an expectant father whose unborn child is suddenly lost. Why wouldn't the board reward him with their electoral votes; this after all would ease his pain.

He prepared himself to face Natalie with his surprising grief. After all, he isn't supposed to know anything about this. So, he will have the pleasure of watching his wife struggle as she tries to tell him that she lost their baby; all along knowing that it was her lover's. This may be the punishment she needs to get her back on track to his future goals.

Into Natalie's room, he went and the door closed behind him. She slept as he walked in and she is alone. A tinged of anger swept over him as he stared at her. He moved towards her. She betrayed him and he is going to make her life with him pure hell.

Natalie opened her eyes and bolted upright from the bed. The sight of Christopher attempting to put his hands around her neck frightened her. She shook her head and saw Christopher standing alongside her bed, smiling at her.

"Bad dream honey?" He said to her almost laughing in his tone.

He has to be careful not to express his true feeling of satisfaction about all of this.

"The worst." She answered him.

"I know you are going through a lot right now. Why didn't you tell me?"

"I couldn't...I didn't have time" Natalie said.

She decided that she is going to attempt to be honest with him as close as she can. They weren't what she thought they were before, but she still wants to keep the peace.

"Honey you can tell me anything. Our child was precious."

Natalie cried. She couldn't help thinking what she has caused her life to be.

How did she get here?

By doing what she thought her parents wanted her to do; it set forth these chains of events further from who she really is and her life with Michael. The man that is before her is what she ended up with because she didn't trust in love. She didn't want to take risk. She had no faith. So she cried for all the things she wished she could say to Christopher. She cried for the lost time with Michael.

She cried especially because every time she tries to love Michael something happens to keep them apart and that frightens her. She felt so defeated.

Sensing that this is his cue to further confused Natalie Christopher begins to cry as well. As he bent his head down away from Natalie's view, he begins to laugh; but sounded as if he is crying. Natalie caught up in the feelings of guilt that she has lied to him, stroked his hair. Her guilt has nothing to do with Christopher but she felt conflicted.

"I am so sorry Christopher. I really am."

\*\*\*\*

Get it together, Veronica Lane thought in her mind. Just keep your mind on what you are doing and what you have to accomplish. Your child depends on you and you have to be strong. Ignore him, ignore what he does and most of all refuse him the next time. You don't have to do what he says there is another way.

This is what rummaged around in her head all the time now. This is what she going to face every day for the rest of her career? These assaults from Sebastian Black were not going to happen again. He will be stopped because she has more than herself to worry about; she has her son.

Strength began to build in the heart of Veronica as she thought of how she is going to turn this all around. His abuse of her will discontinue and if not he'll wish that he did.

The rumors that are floating around about him are true. He is a womanizer who will defile anything that he is attracted to and he is a sadist. How did she let him touch her like that and do those things? What was she thinking of when she succumbed to him? Did she think that if she did what he wanted that she would be free of him? That's it, she wasn't thinking. She wasn't thinking that once he conquered her; that he would never stop his abuse. Sebastian Black is evil.

****

It wasn't that she is getting tired of meeting him outside of the precinct, she just felt out of place. Instantly she reminded herself of the first time she was at this precinct. She was, brought in for disturbing the peace charges after her fight with Abigail. She agreed in her mind that she isn't going to lend too much time thinking about this again; but it is always in the back of her mind. She hasn't told him that and she didn't know why.

Everyone has a past is what Stephen told her. He said that the best thing to do is to appreciate the good and own up to the bad. Sometimes people have to own up to the bad with their lives which is something that she doesn't plan to do. That's the reason why she is so hooked on him and she has no desire to go back to work. He is very comforting to her.

Before, she couldn't see herself thinking of anything other than work. Her career was all she could focus on. Especially since she took great strides and risks in the past to make sure that she got where she needed to be. She was the fast moving Mona Daniels and now she's finding out that her desire in life is to be in love. That is such a small thing she thought, but it's a big thing to her.

It took being prey to a criminal and a killer to finally, see the light. Not to mention what happened recently to Michael and Natalie. They were on their way and now this setback. How did Gellar not see this? He isn't the most brilliant doctor she has known but he knows his medicine. He isn't just this fly by night doctor just getting by on luck; he actually knows what he's doing. So again she questions why he didn't know that Natalie was heading towards a miscarriage.

She got out of the car and headed toward the entrance to the precinct. She is going to surprise Stephen and learn a little more about Dr. Monarch's murder.

Once she got to the steps of the front entrance, she looked down the street and Stephen appeared. She saw him talking and walking with an officer.

As the two of them got close enough to her, Mona saw that she recognized the officer. He was the one that arrested her the night she fought Abigail. She instantly turned her head but that made it too obvious so she turned to face them again.

"Thanks officer I'll keep that in mind. Mona hey, I'm sorry I'm a little late. I just got off work." Stephen said as he walked up to her twisting his ring, as usual.

The more Mona sees him doing it the more she thought how obsessed he is with it. She always mean to ask him about it but forgets until she sees him do it again. For sure later, she is going to asked him. Really it isn't such a big deal she thought just annoying a little. It's just a little quirk like the one all people have.

"Hi Stephen, hello officer…"

"Good evening Ms. Daniels, good to see you again." The officer said as he passed by her.

Thank God, he just kept on walking. Now that he has seen her with Stephen; she is sure that he will give him a hard time the next time he sees him. She had better tell him before he's caught off guard. Not that it makes any difference but she felt that she needed to be more honest with Stephen. It's his way almost as if he already knows her. It was as if they had been lovers in another lifetime. She is falling in love and this is new, yet familiar.

"So how do you know Officer Brewer?"

"I've been to this precinct a few months ago. The woman who was stalking me setup my friend's wife and we ended up here. It's a long story but nothing came of it."

"Oh that's what he meant by saying he hopes you don't go ballistic." He laughs.

"Not funny."

"It is."

"Well you and your coworker are laughing by yourselves. Instead of being so funny can you tell me how far you've gotten on the Paul Monarch case?"

Stephen paused and the smile left his face.

"How many times are you going to ask me about that? You know that I can't tell you much about that case. All I can say is that there is nothing new. We are checking all our leads but it seems as though this might be a cold case, with no leads."

"I can't believe that Paul was murder and his murderer could be anywhere in Chicago right now. He could be watching me at this very moment."

"Why do you believe that it's a man? From what I understand because of the type of murder; it was very personal."

"So?"

"It could be a crime of passion; a female, an ex or something."

Mona didn't want to hear that, not again. She didn't want to believe that once again there is a crazy woman running around Chicago bloodthirsty. Because the woman could possibly be bloodthirsty with, revenge to kill her.

"What is the likelihood of two people in same department being murdered around the same time and it not be related?" She asked urgently. "I know that the police thought that Craig McNair was murdered by Kimberly Stanford; but I believe now that it might be someone else."

"Well at the time we only had facts that Kimberly was the last one seen with McNair. They were at the pub that is a few miles away from Cultrax. We don't know that she was at Cultrax the night of the murder because the security footage went missing."

"I know the news reported all that. What else did you guys find out?"

"Not much. Maybe I can introduce this theory to the lead detective on this case and maybe we can get a fresh lead. Who knows the killer may get just what he deserves quicker than he thinks."

"I hope so."

"By the way, I came by your condo yesterday afternoon. I was going to surprise you but you ran out of your building so fast. Who were those two people you were arguing with?"

Mona looked at him with utter fear. This is what she was afraid of her shady past affecting her present. Kurt and Diana are dangerous and she needs to do something to steer clear from them. What can she tell him a police detective that scrutinizes everything? Just tell him the truth.

"They were two pesky salespersons that were nothing but trouble."

# CHAPTER

## SIX

A few weeks later it seemed that after all that has happened to her; Natalie felt that she has lost a little of her dignity. Here she is about to fight over this man with a woman who has become her nemesis over the years. It isn't her fault. This was, thrust upon her and she has no choice but to adjust to the assaults that Sonja is throwing.

Earlier, months ago when all of this first happened it was one jab after another from Sonja until she couldn't and wouldn't take it anymore. It's not her fault that Michael is in love with her and no longer in love with Sonja. It's not her fault they've been in love with each other since they met ten years ago. They have been apart for longer than they should've been under the circumstances. Now is the time to correct this awful mistake before any more time passes.

She taunts their love but Natalie wants her to fear it. She wants her to know that the possibility of her losing Michael is near and it will happen. There is no other way that it should be.

Once she drove up in front of the Montgomery home, she realized that she is going into uncharted hostile waters. She didn't know what to expect as she approached the door.

She pushed the doorbell and waited for Sonja to come to the door. She knows she's home because Michael mentioned it when they talked earlier.

Sonja snatched the front door she opened snappishly.

"Where do you get off coming to my house Natalie?" Sonja hissed.

"Hello Sonja." She said calmly.

"You know you have quite a nerve, coming to my house?"

"May I come in?"

"What? Why?"

"It's really time to clear this up."

Sonja stared at Natalie a bit. This woman is pregnant by her husband and now she has the audacity to show up at her front door. There is no end to this woman's arrogance.

"Just right there." Sonja said nastily, motioning to the foyer's living room off to the side of the entrance.

Natalie sat down on the sofa and Sonja on the adjacent loveseat. The two women stared at each other a while before Natalie spoke. Natalie noticed she is getting a lot of that lately.

"This thing with Michael is getting out of hand. Why don't you simply give him up?"

"Really, you're actually sitting in my home telling me to give up on my daughter's father; my husband to you? Why because you're pregnant? I guess you didn't know that I've known about that huh?" Sonja said trying to ambush her.

That really stung Natalie. She wished she could tell her that yes, she is pregnant with Michael's baby, but that would be a lie. She has barely been able to move on from the death of their baby and Sonja says this. However, she didn't need lies to certify Michael's love for her like Sonja does.

"First of all I'm not pregnant. You want to play the victim but you are definitely not. You don't want Michael. I won't speak on your daughter because she is between you and Michael right now. I won't, at least not until Michael and I are permanently together and that will be soon. You need to worry about sharing custody. You won't win Sonja. Michael is already mine." Natalie pressed with her words.

"I should smash your head now and take my chances in the court. How dare you disrespect me and leave our daughter out of your whorish mouth." She hissed. "I don't believe that you are not pregnant because I heard Michael say that you are; but you can have it your way. I know one thing for sure is that if you don't stop seeing Michael I will tell your husband and this time I'll make sure he believes me. You will have your own custody battle to worrying about."

"Well if you do, I will probably lose my husband; which at this point is not a big deal, but not my girls. I guarantee you however will not have your husband either."

Natalie couldn't believe the way her mind thought right now, but she is upset. This woman has stolen her life and now she sits here unwilling to accept defeat. Michael told her that he loves her and that is good enough for her to rely on. It is a done deal and she is going to fight for him or at least fight to be with him.

"I think that you better get out of my house before I do something to you that will make Michael hate me for life. Though, it won't matter to me because no one is going to condemn a woman, who is defending her home from a deranged doctor threatening to take her husband." Sonja warned her.

"And you think that I'm concerned right now. This is the fourth time that you have threatened me but I haven't seen you make any moves yet."

"Oh sure, I'm going to hit a pregnant woman and end up in jail. You won't get rid of me that easily. Besides, I won't need to stoop that low Natalie. Michael will never abandon his daughter, which means he won't abandon me either; so now you can leave, pest."

Sonja got up out of her seat and walked to the door. She opened it and waited for Natalie to get out of her seat to leave. Natalie got out of her seat and proceeded to the door as well. When she got there, she turned and faced Sonja.

"You know I can't just let you have the last word. I know that Michael is a good father, so you are correct; he would never abandon his child. But he won't have to because remember I love children and unlike you; I will support him in everything that he wants to do." Natalie said with a smile as she walked out onto the cement stoop of the house. She laughed, as she kept right on walking feeling the intenseness from Sonja's eyes in her back.

The feeling mounted in Sonja so much she wanted to scream. She wanted to hurt someone right now and of course, it is Natalie. No, she isn't going to play that kind of game with Natalie that would make her notorious; she liked the subtle approach. What is she going to do?

\*\*\*\*

The next day during a live early morning taping, Michael is backstage as Deena Williams does her opening monologue for her show. They have received solid ratings lately. Michael spent his college life devoted to achieving this goal to be an executive producer. As a bonus, he is the creator of the show as well. *Life Talk with Deena Williams* is steadfastly becoming a bona fide hit and just before the fall season. He has everything to be happy and thankful for.

So, why does he feel so empty?

He couldn't answer it; but he knew the answer. He knew that it is because Natalie's still in pain. He's in pain too but he couldn't think about himself right now Natalie is all that mattered.

It has been a week and a half since she left the hospital and just as long that she has spoken to him. He's been calling her but she hasn't answered his calls. There was no way he was going to admit what he's thinking cause he knows that it's not possible. It's no way she could abandon him and reconcile back with her husband. That is not possible. No Natalie would tell him that.

"Before we welcome our first guest, you know it's time for *Deena's Phone Chat*. In case you're new to the *Deena Williams Show* this is the portion of the show where I have viewers call in with hot topics or for some advice; to discuss.

---Caller you're on the line…

---Hi Deena, I'm so glad to reach you…

---Hi caller what's your name?

---Natalie Stanford…"

Backstage Michael almost fell from his chair, as he instantly knew the name is not a coincidence. There is no way it could be her, Kimberly is at Chicago Mental. It is someone else that he knows. He immediately ran to the nearest phone. He picked it up and dialed the operator.

"Yes. How can I get a phone call traced, now? Yes…"

"----Well Natalie what is your reason for calling?

----I want to know what I can do about a problem I'm having with my husband…

----Ok, what is going on?

----Well it seems that he is having an affair with the woman that use to be my best friend. Well we haven't been friends for a longtime but I just found out that they've been sleeping together. Then just recently, I found out that she's pregnant.

----Oh my, let's break this down…."

****

In his office, Michael finally managed to convince the operator that he needed the phone line the show is using traced. They traced the phone call. They gave him the number where the call was coming from. His stomach felt like a knot instantly pushed in there.

It was from his home number.

****

Halfway across town at the Montgomery's, suburban home. The back door opens and a woman walks out of it. She climbed into the parked car in the rear of the home and drove off.

****

Later on that day at local radio station 95.8 WGBB, Sebastian is in his office. He sat back relaxing before he goes home to his home with Abigail. He decided to move back after Abigail begged him for another chance. It looks like the counseling session with the new quack is working out. She's back to her senses. She doesn't even call herself Ambrosia anymore. He got a moving crew to move him from the condo back to his home in less than twenty-four hours. That made Abigail so happy that she treated him to best sex he's had since Veronica.

The radio program went well today but he's going to have to do something about Veronica. He thought that once she relaxed with a little bit; of his sexual healing, she would be better at the job. Now it seems as if she hates him.

It is nothing that he did. He just simply told her that she has to work harder at her job and that included satisfying him. He surely enjoyed what she has to offer. He knows he doesn't call her Hot Cinnamon for nothing.

This is much easier than what went on with the office temp a few weeks ago. She literally broke down crying at the front desk when she saw him the next day at work. He doesn't know why she was so upset. What did she think would happen after he took her out? He's not into charity or friendly dates. When he takes a chick out she has to give him what he wants. She tried to resist him and he gave her a little extra coaxing the Morning Lover way. She didn't scratch him too deep from her excitement.

She hasn't been back since that day after their date when she broke down in the office; but Sebastian knows how to reach her. No woman stays too far away from the Sebastian experience if he wants more. He always gets what he wants from a woman.

Looking at the time he decided to get going so that he could meet a late lunch date, he recently set up.

As he walked out into the outer offices from his office, he saw Veronica talking to Raina. He winked at her and she turned her head. Raina looked at her curiously and then towards Sebastian until he disappeared around the corner to the main hallway.

"Are you alright Veronica?" She asked.

"Yes. I just can't stand that man." Veronica said almost as if she was going to scream.

"Well at least I saved your job for you."

Veronica looked at Raina. She wanted to slug her in the face. She is such an idiot. She has no idea what she's gone through to save her own job. How dare she say that to her.

"I have to go Raina. I have something to do."

She quickly left Raina standing there, bewildered by her sudden departure.

****

Once the elevator went all the way to the lower level Sebastian walked off it. Then he boarded another elevator to take down to the garage. He rode it to the third parking level. He exited that elevator and walked further down within the tier-parking garage to where he parked his Mercedes.

This is really an inconvenience. His permanent parking level was being painted and repaved. Out of the goodness of his heart, he didn't have the other parkers to remove their cars so he could get a closer parking space on a higher level. To think that some people think he's self-centered.

As he continued to his car, he could hear that there was someone else on the garage level with him. It sounded like a woman from the sound of the high heels. Maybe he should turn around and go back to meet her. That's when he heard the sound of steps closer and then the sounds stopped. He heard the door of a car open up and then he heard a car motor turn on.

He continued to his car. She is probably someone that he has scored with already anyway.

Once he got to his car, he pushed the remote on his keys and unlocked his driver side door. Then he leaned over the open door towards the window shield to remove a parking slip from it. How many times has he told the damn parking attendants not to touch his car with those ridiculous parking slips? He pays monthly so he wouldn't get one. So that means he's getting someone else's crap. Somebody's about to be fired.

In that, instant he felt the hard object hit across his back.

He dropped to his knees from the blunt force and felt the pain of the hit. He became dazed and he tried to turn around to look back. Then came the next hit and then again and again, repeatedly. All Sebastian could think about is that he's being, beaten multiple times until he finally passed out from the assault.

****

"I'm telling you Michael all of Chicago heard that evil wife of yours. Your show is more popular than you think." Mona said to Michael as they drove together through the streets of Chicago.

"I know Mona but it's not that bad. Nobody's going to relate that to me. Deena made sure that she indicated the call came from out of town after I had Shanna slide her, a note. The audience and the whole country believed her. As far as they know Natalie Stanford lives in Denver or somewhere far." Michael said with confidence.

"I still think you should approach her about this. Sonja should not have called your show pretending to be Natalie."

"Well she didn't really say her real name it was a combination with Kimberly's."

"Yeah, yeah, yeah, minor details that's all just minor details. This woman is going to drive you insane. Now you are making excuses for her. Next you will be doing her bidding."

"Not possible."

"We'll see."

"Why are we on this end of town?"

"I wanted to work out a theory that I've been thinking about. Here we are, Chicago Mental Hospital."

"Are we here to see Kimberly? I don't think that's a good idea."

Of all the people in the world, that Michael wanted to see, Kimberly is not one of them. Although he felt sorry for her he hadn't forgot the cruel way she killed JC. She lured him into her grasp; into a false relationship for months and slowly gave him Meth. She reintroduced his addiction to him. Then she killed him while all the time making him think he had lost his mind.

He is not in the mood to see her. He could kill her for what she did.

"Michael, ever since I had that conversation with Stephen about who really may have killed Craig; I've been wondering. Suppose it's someone else that's doing this? What if it has to do with the new drug we developed? Remember Jackson was acting alone before he met up with Kimberly, but he could've had a partner. Someone that laid low until now a male or female. They may have killed him at that hotel. Remember you thought he was murdered. Maybe they attempted to get more information from Paul that he or she couldn't get from Craig. The police and all of us just really assumed that Kimberly did this; but we really don't know for sure. Even Stephen admitted that it could be a possibility that she didn't do it. He did say it could be a male."

"And what do you expect Kimberly to do, tell you the current killer's name?"

"Yes, that's exactly what I expect her to do. Let's go inside."

The two of them went inside of the mental hospital and arranged to see Kimberly. They were waiting a long time until Dr. Murphy approached them.

"Hello, I am Dr. Murphy. I understand you want to see patient, Kimberly Stanford?"

"Yes doctor. I'm conducting a police investigating…" Mona said cutting her eye to Michael.

She knew that if she didn't say that she is with the police they wouldn't get in.

"You are with the police?" The doctor asked.

"No we're…" Michael said trying to get his words out.

"We're detectives, is what Detective Montgomery is saying. I'm Detective Dunn of 2nd Precinct." She said interrupting.

Mona flashed the doctor a badge. She lifted it from Stephen's belongings when they were together at her place. She knew she had to grab it just for this occasion because she didn't want to be, turned away from seeing Kimberly.

"This is a police matter and we could really use your help and Kimberly's."

"By all means Detectives, I'll do whatever I can, but Ms. Stanford is in a coma. She has been for a while now. Somehow, she was given the wrong medication. There is an inquiry going on right now and when we know more so will the police."

"Are you saying someone tried to kill her?"

"No, more like a mistake. So I guess we can't help you…"

"So can we still see her?"

Michael looked at Mona carefully. What is she hoping to find out now? The doctor said that Kimberly is comatose or does she, not believe the doctor?

****

It was a challenge to get through her first day back to work since losing her baby. Natalie got through the workday and greeted each child the way she has ever since she started her career with a smile.

She felt that she could no longer stay at home because that was driving her insane. She knew better than to dwell on these medical things. She is a woman of medicine.

She hasn't spoken to Michael in almost two weeks. She just didn't want to be, reminded of his pain while she is dealing with hers. Is this how it is going to be with the two of them, never speaking about the bad? She didn't think that would occur; but it is strange that the one person that she should have ran to is the person she stays away.

Another reason for wanting to get away from home is the fact that Christopher is becoming increasingly annoying. His constant pampering is too overwhelming and his attempt to be affectionate seems rehearsed. She is glad that she didn't fall for it when he tried to lure her into bed. She didn't want to make that mistake again; because if she is sure of one thing is that she is going to leave him.

Seeing her girls was one of the highlights of her time off. Even though it meant being in close proximity to Christopher, she is able to deal with it.

She looked at the time and it was nearing the end of the workday. There were no more appointments because the office closed an hour ago. This is the time that she would have a cup of coffee with Janice and talk about the latest gossip. She hasn't seen Janice since that day in her office and nor has Janice called to see how, she was doing.

Before her loss, she was determined to get, to the bottom of Janice's strange behavior. This is something that she is going to continue and not let go, not for a longshot. It is clear to her that Janice has been lying to her. She is hiding something and Natalie needed to keep an eye on her.

**** 

Mona and Michael arrived on the floor Kimberly is kept. Dr. Murphy led the way and made all of the necessary arrangements so they wouldn't be, interrupted.

It made her cringe a little as; she walked by some of the mental patients that were being escorted through the hallway. She hadn't realized prior to coming to this floor that she would see as many patients about. She imagined they all would be, locked in their rooms.

As they walked around the corner towards the end of the hallway, Michael thought this is always how it is in horror movies. Why does the room you want to go to always is at the end of the hallway? This is too creepy, creepy.

They continued on their way. They were walking pass a young woman who sat in a wheel chair being prepared for transport. She saw Mona and jumped out of her chair.

"It's her, it's her; I'll kill you. I'll kill you. You took my baby; you took her away from us." She screamed at Mona while trying to claw at her face.

"Mrs. Stevens, stop. Let her go. Stop…" the orderly said to the woman.

Mona fought her off but the woman just kept going at her as the orderly tried to control her.

"I'm going to kill you vile whore, tramp, harlot, trash…you will die."

More orderlies came running to subdue the excited woman. Once the third man joined the other two, they were able to get her into the wheel chair. They strapped her down.

"She's a murderer, a murderer, a murderer, a murderer, a murderer…" She continued to yell and gyrate as the doctor injected her with a sedative and she started to calm down. "You will pay for this…" She said weakly never taking her eyes off Mona. She continued a bit more until she passed out.

"Mona, are you alright? You aren't hurt are you?" Michael asked her.

"Yes I'm all right, just a little bit shaken. I knew we wouldn't get out of here without something weird going on."

"You must have triggered some forgotten memory Detective Dunn, Mrs. Stevens is usually quite docile since she was committed by her husband. Her husband used to be a pharmacist here. They lost their child to some illness many years ago and it drove her emotional state over the edge. She keeps on about some murderous woman and poison. This is really the first time that she's ever associated someone to her psychosis. I'm sorry about that. We have to make sure that this doesn't happen again." Dr. Murphy said. "Do you still want to see Ms. Stanford?"

"Of course doctor." Mona said firmly.

Inside of Kimberly's room, they all gathered. She is indeed, as the doctor said lying in a deep coma state. She laid on the bed as if she was already dead. Michael went nearest to her and looked at her. It is the first time he's seen her since the attempt on their lives nearly three months ago. She looked as though she is full of peace.

"So Dr. Murphy has she ever been conscious?"

"Yes Detective Montgomery, a time after she was brought here from the hospital. She was actually doing quite well until the mishap with the meds."

"Are you her physician?" Michael asked.

"No I'm just on the team; her doctor is still Dr. Janice Edwards."

The two of them looked at the doctor in shock. For Michael it is becoming all too clear what has happened because he knew the other missing pieces that Dr. Murphy didn't know. He was there when a presumably insane Kimberly attempted to gun them down but she couldn't do it. She said she was making her do it. No one else seems to remember that confession but he knows what he heard. Janice was making her; controlling her.

If that were true, that would mean that Janice sent her to kill them. Why would she do that? They barely knew her in college. That is the only thing that is not making any sense out of all of this. What is the motive?

"This is really getting complicated." Michael said.

"What's complicated about it Michael?" Mona asked curiously.

Before he could answer, Janice stirred a little in the bed.

"Michael did you see that, Kimberly moved?"

"I did. She could be waking."

Again, Janice stirred and with her eyes closed, she began to speak.

"Michael, not Kimberly, not Kimberly, Switched," Janice, mumbled groggily. "Still in danger…she will kill again…"

Then the woman fell back unconscious.

"What did she say?" Mona asked.

****

This is her second trip to her car and Natalie is getting very curious as to what she's carrying in the boxes. They looked like files and other important papers that she didn't think were ethical for Janice to take home. It isn't a big deal but because Janice is being so aloof these days; she couldn't be too sure.

It is afterhours at the hospital. The hustle and bustle of the busy day is at its conclusion. Natalie knew this would be an opportune time to search Janice's office. She would slip in the office undetected and hide from her. It would be good to wait until after she leaves if she could. She didn't really know why she wanted to do that but something about Janice is not right. They really, never hashed out what they were talking about to Natalie's satisfaction. It just seemed as if she is playing with Natalie and playing the victim.

If she could find something, no matter how small that would shed some light on all of this.

Janice was exiting for the third time and so she waited.

**** 

At Chicago Memorial Sebastian settled back in his hospital bed and decided that he might as well make the best of it. The hospital staff gave him a little semi-celebrity treatment. Mainly because this is, his second stay here not because he is a semi-celebrity. It's fortunate that he didn't have any broken bones. The assailant took it easy on Sebastian and didn't cave his head in. It is just luck they say that another woman who saw a little of the attack screamed and ran off the assailant.

Once again, in a mere matter of months he is right back at Chicago Memorial Hospital with a few broken ribs and two fractured arms. He is in pain and couldn't for the life of him figure who would do this to him. The police said that he wasn't, robbed and that the assailant had plenty of time to take things before he was run off. It seems to them that it was personal like; some of the other crimes that were occurring in his circle lately. It was just a month ago, that Mona's coworker was brutality murdered in his office. This was aside the murders that, Kimberly committed.

He knows that word has gotten around he's here and he expected to see Michael and Mona; but they weren't here yet.

He hasn't seen his friends much lately. They usually got together every Thursday night to play poker but that has dwindled away. Natalie is the only thing on Michael mind lately. They've gone silent since the death of their child. Mona is just as bad. She may never go back to work and now that she has that new boyfriend, she's been hard to catch up with.

Things have really changed this year with them. He couldn't say that it has just come about because it seems as if the others have written him off since finding out about

Kimberly. Well damn, so the little tart felt a certain way about their night together. She knows she wanted it. Who comes to some guy's apartment in the middle of the night, drinking and not expect sex.

She really turned things around on him, Sebastian thought. Even though she claimed she was there to see Michael, she knew he wasn't there. She placed herself in the situation for Sebastian to make a move on her. Then when she got him hook she wanted to back out. What was she thinking; you don't make a bargain with the devil and then say never mind. Though he doesn't consider himself the devil, really he fashions himself as a Greek god to all women.

He settled back into his hospital bed and thought about the pretty nurse that seemed to be giving him extra care. He wondered if she would be interested in giving him a sponge bath.

# CHAPTER
## SEVEN

The next morning, bright and early, Chicago Memorial is bustling with multiple activities. It rained in the early morning hours just before daybreak and that produced many car crashes in the city. That meant many injuries, whining patients and that Dr. Austin didn't care for. He had gone down to emergency to handle it all. Now he finally has a chance to get a break in his office.

It is overwhelming to Dr. Austin. It's probably due to the fact that by now Dr. Bower should have contacted him with good news.

His life didn't stop. He made the bargain and he expected to be, compensated with some type of career move. It wasn't really ironed out it just was understood that they were exchanging favors. Well Gellar is ready now. Reaching for the phone, he dialed the number to Dr. Christopher Bower's office.

"Yes what is it Gellar?" Christopher said.

He sounded annoyed that the other doctor called him.

"Well I'll be direct. I did what you asked and I'm more than ready for you to compensate me."

"I don't follow you. I said that I would help you and I did. I submitted your name in the hat for Dr. Inka's medical team. He should be contacting you soon."

"Are you serious? I could have done that with my eyes closed. That's not a promotion or some compensation; that is a transfer to a shitty medical team that is riddled with issues. I might as well go back to Lennox." The other doctor spouted.

"Gellar, I did you as much of a favor as I could at this time. If something comes up, I will get back to you…" Christopher said attempting to dismiss the other doctor.

"This wasn't a favor it was a job I did for you. Look, I'm a desperate man right now with nothing to lose I thought you understood that? I see that I have made the wrong move allying myself with you. Maybe if I ally myself with someone that would like to know why the candidate for COS had his wife's baby aborted; I can get what is due to me." He paused and waited for the thought to sink into Christopher's mind.

He wasn't going to give up this chance to make the kind of money he knows he could make by; being in a high-level hospital position. At this point in his career, he wants to push papers and make frivolous decision leaving all that hands on medical stuff to the young.

"Oh I see." Christopher said steadily. "Looks like we need to see about getting you what is due, then."

****

A few hours later in his office, Dr. Austin knew his choice is clear he has to take matters into his own hand. He decided that he definitely couldn't trust in what Christopher Bower said to him earlier.

After the threat, of course that arrogant son of a bastard wanted to cough up some new ventures. Some sounded impressive to Dr. Austin but he couldn't take the chance. He already proved to him that he couldn't be trusted. So, he'll strike a bargain with his old cu padre and see if he can't get his fortune on that end. This man will deal with him in his favor he knows it. Most people who have something to hide will do most anything to keep it hidden in the dark.

Right on cue the phone in his office rang and he quickly picked it up.

"Thank you for returning my call so quickly, Warfield. We have a lot to talk about, the two of us. And oh by the way Diana and Kurt are in town, just FYI."

****

Later Mr. Final sat at alone in his car in the dim light of a garage.

What a stroke of luck to have found out this new information. The more the merrier.

Things were moving slowly but finding out that two more targets have just come to the city, upped up the ante. Two people that have just as much to do with his downfall as the, prime target. His hate for the one who cost him so much is enough to share with those others. They destroyed his life and now he has a game to play so they won't be able to do it again.

He pulled out the individual pictures that he made of each of his intended victims. He scanned them all with his eyes as they sat in a bunch on the front seat of his car. Which one will be the next he thought? It was just that simple as that, pick a picture. Just point or tap and instantly the decision, is made.

Doing just that, he pointed to the picture of the next victim.

Now is the choice of how they were going to die. What operation is he going to perform on them? He has to make it look a little less like a crime or personal hate this time; and more like a random thing.

Definitely, he will have to tie up any loose ends as well.

****

For his second day at Chicago Memorial Hospital, Sebastian is restless. He spent an entire night at the hospital and no one but Abigail and Raina came to see him. Where are Mona and Michael? The two of them haven't even called him. Abagail insured him that she left the message that he is in the hospital on their cell phones, but no calls. He thought that at least first thing this morning they would have shown up.

He isn't sure what is going on but something heavy must be going on for neither of them to call or at least text even.

This is a happy time for Abigail he thought because this is what she wants, just the two of them. Of course, she didn't mind Raina because she knows that she is only a coworker. There is no threat of Sebastian spending too much time with her, but that is Abigail's thinking not his. What he is thinking is that he doesn't want to go to that stupid session with that counselor; that Abigail set up. There's nothing that quack chick can tell him that will help his relationship because; he's going to do what he wants anyway. It's Abigail, which needs to be controlled.

The door to his hospital room opened and he half expected Abigail to come waltzing right on cue. It wasn't it's Mona. She came in with all smiles but he could tell that she is miles away from here. What is going on, he thought?

"My, my big boy you are always in this joint, huh?" Mona said jokingly shaking her head playfully.

"Well this is only time that I can get some attention from my friends. Seems that I didn't get the memo that we don't get together on Thursday nights anymore. My poker game is rusty."

"It's been something lately and I don't know when it's going to let up. You heard about Paul Monarch?"

"Yes that's tragic. I was meaning to ask you about that," he said evenly.

Mona began to feel awkward. They hadn't talked to each other in such a long while that she found it difficult to talk to him. So, she decided to change the subject.

"Who did this to you?"

"I have no idea."

"Well what did the police say?"

"Nothing."

"So you're in the dark?"

"I guess."

He began to frustrate her and she didn't know why. Something compelled her to make peace of this situation, to, just make peace.

"Sebastian come on, this is Mona you're talking to not crazy Abigail. I'm not judging you on anything."

"Okay so what's with the 3rd degree? I said there is no word on who attacked me."

"And I know you're lying. When you lie to me like this that means a female is involve. So this female had her brother rough you up or something?" she said amusingly.

"That's funny to you that I almost got my skull caved in, right at my place of work. You think that little of me don't you?" He said to her seriously.

"Aww Sebastian, basically you have been having nothing but rotten luck lately with women because you don't know how to keep it in your pants. Admit it there's someone at work."

She sounded a lot like Michael. For a minute, he swore he hears him speaking through her. How he can sound so matter-of-factly righteous and of course he isn't.

He thought about what Mona said. He did think that he heard high heels walking behind him just before his mind went blank. Veronica Lane is pissed off enough to do something like this to him so it has to be her. The little slut deserved the humiliation he gave her for being so mouthy. Nobody tells him what to say over the air. He plans to use her once a week until he's tired of her. Then when he's gets bored with her, he's going to fire her overbearing ass.

"Well yeah, there's Veronica Lane."

"The one, that's on the air with you?"

"Yeah that one."

"What did you do to her to piss her off that you would think she would do this?"

"I treated her like a queen, ha, ha."

"You still think that you can do anything to these women these days and get away with it? It's not like the college days when you got away with your abuse. You just barely missed being killed by Kimberly."

"Veronica Lane and all those others were just begging to be with me. They were reluctant, probably shy. I just simply helped them make that hard decision. It's better than sitting around waiting on those twats to cut through all those scruples they think they have."

"Sebastian you assaulted those women. You have to face that fact. You need help. I'm your friend and I care about you. One of these days something worse than a few bruises and sprains is going to happen. One of those women is actually going to do you in."

"You know I'm really tired of your self-righteous bullshit right now. Kimberly is a lying bitch and she is going to get hers for it. And I'm surprised at you. You think that just getting a new police detective boyfriend can change all your evil deeds; well it doesn't. You don't know this but I remember when you used to work at Lennox Laboratories. I know all about the dirty little crap you used to do there and you know what, I never judged you. I just felt like you were doing what you were doing to survive. Just like me."

He wouldn't tell her but where did she think he got his supplies from when he use to peddle his drugs. Detroit was always the best place for that kind of activity to buy and sell. Lennox Laboratories was the hot bed for what he needed. That's where he saw her and where they both share some mutual associates.

"It's not the same thing; you destroy lives."

"And you didn't?"

"To hell with you Sebastian that really hurt," she shot back at him. "I see why Michael is avoiding you."

She wished she hadn't said the part about Michael. Those were her thoughts, Michael never spoke to her about that.

In her own psyche he struck a nerve. What she had to do long ago wasn't her fault, she thought but then again she knew it was. Everything was wrong but she turned a blind eye to, it. All that mattered to her then was her own self-preservation. She has run from her past all these years, even at one time forgetting it all together. However as fast as she has ran in her mind she could never forget Lennox Laboratories.

Sebastian watched Mona dash out of his room and smiled. Next time she'll know if she dishes it out she's gonna have to take it.

Well then, to hell with her and Mic, he thought as he got out of his bed, still in pain. He is tired of being a helpless target for Kimberly, for Veronica; and any other so-called victim. He's going to do something about it. He slipped on his pants and exited the room.

\*\*\*\*

Quickly she moved through the halls of Chicago Memorial not really going anywhere. She just knew she should to get away from Sebastian. She was so angry with him she could have killed him in his bed. What's happened to him, Mona thought? He used to be fun but now he is all wrong. There is something dark about him. It's almost as if that bullet that went in his leg killed him and this soulless Sebastian thing is walking around now.

At the elevator, she pushed the down button to call the elevator to her floor. The door instantly opened up.

"I figured you would be visiting your friend." Stephen said as he exited the elevator and embraced her.

"Stephen." She said as she relaxed in his embrace. "What are you doing here?"

"I came here once I heard the police dispatch. There's been a murder here."

"What? Who?" Mona said gasping her breath.

"Some doctor named Gellar Austin."

****

As he parked his car in a space at the hospital's garage, Michael dialed Natalie's cell number. They have been playing phone tag with each other for the last past two days and that unnerved him. At least they communicated. That showed him that she wasn't trying to get away from him. When they were together last, over two weeks ago it was brief and rushed. It was not enough time to mourn for their baby to get through it together. They had to put on their happy faces and continue without each other. Their relationship is filled with roadblocks because they refused to be selfish people. Instead of just taking their love and making, the necessary moves to be together, they deal with their spouses. Their children are young and they can make the adjustment as long as the stay together. Instead, they play it safe and that frustrated him.

"Michael, so you do still live in Chicago." She joked with him trying to make light of their situation.

"Hey beautiful, what have you been doing lately?"

"The usual hustle and bustle; I'm getting myself back to my daily routine. Sorry I haven't been attentive lately."

"It can't be helped, I know. As much as I want to fill my days with you, I know that we are in something that's just slightly off. All I know is that I can't stop filling my mind with you, Natalie Vincent."

This is what makes it hard when she tries to search her mind for what is logical. She knows that she should not have gone this far with Michael but she has not felt so alive in all her life. If she could reverse it, go back to before they crossed the line to here, she would have made choices that were more logical. It wouldn't have been as fast but right or wrong, logical or illogical it's done and that can't change.

"Michael Montgomery you do know what to say. I fall in love every time I talk to you."

"Here's hoping, beautiful."

This is the way he likes them to be in this enchantment. He always felt more than an ordinary man did; with everything about him, being amplified tenfold when he was with her. He always felt the electricity between them.

"Are you in your office because I'm at the hospital right now?"

"No, I'm away downtown at a meeting. I was on break when you called. It looks like it's going be a late one. Why are you at the hospital?"

"Oh, I'm sorry I thought Mona would have told you. I'm here to see Sebastian. Once again he's taking up residence here."

"I didn't know. Well judging from your humor it doesn't seem to be serious; is it?"

"Well not on the surface, some broken ribs, but who knows. He was attacked by someone with a, bat. It sounds like it was an attempted mugging or possibly a carjacking."

"Are you two okay?"

"What makes you say that?"

"It's just something I noticed."

"Well a lot of things have gone on and I guess I sort of blame him for it. If anything had happened to you I..."

"Michael you can't blame Sebastian for all that happened. Kimberly's traumas happened long before she met Sebastian. What he done was definitely heinous but she was already unstable."

"No Natalie it was him. He was the catalyst to what happened to JC. When he assaulted Kimberly that put us all in danger because, she was unstable."

"Yeah I agree but I think...oh Michael time for me to go back to the meeting. I'll catch up with you later okay. I'll call you tonight. I love you."

"I love you too."

They hung up with each other and Michael suddenly realized he's in the lobby. That's when he saw Dr. Janice Edwards board the elevator and the doors closed. It's now or never that he speaks with her. Her elevator is going up. She is probably going back to her office. He has many questions that he wanted to ask her and especially what Kimberly said; when Mona and he were at the mental hospital.

He boarded the other elevator that opened. He pushed the button to the floor her office is located.

****

"I still can't believe Gellar Austin is dead." Mona said in disbelief. "I just saw him a few weeks ago. How?"

"Someone just slit his throat." Stephen said matter-of-factly.

It registered with Mona, the sound of his nonchalant tone. However, he is after all a police detective she has to remind herself. He must see this kind of thing on a regular basis. Still she wished he could sound a bit more concern for life.

They were standing down the hall, on the eleventh floor. It's on the other end from where the police who have just arrived had cordoned off the area. The place is swarming with officers uniformed and plain clothes.

"Am I keeping you from the scene Stephen?"

"No I've already been in. There's not much to it. It's murder, plain and simple. Right now forensics is going over his office and then the real investigation will begin. You really look shook up, did you know him personally?"

"Yes and no. When I first started my career, we used to run into each other a lot. Enough to know each other on a first name basis; but that was so long ago it doesn't seem worth mentioning."

She felt that's all she should say about the connection between Gellar and she. She didn't want to become a suspect.

"Everything's worth mentioning. When you miss the little subtle things people say and do, you miss certain clues that can make a difference between life and death."

There he goes again, Mona thought. For a man as loving as Stephen, almost to a fault, he can be morbid and cold at times. She was new to the inner workings of law enforcement. Actually, she never gave it a single thought how it affects those who work in it. She is trying to see what could ease that piece of him. It's only because she could feel that he is truly, affected by his job.

"Mona, Mona Daniels?" She heard the solemn female voice from behind and turned.

"Sabrina." Mona responded.

She recognized her as being Gellar Austin's physician assistant.

"I just can't believe the Doctor was murdered. It is so horrific. When I found him, he was laying back in his chair with his head cut open from the top. Portions of his brain were lying over his desk. It was disgusting. His throat was, cut deep. Even being a nurse it is almost too much to take. I almost fainted. Who could have done such a thing?"

Is it Mona or did Sabrina sound a little non-caring about what just happened to Gellar? What is going on with everyone? Why is everyone so cold these days? Maybe it's her. Maybe what happened to her months ago is just starting to catch up with her and making her suspicious.

Stephen laughed in his mind. Suspect number one he thought. This is going to be easy.

"Poor Gellar," Mona said.

"Yes it is terrible, especially the words written all over him. It's just creepy."

"What words?"

"On his forehead it had the word, '**think**' and under his neck '**mute**'. Then on the desk on a piece of paper it read '**I'm closer now**', all in bold black lettering. I heard the detectives say that there were similar homicides like this one at Cultrax. You work there right?"

Mona ignored the question.

"Other detectives, you mean Detective Dunn and someone else? This is Detective Dunn." Mona motioned to Stephen.

"No I mean those two over there." Sabrina said eying Stephen casually, motioning to the detectives that were standing a little ways from Dr. Austin's office.

"Stephen those other detectives, who are they?"

"Mona can I talk to you for a minute alone," Stephen said to her politely while grabbing her arm.

The two of them walked off hurriedly down the hallway. Sabrina watched them closely. She didn't know that he is with the police. Well it doesn't matter, she still said what she supposed to she thought. Sabrina walked off towards Dr. Austin's office. She watched as the coroners brought out Dr. Austin's body.

"Did you remember to put it there before the police came, Sabrina?" a doctor said coming up from behind her.

"Oh, Dr. Warfield, you startled me." Sabrina said relaxing herself again. "Yes I did, but I don't know why it would be important now. His death changes everything doesn't it?"

"It does. It makes all of this much easier than our previous plan. Was that Mona Daniels, I saw you talking to? I have to talk to her."

"Yes."

"Who is that man with her, he looks familiar? Is he another doctor?"

"No he's a police detective."

****

Stephen led Mona into one of the small canteen areas on the floor. She saw the look in his eyes that he is upset; but she didn't know what's wrong.

"Stephen what's wrong? Why did you rush me off like that?"

"You don't know why? It's because you are too causal with the knowledge that I am a police detective. A crime was committed out there and she may be involved. By announcing me, you ruin my chances of ever getting a spontaneous reaction from her again. She was spilling a lot of info. Sometimes a killer will tell too much of a crime scene, when they think they're too clever. I thought I heard her say something that couldn't be known by anyone but someone who has been in that office. I need you to be a more discreet and leave police business to the police. Which brings me to my, next problem with you. Do you know it's a felony to impersonate a police detective?" He said to her seriously.

She looked at Stephen innocently. How did he know what she did? He is truly a detective.

"I didn't know that. I'll be sure to remember that if I decide to impersonate one." She said coyly.

"I'm not joking Mona. Dr. Murphy called the police precinct looking to speak to you. He was shock when I answered the phone. Of course, I heard the story that you and your detective friend visited Chicago Mental Hospital using my shield. I could have you arrested."

"And then who will you have dinner with or share a bed?" She joked.

Then she noticed that he didn't laugh.

"Alright, I get it. Stay in my own lane and out of yours. I was desperate. I needed to know what Kimberly knew and I'm still in the dark. The police are not a lot of help. Then some crazed, mental woman at the facility attacked me. I was surely punished."

"Not as much as you're going to be…" He said to her and she stared back at him confusedly. "Yes, if you keep on playing lady cop. Look I have to go back to the precinct so I'll see you maybe later?"

"You bet, call me."

Mona noticed as Stephen walked off it was in a huff. He still seemed agitated and even more now. Okay maybe she went too far this time but she couldn't help it. Mona Daniels always does what she wants.

****

It took him a few minutes to gather his nerve as he stood in front of the office door, but he has to get some answers. Michael opened the door to Dr. Janice Edwards' reception area of her office suite. He expected the receptionist to be there but no one is in the office. He went to knock on the door that led further back to another office he presumed.

Instantly the door opened and out walked Dr. Edwards.

"Michael Montgomery. How are you?" she said as if she had been waiting for him to enter the office.

Actually she was. She most recently installed a mini camera in her office and down the corridors. This way she could see what's happening around her office. She saw Michael on the monitor as he came down the hall.

"Hello Dr. Edwards, I'm fine."

"Oh you've come to see me that's good."

"Yes, but we've never met."

"Michael you were dating my cousin, Kimberly in college. Yes we never met but I was sure that Natalie told you by now that we are friends."

Kimberly is so thrilled right now, that Michael has no clue that she is not Janice.

"Well Natalie did mention something but no details."

Michael didn't know that this encounter was going to be so difficult. In his mind, he had all of the words that he wanted to say to Janice and now he froze. He didn't know what to say to her. She didn't seem like this conniving sinister psychiatrist that her actions made her out to be.

"Why are you here?"

"I came to talk to you a moment if you have the time."

"I always have time for you Michael." She said as she turned to go back into her office.

Michael shook his head at her candor and followed in behind her. She is real peculiar and confusing in what she is saying. It is almost as if the two of them have a budding friendship.

"So what did you want to talk to me about?" She said as she sat down.

"Who are you?" Michael said not believing that he said it. The words just tumbled out of his mouth.

"I don't believe I understand the question." Kimberly said trying to be coy.

Something about her response triggered a memory or something within his mind. It's a memory of how she was when they were in college. She was always trying to be witty and in control.

"Kimberly."

"What about her Michael."

"You, I think you're her."

"We are close cousins, first to be exact. We're almost like sisters. But I don't have mental issues." She laughed.

It is incredible how much she begin to manifest Kimberly's persona. She did have a point; family can act the same. She certainly looked like the Kimberly he once knew, similar. He couldn't say anything or gather his thought; once again another twist.

"Michael," she said as she got out of her chair and went to her file cabinet. She retrieved something he couldn't see. "Why don't we step back a minute. I want to make sure that you truly know who I am. That I'm not trying to hurt you."

She walked back to her desk and sat down. Then she jumped up immediately and headed to the door of her office. She opened it quickly as Michael watched her. Looking out in the outer office, she went out of it.

He heard the outer door open and close. Michael heard her talking to another woman. He couldn't quite hear what they were saying their voices were muffled. However, the other voice sounded very familiar.

While he waited, he busied himself by looking at the upside down files on her on her desk. He read the names upside down and wondered why she hadn't put them away when he came in her office. Then he felt the pinch on his neck and instantly everything went fuzzy.

****

He isn't quite sure that he is walking but Michael felt himself moving. He couldn't figure out where he was or where he's going to but he's moving, moving down, down. The voice next to him talked to him guiding him but he couldn't tell what the voice said. However, he obeyed the voice. He only knew that the voice sounded familiar. It sounded like Sonja's voice. He just kept moving until his thoughts became so fuzzy. Instantly it felt as if he was falling and then he wasn't; there was a lot of pain, he felt that. It all seemed like a bad dream. When the cool temperature hit his face, everything became, distorted.

# CHAPTER

## EIGHT

It has gotten late and Mona thought that she has spent too much time here at the hospital on the eleventh floor. She was still near Dr. Gellar's office in the employees' lounge, alone. She had thought about going to see Natalie in her office until she found out that Natalie isn't at the hospital. She just couldn't move. She didn't know why she stayed here so long; Gellar Austin wasn't a friend. It's because this is the second person to be murdered that is, connected to her; and it's beginning to look like more than a coincidence. Both Gellar and Paul were a part of the Lennox thing with her and then there's Diana and Kurt. They just showed up all of a sudden and now the murders. Could they be the ones?

How can a murder be committed in the day at a busy hospital?

She didn't notice that someone walked into the lounge. She was lost in her thoughts and didn't pay any attention until he sat down beside her.

"Are you alright Mona?" He asked his voice not really sounding to concern for her.

"Bradley Warfield, you are feeling concern for me?" She asked him in false disbelief.

The two of them have not always gotten along during their time knowing each other. Dr. Warfield has been a doctor at Chicago Memorial for five years now and for some strange reason he is likable by the upper echelons. It doesn't hurt that he's knowledgeable about medicine as well. That's why he's the other contender for the new Chief of Staff position. The same position Natalie's husband, Christopher wants so badly.

Mona doesn't understand it because she knows how he truly is and how money is always an object with him. His greed is only, outweighed by his uncontrollable anger and that Mona has seen first-hand. It's almost uncomfortable sitting this close to him right now.

She suspects that he is only friendly like this because she could blow the lid off his career if she so chooses to. He is another one that was in on what they all did at Lennox. She remembered his protests on everything that they did, however he enjoyed the spoils. He always tried to appear as the outsider of their group while maintaining his allegiance when it came to the money. He even tried not to be linked with them when things almost hit a brick wall and the police were on their heels.

So why this sudden interest to, show this concern for her feelings?

"Mona you have always been what I like to consider a friend. After all we've gone through during our times together at Lennox, I would think you would agree. I'm surprised that we have not connected sooner than this because I've seen you around this hospital on occasion. I guess death does bring people together."

"A lot has changed Bradley and frankly I don't believe you. I don't believe that you are as sincere as you would like me to believe. My memory is not failing me and I remember you as one of the biggest assholes I've have ever met. They don't call you Dr. War for nothing around here. You may shine for the upper echelons, because they don't really know you. The staff that works under you, however knows like I know that you are war in every sense of the word."

Dr. Warfield let Mona's words sink in slowly before he responded. The witch, he thought. How dare she act like she, has gathered a backbone in these past six years. He could squash her in one fell swoop. He truly is, this Dr. War that he knows the grunt staff calls him and they had best beware of him.

"I see that I can't be reasonable with you; as always. So be it. Let me just say this to you. Two deaths within our own little Lennox community means to me that we should be a bit more concern. It also means that we should bond together and pull our resources to find out if we are becoming targets."

"I don't care what you think or what you suggest." She said not looking at him.

The disgust resonating in her voice as well as the fear.

He stood and then stood over her.

"Your problem is just like the rest of your bunch. You were then and you are now; too careless and frivolous. You, especially because you got personally involved with, shall we say our customers. There is too much they know about you."

"Leave me alone Bradley. I'm not interested in your fear infesting tactics. I'm alone and I will remain alone."

"So be it. However, I will issue you a warning you can relay to the others. Keep my name out of your mouths.

Keep your distance from me and stay far away; because I will stop anyone who stands in the way of my success as the new COS. Don't be foolish and think that I will not."

It wasn't what he said that caused Mona to turn and look up at his face. His tone sounded sinister. As she looked into his eyes, she saw a murderous indignation towards her and she felt herself draw back from him. Her heart began to beat fast. He then turned with a devious smile and left her in the lounge alone.

She watched him steadily as he left the lounge and her heart slowed down from beating fast. Mona for first time in her life is in fear for it. Suddenly she began to think in her fear and her thoughts begin to focus on the man that just left her presence.

Bradley Warfield has to be the killer, plain and simple; it is too obvious with his threats and all. He is all but telling her that she should side with him or he will kill her. She has to get the hell out of this hospital and think of what she should do to protect herself; she could be next. He hates her and the last person who hated her almost killed her.

****

It was a few hours later when Mona got home and she decided that she wasn't going make herself available for Stephen tonight. She's had too much of people for today and she doubts that even he could make her feel comfortable. She just needed a good night sleep then everything will be clearer in the morning and she can stop shaking.

Her cell phone rang and even though she thought to herself that she shouldn't answer it, she did anyway. It may be an important call.

"Yes."

"Detective Dunn?" the man asked.

"Yes, why yes how may I help you?" she responded once she realized that it was Dr. Murphy.

"I just call to let you know the latest on Kimberly Stanford. She's dead."

"What are you saying?"

"I said that Ms. Stanford was murdered tonight."

"Why wasn't I called immediately?"

"Our hospital I assumed wasn't in the vicinity of your precinct and that's why the other detectives showed up with the police. I mentioned you and they said you weren't with their precinct."

"Well what did you want when you called my precinct looking for me?" She asked slowly because she was taking a risk by reminding him that he spoken to the real Detective Dunn. She is going to cross that bridge when he recalls that Detective Dunn is a man.

"I haven't called your precinct. I don't even have the number or its location; remember you gave me your personal cell? Is there something wrong?"

"I did…and no, I was mistaken," she said as she recovered.

Why would Stephen lie to her like that? He is probably trying to scare her into not using his credentials as an alias again. He is too clever.

"So how was Kimberly murdered?" she asked hoping she didn't sound as relieved as she is to hear the news.

"The orderly here says that a man dress as a doctor was seen hurrying from her room to the stairway. We reviewed the cameras but we couldn't see his face. He slipped into her room in plain view from the stairway, strangled her and then slipped right back out the same way. He had keycard access to the stairway. Do you want me to send a copy of the video footage to your precinct?"

"No that's okay. The detectives in your district will handle it from here. My portion of my investigation ended when you called me. Thank you Dr. Murphy." Mona said hanging up from the call.

Kimberly Stanford is dead. As much as she shouldn't celebrate a murder, she is glad to be, rid of her. She actually lived in silent fear thinking that Kimberly would break out of the mental hospital and be hovering over her as she slept. This means she will get goodnight sleep, tonight. She thought about calling Michael, Natalie and Sebastian and then thought against it. As much as everyone deserved a good night sleep, she didn't want to stay awake any longer.

**** 

The next morning Mona started the weekend fresh and early after her good night sleep. She started her morning notifications of what she thought is the best news since she was clear of the charges; trade secret misappropriation. She dodged a ten-year sentence and restitution repayment. She didn't do it after all.

Mona called Michael first but he didn't answer his cell phone. She didn't want to call his house phone in fear she may encounter Sonja. She's been quiet lately, since her match with Natalie. No one knows what she been up to lately but Mona is sure that when she does resurface she is going to be a pain in the ass. She called Natalie next and she was too busy this early in the morning at her office to talk. Mona decided to hold the information about Kimberly from her. First, she didn't want to distract her from her patients and second she wants to get her full reaction when she tells her.

She decided to call Sebastian and tell him. She is still a little peeved from what he said to her yesterday. She thought about it however. She felt that they have been friends for far too long to let something as petty as words interfere with their friendship. Once she talks to him, she will tell him how she felt about what he said to her and make him apologize to her and they will be good.

She dialed his number.

The cellphone rang a little and before it went completely over to voicemail, it connected the call, when it was, answered.

"Sebastian, are you sleep or something, speak up." She yelled into the phone.

"Mona, this is Abigail. Sebastian is asleep right now."

Other than Sonja this is another person that Mona didn't care to speak to but she is the lessor of the two evils.

"Oh hey, Abigail, I guess the hospital finally got Sebastian to take his pain medicine? How are you?" she asked trying to be polite.

"I'm fine," she said. "But no Sebastian is tired from walking out of the hospital last night. It took him almost two hours to get home he was in so much pain. Maybe when you talk to him you can get him to go back to, the hospital to readmit himself."

"Oh, okay. Well ask him to give me a call if you don't mind."

Mona didn't wait for the other woman to say anything; she was lost in instant thought. Why did Sebastian leave the hospital last night without being, officially discharged? What did he do to take two hours to get home? Abigail said he got in two hours late from leaving the hospital. Could he have gone off and killed Kimberly? That is more than enough time to pull off what happened to Kimberly. Aww, Sebastian, Mona thought, this is not going to be good.

Michael, she had better call Michael.

**** 

Sitting in Dr. Janice Edwards' office Kimberly sat at her desk crying wildly and she didn't know why. After all that has occurred and her, own personal struggles; is this really it? She didn't think that it was fair that Janice had to die this way. Since she hadn't been killed by the drugs Kimberly administered to her, she has gotten used to her being silently around. Now what is she going to do? She is all alone. No one is, left to care for her. Janice was her last hope.

Who could have done such a thing she thought? Who is responsible? Deep down inside she knew the answer because of the manner of how she was killed, strangulation. She knew of only one person who hates her that much that he would want to kill her, Sebastian Black.

He would do this thing to silence her for the last time and he did. However, he mistakenly killed the wrong woman and he will regret that mistake dearly. She will strike at him tonight and she can hardly wait. It is going to be over, tonight. The rage in her beginning to mount and she began to taste the blood of her bottom lip as she bit into it. When she realized what she was doing, she stopped and began to pound her fist hard. Then her thoughts shifted and she realized that all is, not lost.

At least she has her prize possession and no one will take that from her until she's ready to release it.

****

Later that day Mona conversed with Natalie over the phone. She found it hard to believe what Mona told her about Dr. Gellar Austin. She had just seen him several weeks ago and has chosen to start seeing another doctor. Even though she didn't blame him for her loss she still couldn't quite get pass the thought that he could have done more. It wasn't her way not to be compassionate about his murder but she guessed it has not sunk into her mind yet.

Once Mona felt that Natalie isn't really going to dwell on Gellar's death that long; she told her about what really is the reason for her call; Kimberly's murder.

"I don't believe it," Natalie said in skepticism. "It has to be a mistake."

"No I spoke to her doctor directly at the mental hospital myself."

"Do they know who killed her?"

"No, I don't have any details."

Mona decided not to talk to Natalie about her theory. It was already too much going on and adding Sebastian to the mix might not be wise. He may get nervous and start talking about Lennox.

"Why did he call you specifically to tell you that; that's odd?" Natalie asked inquisitively.

"Natalie you seem to underestimate your best friend all the time. Didn't Michael tell you how we infiltrated the hospital under the guise of being detectives?"

"No he spared me of that because he knew what I would say," she said knowingly.

"Well don't be so hard on Michael, he didn't have a choice to go along with the act. I sort of forced him. You know in for a penny, in for a pound. By the way, did you hear from him today? I've tried to call him."

"No I haven't, not since earlier morning yesterday. He was at the hospital visiting Sebastian."

"Well he didn't make it because Sebastian was all in an uproar. I stayed until visiting hours were over and was at the hospital late, because of Gellar."

"That's kind of strange don't you think, Mona?"

"Yeah it is. Let's give him another call."

****

Sebastian insisted on returning to his normal life even though he is in serious pain. He decided to go out for the evening with Abigail and they just returned home. He pulled his car into his driveway to put it in the garage. He noticed the thick nails on the driveway as his headlights shined of them as it hit them. They were directly in front of the car's path. He slammed his brakes to avoid them.

Damn neighborhood kids, Sebastian thought. All of the money in this neighborhood and these damn kids; don't have anything else better to do than try to flatten tires. The kids didn't like him in his neighborhood only because they always wanted to trample all over his yard. Sebastian Black's property is not a fun park.

"These damn kids. Suppose I drove over all those nails and flattened all of my tires?" He said angrily to Abigail.

"Well how do you know that kids did it? I mean it could have been anybody including an adult." Abigail said, not wanting to start of another confrontation with Sebastian, like earlier.

They were having a simple dinner out. She brought of the fact that they have not been to their first counseling session together. She only wanted to get them back on track of what they agreed on, which was to see Dr. Tanner. Sebastian accused her of trying to make him feel guilty about Mona and trying to control him. That is not true. She only wanted to get their marriage back on track and for him to get help for his treatment of women.

There are parts of his personality that are dark and she sees it. It's as if he has two personalities. The one she sees and the evil one that others see. Before she thought that, she wanted another persona when she wanted everyone to call her Ambrosia but she's passed that now. All she wants now is a happy life with her husband and she thinks she can get that with the help of Dr. Tanner's assistance.

For example, the doctor suggested to her that she talk to Sebastian about his addictions to carry out violence against women. She figures that it would help him to forgive himself. The more he repressed his deeds the more he would perform these acts. She tried to get this across to him and he rejected it and rejected her. Then they fought verbally, explosively. Now it looks like she may have said the wrong thing again.

"Abigail can you do anything else but criticize me?" Sebastian yelled at her.

"Sebastian I think that you have taken this thing too far. Now, I have listened to you go on for two hours now about really nothing, and I'm tired of it. I have been trying to get this marriage back on the right track and all you do is complain. So I think I'm going into the house now. I'm going to take a hot bath and forget about you."

Sebastian watched as Abigail got out of the vehicle and walked up the driveway. She even kicked a couple of nails when she passed through them. He just shook his head. He got out of the car and walked around to the front of it. He cursed as he seen all of the nails that were sitting in front of his car and bent down to pick them up one by one.

As Sebastian picked up the nails he heard a car approaching. Before he could look up, the car jump the curb and he saw the flashing lights heading towards him. Without thinking and only going by instinct for survival Sebastian dove out of the way, landing in the grass beside his car.

The car did not stop and Sebastian really couldn't get a clear view of what kind of car it was. The car, haven't entered on one side of the grassy yard exited to the other side; leaving trails of tire marks through the law as it sped off. Sebastian looked on grabbing his body as pain hit it violently. Abigail came out of the house running towards him to check to see if he was okay and he just waved her off. This is another attempt on his life thought. Veronica Lane is going to pay for this.

# CHAPTER

## NINE

It has been exactly one week to the day since Natalie and Mona spent the bulk of their day last week; trying to get in touch with Michael. It isn't like Michael not to keep in touch. Sure, they had that two-week gap but that was something else. This is very different. Something is terribly wrong and she is getting scared. Natalie chastised herself because she should have thought about contacting Sonja sooner. If anybody, she can shed some light on this. She just thought that she could simply avoid her. She felt she knew what kind of reaction she would get from Sonja regarding Michael. Now however, this has become serious because this is different; and she will be damn if she lets Sonja keep her from finding out where he is.

Mona said that Sebastian hadn't heard from him either; but that wasn't unusual because the two of them seemed to be going through a Cold War. Mona said that was Sebastian's words not hers. What has really been going on is that they've both been busy with their careers and haven't had a chance to catch up with each other. Natalie knows for fact that Michael was at the hospital to see Sebastian the day Gellar Austin was, killed. That was the last time she talked to him. Is Michael, somehow involved? Did he see the killer and the killer did something to him?

She let herself think the worst against her better judgment.

Four days ago, while she was at work she checked the garage to see of Michael's car was still there. It wasn't so it relieved her but only just so.

Where are you Michael, she thought?

****

As he sat and listened to the police officer talk to him in his home, Sebastian couldn't believe what he heard. He thought that the police were coming to follow-up on his complaint he filed against Veronica Lane; for attempting to run him over in his yard last week. Instead, they were asking him his whereabouts on the night that Kimberly Stanford; was murdered at Chicago Mental Hospital.

It pissed him off that they would even ask him. It took away from the enjoyment he wanted to feel about her death. If you asked him, the psycho got what she deserved running around Chicago killing people. She killed JC without a second thought. What did she expect would happen to her?

Even though he didn't commit the murder he would have gladly did it himself if he thought of it. Also if he thought he could get away with it.

He looked over at Abigail who has been quiet the whole time the officer has been there.

"It's just incredible that you guys can come to me with this ridiculous allegation. I was nearly killed twice and does anyone know about that?"

"Mr. Black we are only acting on a tip. You did just leave the hospital that night without being, officially discharged. There's the two hours timeline that you said it took you to get home. A timeline that was verified by your wife before we talked to you. That calls for us to investigate. If you factor all that in together you would expect the same thing. You do have prior history with the decease. As for your attacks, we've been working on that Mr. Black but each time you were unable…well let's just say it's a lack of information. However, we are doing the best that we can. We'll have to get back with you on that."

"This is what I pay my taxes for? Well am I going to jail or are you guys through questioning me? I know, you will you wait until I'm dead and then I'll get some help."

"Sebastian, please," Abigail said chastising him.

"Mr. Black, someone will call you tomorrow to get an official report," the police officer said as he walked towards the door of the Blacks' home. "And we'll have a car come by frequently for a while."

"Sure, like hell."

"Thank you officer and have a good evening." Abigail said to the police officer making up for Sebastian lack of courtesy as she walked him to the door.

Once the officer went out of the front door Abigail turned to see a disapproving Sebastian glaring at her.

"One of these days you will get a backbone. I hope I live to see it." He said as he walked away.

****

This will be third time Natalie has come to the Montgomery home. The first time she never went inside. The second time she came here, she thought it would be the last but here she is again. She dreaded ringing the doorbell because she really didn't have any patience for Sonja's antics.

She waited once she rang the doorbell not really knowing that Sonja is even home. Then she heard the shuffling from inside.

"Oh come on. You've got to be kidding." She heard Sonja scream on the other side of the closed door.

However it opened and there stood Sonja.

"You've got your nerve coming here again. You have got to be either, the boldest woman I have ever met or just plain stupid; or are you hard of hearing? I thought I told you I never wanted to see you here again, ever." Sonja said contemptibly.

"Sorry, I don't recall," Natalie, said not resisting displaying her disgust for the other woman as well. "However this is important and once you answer my question I will leave and definitely not come back."

There was an awkward silence and then Sonja motioned Natalie inside the house.

"Make it quick. What do you want?"

"Where is Michael?" Natalie asked reluctantly.

"I knew it," Sonja screamed. "I knew you would do something like this. You are a witch."

"What are you talking about? I just asked where Michael is."

"You know damn well where he is. He's been with you all week tramp and I am tired of it. Not only does he run off with you; abandoning me but he's also abandoning our daughter. Did the two of you ever think about that, huh?"

"Sonja," Natalie screamed. "Calm the hell down. I don't know what you think but I have not seen or heard from Michael for a whole week. He was at the hospital to see Sebastian and called me, then that was it. Michael is missing."

"No he is not Natalie. You know you're becoming a big filthy lair as well as trashy home wrecking slut." Sonja said as she walked over to the small desk they keep at the entrance.

Natalie kept her eye on Sonja just in case the woman tries to strike at her with some object.

"The next, time the two of you plan a getaway make sure you talk it over so that the lie will be straight." She said as she handed a piece of paper over to Natalie.

Reluctantly, Natalie took the paper from her hand and began to read it in her mind.

*·Sonja I can't stay here anymore I got to follow my heart. We are not good together. I'm going out of town for a little while to get my thoughts together. I have taken a leave of absence from the station. I don't know how long I will be. Everything will still be paid so don't call me about that because I won't take your calls, Michael.·*

"All this made you believe that he was out of town with me? What a dumb…Michael is missing Sonja, get it through your thick head. You need to wake up and call the police. If you don't I will."

"Get out of my house lair. You and my husband can go to hell. I'm glad he's gone, it will save me the problem of throwing him out." She said to Natalie as she opened the door for her to leave. "If you come back here I will do something to you that you won't like."

Walking out of the house Natalie just shook her head. Could Sonja be that jaded by her hate for her that she doesn't see the truth? Michael is missing. He could be…no she isn't going to think about it as she burst into tears. She is beginning to feel the full affect the something terrible is going on and she felt helpless.

She got into her car still, teary eyed as she dialed on her cellphone.

"Mona," She screamed. "He's gone. Something is wrong. We have to go to the police. Tell Stephen please. Help me."

****

The next day Natalie sat in her office in a trance. She probably shouldn't have come in because she was still upset. Michael could be dead and everyone is dragging their feet to find him.

She ended up going over to Mona's last night and Stephen was just getting there when she arrived. Instead of Mona, she was the one who told him the run-down of the week and how she determined that something is wrong. She spoke of the note that Sonja let her read and her reluctance to believe that Michael is missing.

Stephen told her that he would take the report and someone would get on the case soon. In addition, he would personally go out to the Montgomery home and speak with Sonja. Natalie felt better and it eased her mind a little. She still didn't know what's up with Michael. She will remain this way until she physically sees him again.

The phone to Natalie's office rang and she pushed the speakerphone to answer it.

"Yes Kelly."

"Dr. Warfield is here to see you."

"Bradley Warfield? Yes send him in."

Natalie didn't know what to think of this visit. The great Dr. War wants to see her and she couldn't imagine what it would be about. She knew it didn't have anything to do with Michael because he doesn't know about that; at least that's what she thinks.

"Natalie, how are you?" Dr. Warfield said pleasantly as he walked into her office.

"I'm good Bradley. Just a little puzzled as to what brings you to this side of the hospital today." She said evenly.

They weren't really that aquatinted and from what Natalie knew of him she didn't really care for. He is pompous, arrogant and disrespectful; sort of like Gellar but she overlooked him because he was a friend.

"Well Natalie, I know we have not been in the same circles of this hospital, but I do value you as an excellent doctor. I look forward to working with you in the coming days once I'm Chief of Staff."

Wow, Natalie thought, talk about a two-headed coin. She didn't think that she would ever meet anyone more arrogant than Christopher. She hasn't thought about the COS position for a while. They were both covenanting that job.

"Well I wish you all the best, Bradley. Now before I get called away."

"I think when I discuss this with you; you will have to clear your schedule for a few days. This is very disheartening."

Natalie didn't say a word. She just listened to his tone as he told her of what Dr. Austin did to her. As he spoke the words, she kept looking away from him. She was trying to resist the thought that Bradley Warfield; somehow enjoyed telling her this painful story about how Gellar Austin killed her baby. It is incredible and very heinous but something told her deep down in her gut that it's true. The sickening feeling almost overwhelmed her as she thought about how she never really believed that her baby's death was natural.

It was the tone that Gellar often used that, betrayed his true feelings; that he was amused about what happen to her. There was no remorse that, she saw in his eyes either. Now that she has this to consider she could see why all this made sense to her. Why did he do it? What did he have to gain from this?

The more she questioned her mind trying to get a rational reason why a prominent doctor and close colleague would; abort the child of another doctor is beyond her. She is angry and it is a good thing that Gellar is dead for his sake.

"Why did he do it?" she asked silently.

Dr. Warfield watched her carefully. She is where he needed her to be at this moment on the verge. However, he could not divulge the whole scenario or she will drag this hospital down with her vengeance. He needed the hospital to be pristine when he takes over it.

"It's not clear what the motive is yet however he wasn't acting alone; and the identity of that person is not known."

"I need to see what evidence that you have that Gellar did this. I can't believe that he…" She paused.

The flash of the last examination before the she lost the baby came across her mind. She wasn't thinking straight but that thought is, embedded clearly in her thoughts. She found herself lately going over that day trying to figure out what happened to cause the miscarriage. She thought she lost the baby because of her argument with Janice. She never told Michael that she went to see her because she didn't want him to blame her for all of this. Even though she knew that, he wouldn't outwardly, but she didn't want to deal with the blame she would eventually put on herself.

It was Gellar after all. The shots and the ultrasound pictures; Sabrina was right they did belong to another woman. How stupid she was to just go along with that quack? She is a doctor for God's sake. How could she have let her guard down so low to go against her better judgment?

"Natalie I'll provide you with anything you want." He said as he left her office.

Natalie turned the chair she sat in around to face the window that is behind her.

Then she just cried.

****

Dr. Warfield emerged out of Natalie's office into the corridor very pleased with himself. He wanted to feel passion for the woman but he just found himself pitying her. She is after all weak. She's not aware of the agendas that go on in this medical community and what is needed to be on top. There is always a lot of money to be made and of course the prestige. How could anyone resist prestige of being the one that makes the decision whether you live or die?

"I told Kurt that I saw you come this way. You move exceptionally fast for a man of your age." Diana said playfully walking up from behind Dr. Warfield.

Diana Martin he thought and Kurt Brenner has to be with her. He didn't readily turn around electing to stage an attempt to be in control of this confrontation that he knew would be, eventual. Once he placed enough time in between Diana's words and his reaction he turned around.

"Bradley Warfield, man you are a sight for sore eyes as they say." Kurt said mockingly.

"Diana, Kurt. What brings the happy couple here to Chicago Hospital?" He said in response trying to be cordial.

"We are trying to get the old gang together for a reunion..." Diana said aloud then being, cut off by Dr. Warfield.

"Keep your voice down. This is a hospital not the busy streets." He said aggressively grabbing her arm.

He could really care about the acoustics of the hospital; he didn't want her to be overheard.

Kurt went to separate Dr. Warfield from Diana's arm. However, the doctor removed it before he could fully react.

"As I was saying," she said in a lower voice. "We are trying to reconnect with our friends. There's lots of money to be made here in this gleaming city and by the looks of it, the four of you have been doing excellent in your new lives. We want to be a part of it, Kurt and me."

"You want to be a part of death?"

"What are you talking about Bradley?" Diana asked.

"Yeah what kind of scare tactic is this; you have so many." Kurt blurted out.

"Well it seems the two of you have maintained your position as the dumbest of our sextet. Let me spell it out this way. It may have been better if you two had stayed in bankrupted Detroit instead of trekking all the way over here to Chicago to be murdered."

"Does everything with you have to have a buildup? No one wants to hear you hold court. What, the hell are you talking about? Why would we be, murdered coming here? Are you threatening us because if you are I..." Kurt said to him as a warning.

"Are you ready for it? Paul Monarch and Gellar Austin are dead ta-da. Murdered in cold blood at their workplaces and you two are next." He laughed.

"What...? What are you saying? Mona didn't say a thing to us. When did this happen?"

"Kurt my friend, Mona Daniels detests us all and it's no wonder why you two weren't told. No one wants to be, bothered by you. She was probably hoping you would get murder next and you will. You two are so predictable a random amateur killer can catch you off guard."

"Not too much of an amateur that we don't know we have an ace-in-the-hole named Dr. War. He's our meal ticket to fly." Kurt mocked.

Before the other two could react to his attack Dr. Warfield slammed, Kurt against the wall with a hard impact. It caused a nurse from the opposite end of the hall to look down the hall towards them. Diana put a hand on his shoulder and he turned to look at her. Dr. Warfield released Kurt and backed off slapping him playfully on the cheek a couple of times while grinning.

"You presume too much; the both of you." He said looking at Diana then back to Kurt. "Don't stand in my way and don't threaten me again or you may just be next." He said staring intensely into Kurt's eyes. "Don't contact me again."

Walking off Dr. Warfield punched the wall with his fist as Diana and Kurt looked on. They were in shock.

"So what do we do now, Kurt?"

"We'll find a lessor target to control. This one's a killer."

# CHAPTER
## TEN

How could it get any better? Christopher still couldn't believe his fortune as he held the gold name plate in his hands. This is a sign that his road is paved in gold with the, Chief of Staff title newly engraved on it. Now that Gellar Austin is dead, he didn't have to lift a finger to do anything else. All the loose ends are tied up. It's great news. Just before his death, Gellar threatened him that he would reveal what they had done. That was a definite violation of the agreement. Well you know what they say about karma.

He is in his office working on his document. The board is going to announce their choice soon and he is sure it will be him. He just had a few more paragraphs he wanted to add to his acceptance speech. The board always wants an elegant and brilliant speech when a position is, selected. It will be in front of the entire invitees and he wants the boost a good speech would bring him.

His office door suddenly opened quickly and it shocked him. After all, when people are allowed in his office it is usually after they've been, announced.

Natalie knew as she abruptly walked into his office that Christopher wanted all visitors to be, announced. This is one more of his rules that he always seemed to enforce. It is a rule she felt didn't apply to his wife. She is not in any mood to appease his silly whims any longer. They are coming to a head, he and she and it is time that she told him that. It no longer matters that she is the wife of the prominent Dr. Christopher Bower. Now she has additional new evidence to why Gellar Austin purposely aborted her unborn child to further his career.

"I'm busy Natalie." He said to her seriously, not really looking up to acknowledge her fully.

"I know Christopher I am too. I'm busy trying to figure out how I'm going to make you pay for what you've done."

That caused Christopher to pause what he was doing and look at her more intently. What does she know he thought?

"I have been nothing but attentive to you while you were going through what you were going through. I helped you get back to your regular life." He said, his voice beginning to betray his concern.

"That's really funny right, your unusual concern. I found it strange, very strange that you would do that being as busy as you say are and all. Also because of how selfish and self-involved you are. I didn't really get the answer until Gellar was murdered. There it was the answer. Why would Gellar Austin who I've known for a while now want to kill my child? Well like everything else that goes on in this hospital, you are involved. Gellar had a selfish need and you have what he needed."

"I don't follow you Natalie."

"Come off it Christopher the jig is up and so is our time together. As angry, as I am about the baby, I am happier; I'm done with you. Michael is right, you don't care about me," She blurted out that too quickly because she didn't intend to say all of that. However, it is out now. What else did she have to lose anyway? "You only care that you can live through me. I'm what makes you who you are 'the perfect husband'. Well what would the fans of the great Dr. Christopher Bower, COS think about a husband that would have a baby killed?"

"This is insane. I knew you were having an affair. Even though that baby could be this Michael, I stood by you Natalie. I could have blown you out of the water but I didn't. I don't know what you're talking about."

"Christopher, your time is up! Gellar Austin kept his plans written down. Your name is everywhere in his notes. It's taking all my strength not to throw something at you right now. What you did is heinous and I will see that you are punished. First thing, I want you to leave my house and second, I want a divorce with full custody of my children."

"What? I'm not leaving. You leave; you're the one having an affair. But you leave after I'm selected as COS." He insisted.

"Excuse me that wasn't a request that was a damn directive. You will do what I say and by tonight or I will be in the Chairman of the Board's office at the crack of, dawn. I'm sure Mr. Markell will be interested in what you've been doing in the name of this good hospital. I should have you arrested and sue this hospital. All I want to know is why did you kill a child that could have been yours? What father does that?" Natalie raised her voice at him trying not to get blindly upset.

Christopher didn't dare speak another word. Of course, he wouldn't tell her an answer to her questions. He has to have that COS position even if it means the end of his marriage and giving up his daughters; they can adjust. He has worked hard all his life for this position. This is what his father and his two uncles became during their time as doctors at their hospitals. His father always pushed him in the direction of the medical field and it paid off. He always told him that it would be rewarding to him if he succeed in this. It will be more rewarding than having a family and friends. It will and it can. The Chief position must be his.

When he didn't say anything else, Natalie turned and walked out. Mission accomplished she thought to herself. When she opened and closed the door to his office, she realized that she has just freed herself and her life is now beginning. However, she will never forget her baby.

It was clear that she needed control over her own life before she lost her mind. She wasn't happy and she didn't care anymore about what is right for others. She did what she should have done when Michael came back in her life and for doing it, she is happy.

****

Later at Mona's condo she has unexpected guest.

"Why are you here? I have warned you two. I am not interested in your schemes." she said to Kurt and Diana as the stood boldly in her doorway once she opened the door.

"Mona why the hostility. We only want our fair chance to get on our feet like you?" Kurt said playfully. "Yes we know that we all did agree that when we stopped our little businesses; we would stop communications. We did it to prevent the law from catching up with us and tying us all together; but that has changed. Paul and you were close colleagues before his untimely death. You work at the same hospital as Gellar and then there's our resident Dr. Psycho Bradley Warfield. So really you are all still close knit, so why not Diana and me?" He reasoned.

They were beginning to wear her out. She is after all supposed to be recuperating after her false criminal arrest ordeal and now she has these deaths occurring around her again. It's too much.

"I don't care that you have done your homework. So what, everyone is working near each other. Unintentional circumstance led to the reason why the four of us ended up like that. It is an unintentional circumstance that I will not be repeating; get loss losers."

"Everyone seems to keep telling us that. However you don't seem to understand what we know will hurt each and every one of you." Diana interjected. "All we want is a guaranteed position at your company and we will stay out of your way, Mona. A piece of the pie sort to, speak."

"No Diana that is out of the question," Mona responded simply. "You two don't like to play by the rules; even when it's imperative to do so. You take too many risks and it's just not worth it. You can threaten me with exposure all you would like, but I've seen the inside of jail twice this year and I'm not trying to do a third repeat performance."

"I don't think the stature of limitation is up on the crimes you've already done. Shall we all just step into the light together?" Kurt said disturbingly.

"Whatever."

"I know you Mona all too well. You clean up very well but under the right circumstances, you'll step back down in the mire again. It's all in the right job, so cut the act. Let us in."

There was no reasoning with these two. They were determined to bring nothing but trouble to Mona's already troubled life. She didn't need any help in that department, not with a missing friend and another friend experiencing brutal attacks.

****

Christopher sat at his desk on his computer in his office. He searched the hospital database profusely and still couldn't uncover what he is looking for. He has to find it because he didn't trust Natalie in the state that she's in right now. Her nerves will probably get her to do all sorts of things that will mean the end of his career. Whatever nerves have empowered her enough to admit that she is having an affair, are dangerous. He is sure that she didn't want to do that but her temper got the best of her he guessed. Where is that damn file?

He didn't notice the door to his office opening quietly. His back turned from it. His attention focused squarely on the computer screen in front of him. The man dressed as a doctor came walking up behind him not making a sound. He reached into his pocket and fished around a bit before pulling something out with his hand. He held in his hand the object that he retrieved from his pocket.

"What you're looking for is not there CB, my boy." Dr. Warfield said sarcastically to him.

Without turning around Christopher turned off the computer screen. He got up from his chair and walked around his desk to confront Dr. Warfield.

"Don't you ever knock where you go?" Christopher said. "You know you just cost my physician assistant her job."

"Aww calm the hell down CB. I told the old girl to take a break. I'm sure she's in need of one the way you go on about these days. What the hell is wrong with you anyway, you act like you committed a murder."

"What do you want Bradley? My time is valuable and I don't appreciate the thought of wasting it here playing testosterone games with a, has-been doctor."

"I guess you're entitled to your opinion, but I'd be careful if I were you. It's not every day that you get to step out of line with the new Chief of Staff at Chicago Memorial."

"Bullshit the board wouldn't be that careless as to select a uncover criminal to head their hospital. We both know about that."

"I wouldn't be so quick to speak out of turn sir." He lifted up his hand, the one that held the object he retrieved from his pocket. It was a flash drive. "You might want to take a look this. You can keep it. I have a ton of these things lying around. I lost one, though. It may just have fallen in Mr. Markell's office when I was there last."

"Get the hell out of here, Bradley before I forget that I'm about to be the new COS."

****

"What part of no don't you two understand?" Mona yelled at the two people at her condo. "I've asked you two to leave twenty minutes ago and you just won't move. Do I have to call the police?" She threatened.

"Would you like to use my cellphone?" Diana said handing it in her direction.

Before Mona could answer Diana, her doorbell rang and she got up to answer the door.

"Hey beautiful," Stephen said to Mona cheerfully when she opened the door. "What's going on?"

"Hey you're, right on time. I was just about to call the police."

"Why, what's happening?" He said as he stepped inside her condo and scanned the room.

Kurt saw Stephen's face and instantly bolted out of his seat. Diana followed right behind him. They have been together far too long for her not to read the silent messages that he sends her. If he moves, she moves.

As the two of them passed by Stephen quickly, Diana caught a glimpse of him and quickly scurried to catch up with Kurt.

"Kurt isn't that Dun…"

"Yeah keep it moving so, he doesn't recognize us." He said cutting her off as if the words themselves were slowing them down.

Inside the elevator, Kurt scrambles to close the door.

"Come on, come on, damn it close, elevator door, close."

****

"Those two again Mona, what are they doing here, again?" Stephen said to her sitting down on her sofa and playfully twisting his ring in a circle around the finger it was on.

Mona watched him as he sat down.

"Well they seemed frighten of you. Do you know them?" she asked suspiciously.

"I did ask the question first you know. It's alright though. I'll give you a minute to come up with something to answer with. In the meanwhile, I'll answer your question. I think they were part of a group we busted on a sting operation; I did while I was undercover in Detroit years ago. They're from Detroit right?"

"Yes." Mona said slowly. What group is he talking about?

This is just what she was afraid of happening. Kurt and Diana are bad news and now Stephen is going to ask her how she knows someone like them. What she is going to say, she thought as she began to panic. Visibly he noticed that she was panicking.

"No I'm mistaken they were assisting with the case. That's right they were reluctant to do it. They backed out at the last minute and caused the operation a few costly setbacks. They're not really liked by the Detroit Police Department for that. A couple of characters." He chuckled.

Mona was relieved in a way. At least he didn't know them as being criminals and now her connection to them could be anything she wants them to be. She's always protected by, a thin line. How long will that last?

"So your turn," He said.

"We went to college together the three of us and they are here soliciting a job from me. I know how unprofessional they can be, so I don't want to help them. I have a reputation to be concern about especially after the false accusations. So they've been sort of pressuring me, showing up here unannounced."

"You need me to take care of them?" He said trying to be sincere but it sounded strange to Mona.

What was he going to do break their legs?

"No, I think I can handle it."

Stephen looked at Mona attentively. In his mind, he became suspicious. It's more to why Kurt and Diana are here in Chicago now. Why do they really come here to Mona's home? They could be real trouble and could mess things up him with her. He may have to do something anyway and to rid Mona of them.

With as much beauty she has, she also is very cunning. He of course knows she is lying but said nothing. It wasn't necessary because it just went along with the territory. He knew how she was when he first met her and of course, their time together now has seen no change. He's somewhat partial to the way she behaves, it makes her more attractive; and it makes the hot pursuit worthwhile.

He chuckled to himself at that last thought.

****

"Does the word pest bring to mind the way I feel about the two of you, Kurt?" Dr. Warfield said through the phone.

Kurt called him from the cheap hotel room that Diana and he were staying, at. It wasn't the best accommodations but it is all that they allowed themselves to spend right now. It is until one of these former collaborators of theirs cut them a break. It has been an hour since they returned from Mona's with another angle to their scheme.

"I'm serious we should meet. Things are not right." Kurt said desperately through the phone.

"What things?" he asked impatiently.

"We have to get together to talk about the past and some people from our past. You know the last job Dun…"

The phone line went dead on the other end. Kurt looked at the phone and cursed. This man is incredibly stupid as well as bull headed.

"What Kurt?" Diana asked.

"The asshole hung up the phone. Shit, shit."

"Maybe I should go to the hospital alone, to his office and speak to him. He'll listen to me. He always does."

"Yeah only because you entertain that bastard's attention. Go 'head see what you can do. I'll wait here."

"What do you want me to tell him?"

"Everything."

# CHAPTER
## ELEVEN

It didn't take her long to get to the Chicago Memorial hospital. After she looked up the location of Dr. Bradley Warfield's office from the onscreen directory in the lobby she headed hastily there. It's late but she knew that he is still in his office. At least she would take the chance that he is there. She knows he's trying to be this big thing at this hospital so he's pulling in a lot of late hours. That is his usual MO when he wants something more than life itself.

This was really, funny the way that everything ended up. How before it was Bradley and she that were an item not Kurt. She knew of that running joke that the others used to whisper behind her back; that she was 'everybody's girl'. She however didn't care; she knew that wasn't the case. Bradley Warfield loved her and she had loved him, once. They were great together until Kurt decided to be the competition and she blindly fell for it. Bradley and him became instant rivals and mainly over her.

The two of them never got along; always being on the opposite side of everything that the group did. Neither of them were ever right, often times having to rely on the others to get their schemes done right. However, if she had to chose, if she had a choice, it would be Bradley Warfield easily.

As she got off the elevator to the correct floor, she was surprised how she could move so easily throughout the hospital without arising security. As late, as it is there were still administrative staff working and moving about. No wonder it was easy for someone to come here and murder Gellar Austin leaving no trace. A flash of fear came over her and she reminded herself that she could just as well be in danger as Gellar was. She has to be careful.

She arrived at Dr. Bradley Warfield's office door and she knocked. It's a private office that, he didn't practice out of just his regular office. She tried the doorknob when she didn't get an answer and found that it is unlocked. She paused a little before she walked in not wanting to enter on a murder scene and definitely not wanting to surprise a killer in the act. She continued to walk in. Inside she found the place empty.

Bradley isn't here.

Then she heard someone inside the other room of the office.

\*\*\*\*

It was a mistake to allow Diana to go to the hospital alone. They should stick together while this supposed killer was about. He is after all of them Kurt is sure now. He figured it out too late to warn Diana and her prepaid cellphone was asking for an update of funds. It took a minute before he could transfer the funds over to her cellphone. Now she isn't answering her phone it went straight to voicemail.

He got up from the bed to put on his pants and shirt. It's best he did that because he has to be ready to go after her soon.

Then he heard the knock at the door. The hotel that they were staying at is the lowest of the low, on the west side of the city. No one knew anyone were there, so he didn't understand the tense feeling he is experiencing.

He made his way over to door slowly and opened it. There was no one there. He stepped out into the seedy hallway then looked both ways and saw nothing. Someone did knock on this door. Relax he, thought to himself. It was probably somebody at the wrong door. It did take him a minute to get to answer the door. He went back inside the room and then decided to go see about Diana.

****

Diana is sure she heard the noise coming from the other office space. It must be an adjoining space that the hospital gave the famous Dr. War. How could she not be, drawn to that power again? She is so happy that she would have this chance to be alone with him. Something might just happen. They could reunite. Then Kurt, what will happen to Kurt.

****

He was outside now walking to the train station. Taking public transportation has really put a hitch in many of the strategies that Diana and he planned. He should have rented a car. They had some cash stashed back in Detroit; the money they agreed not to touch until they scored again. It'll take a little time to get to the hospital like this so he looked for a cab.

Blocks ahead up the street, outside of the train station entrance, he looked at the empty taxicab stand. It isn't that late a cab wasn't readily available but who is he fooling. This is the shadiest side of Chicago; he would be surprised if he saw a working, city transit bus.

Only a few blocks away from the train station Kurt realized that it is taking too much time. Diana could be in big trouble by now and he risks her safety by letting her out alone. He has to get to the hospital quick.

Right on that thought a taxicab drove pass him and he flagged it down. It was up a block when it stopped so Kurt had to run to it to catch the cab.

He got in the cab and the driver spoke to him.

"Where can I take you," the cab driver asked Kurt.

"Chicago Memorial, I'm sort of in a hurry."

"Yeah I get it. Sometimes you don't get that much time."

**** 

As she approached the door, Diana thought that she should at least make a noise. That way whoever was there would, reveal themselves. She grabbed the doorknob when a woman emerged from the opened door. She looked like she was relaxing or something. She is dressed in casual clothes.

"Oh hello; I was looking for Dr. Bradley Warfield." She said to the woman.

"Hi I'm Sabrina, the doctor's physician assistant. He's not here." Sabrina said to Diana.

"Are you expecting him soon?"

"Excuse me who are you?"

It was Sabrina's tone that made her simple inquiry seemed as if she is someone more than a doctor's physician assistant. She seemed too interested like why another woman is inquiring about her man. She is obviously protecting his whereabouts. It's very apparent to Diana that she was not going to get too much cooperation.

"I'm Diana, a former business associate. Sabrina, would it be alright to leave a note?" Diana asked relinquishing the battle that is about to begin.

It is no point fighting over a man from her past. He is a man that has shown he is still angry over her decision not to be with him anymore. What would be the result of competing for him now?

"Sure, he'll get it. Like everything else I'll make sure he gets it." She said knowingly and nonchalantly.

****

He should have been at the hospital by now. This route is not the right way the cab is taking him, Kurt felt. These damn cab drivers and their sneaky way of making a buck, is unreal. Any other day would have been entertaining because really, if he felt he was, being carried; he would simply not pay. This is not the first time that Kurt jumped a taxi bill.

"I think you took the wrong way to the hospital, buddy."

"Oh I didn't think you were still going there," the man said.

"I didn't tell you anything differently." Kurt said enraged.

Diana can be in real trouble and this idiot is playing with the meter.

The cab slowed and then came to a halt.

Kurt took a minute before he said anything to the cab driver and looked out the window. The part of town is somewhere that he didn't know and it looked worse than the area he is staying at. It's a lot of rows of abandon buildings and not another car in sight on the street.

"I'm going to have your head for this. Get me to the hospital now." Kurt yelled at the driver.

"Ditto," The cab driver said without turning to address him face to face.

"What? What do you mean ditto?"

"I'm about to have your head." The driver said plainly.

"And I'm concern? Just do what I say." Kurt said back to the man preparing for a physical assault.

"I'm gonna sever your head, Kurt." The man threatened.

"I didn't tell you my name. How do you know my name? This is not funny...I"

Kurt was, cut off instantly when the cab driver brandished a machete; simply holding it up above the seat. Next, the driver turned around and his eyes met Kurt's eyes. In the dim darkness, it didn't take long for Kurt to realize that the driver looked familiar.

He looked like…his thoughts cut off when the man spoke.

"Ready-Set-Go," he said to Kurt warningly.

Kurt took a couple of seconds to internalize what was being, said to him and he shook his head. The driver swung the machete at him as Kurt opened the car door abruptly, got out the car door and ran. He knew from what he saw in this man's eyes that he didn't mean Kurt any good. He also felt a ping of pain on his left arm meaning that he has been; cut by the sharp knife-edge.

Once Kurt ran off a good distance from the cab, he ducked behind one of the abandon apartment building. He felt free to stop running. What is he going to do? As much as it is unlike him, he needed to call the police. He reached for his phone and found it wasn't there. He realized that he must have dropped his cell phone while he was running. He has to keep his wits about him. He checked his arm again and realized that it is just a nick. There is barely any blood. He rested a bit.

****

The man with the machete strolled peacefully down the back street in the direction Kurt ran. The streets were deserted as he expected. This is becoming fun, Mr. Final mused. He thought of how he is going reveal his identity to Kurt and the shock when he truly sees who he is. Maybe he will toy with him as he did Paul Monarch. It's fun to toy with them he supposed as he walked steadily amongst the abandon buildings. It's almost as if he is relaxing and taking a casual stroll. It's clear that Final knew his way around this part of the city.

He continued to scan the block seemingly knowing in what direction to go. He stopped and looked around and that's when Kurt saw him. He hid in the lower basement entrance stairwell of one of the buildings. He ducked safely back down in the stairwell and waited for the other to pass by.

Since he's lost, Kurt decided that he has to make his way back to the parked cab. He at least knew the way he came. Once back, there he could hotwire the car which is another one of his hidden talents that he is proud of possessing. He will get away.

The other passed by and continued down the block a ways. Kurt made his way out of the stairwell and down the street towards the car.

He saw the cab up ahead of him sitting on the slightly illuminated city streets. It is clearly abandoned. That psycho is probably on the other side of the city by now he laughed in his mind. As he approached the cab, he heard a loud crash behind him coming from the alleyway. He only has seconds. He decided to jump into the cab. He hoped that the doors were unlocked.

Instead of jumping into the front seat, which is, locked anyway on the passenger side of the cab, he has no choice but to get into the backseat. The backdoor was unlocked.

Kurt lay down on his back, on the seat of the cab staring up at the ceiling. His planned is that he would just lay there until the other man left the vicinity of where he is. That's if he has doubled back to the cab. He would try to hotwire the car then.

Almost out nowhere, he felt the entire car rock like something fell down on the top of it. Then almost simultaneously, a long knife came cutting through the ceiling of the cab with tremendous force. The knife protruded clearly through the thin-like metal.

Kurt scooted across the seat on his back opening the car door and getting quickly out of the cab. In an instant, he didn't realize or rationalize that whoever is on top of the cab; most likely the deadly driver, would have another weapon.

The moment he stood up to run a machete came across his neck slicing into it deep. He didn't have time enough to turn from it. He heard as he flinched back instinctively from the machete the other's voice.

"A doctor always carries a spare surgical tool." Mr. Final said.

That is all Kurt heard as he fell straight back hitting the sidewalk heavily as he collapsed dead.

Final jumped down from atop the cab and straddled the front of Kurt's chest. He reached into his back pocket and pulled out what looked like a black marker and began to write on his forehead. He wrote the word '**Betrayed**'. He then picked up Kurt's bloodied body and sat him into the backseat. He got in the cab and drove off back the way they came.

****

Later Final pulled the cab in front of the hotel Kurt and Diana are staying at; and parked the vehicle. He started to get out of the vehicle but turned and looked back at Kurt.

"Thanks for the tip Kurt, but I got to say you talk too much. You don't know how to keep your mouth shut," he said.

He got out of the cab and walked off leaving Kurt's lifeless body in the upright position in backseat.

****

As he spoke to Mona on the phone, Stephen found himself twisting his ring again. He is surprised how much he has become obsessed with it, but it truly is his lifeline or better yet, it will be. It is very old and valuable worth more than life itself. He guarded it with his life.

He was preoccupied mostly all the time because of all that is going on. He isn't sure that Mona picked up on it or not. He didn't want it to distract him from making her fall deep in love with him. They were together so much that he is beginning to fall for her too and that is something he didn't think could happen.

Finally, he is going to get everything he deserved and she is going to give it to him.

He didn't want her to discuss with him anything from the past. He just wanted to enjoy the fun he's having with her right now. Dredging up the past would only destroy what the two of them were experiencing now. He wanted to fall in love again and she is reminding him of that. He knew he isn't supposed to feel this way since he vowed he would never mix business with pleasure. She however is always irresistible.

He wanted to be ready; he thought when she finally came to be with him.

"I tried to call you earlier, were you at work? I thought you were off tonight." Mona found herself questioning him irrationally.

"I had an emergency."

"Well you could have awakened me and I could have helped you with it. What was it about?"

"Hey what is this an interrogation? I thought I was the only police detective in this relationship. Now you've gone back to playing policewoman again?" He said jokingly.

"I needed to talk to you and I'm not used to you not answering my calls."

"This is definitely not the real Mona Daniels talking. I hear fear and suspicion. I'm not ready to hear that yet, not from you. I need that spice you always have. What's going on?"

"I have to tell you something about my past," she said with sincerity.

"I don't want to hear it." He protested.

"Stephen I have to get it off my chest. I want to be honest with you."

"I don't want to know Mona. I don't like bringing up the past. I told you that before. I'm here now. We are here now. Let's just enjoy the time we have together without bringing up the past. These days you don't know how much time you may have and in my line of work, there is danger everywhere. So let's not spoil it."

"You sound as if you're going somewhere."

"I'm a realist. I've had to be over the years."

"I don't want anything between us."

"Believe me there will be nothing between us, but us. I guarantee you I will let nothing get in the way of that. You are mine."

Mona smile with delight when Stephen said that to her. Not only did he say what she wanted to hear but also it's how he said it with so much determination. She always knew that he felt strongly about being with her, the way he pursued her. She wished he were with her now to embrace her.

****

When Diana arrived back at their hotel, it surprised her to see the police everywhere. She halted her steps as she saw them surrounding a taxicab and police tape draped everywhere. She decided that she didn't want to be, seen on TV once she saw the news trucks about. She scanned the crowd for Kurt but she knew he loathe this kind of attention as well. No doubt once he found out that the police were about he wouldn't dare show his face.

She went around the crowds that were too busy gawking at what seemed like a person sitting in the back of the cab, dead she presumed. There was another body of a man hanging from the trunk. It's eerie how people seemed drawn to that sort of thing. She picked up her pace and ran inside the hotel.

Once she stepped off the seedy elevator, she saw the police officers instantly as they stood with a hotel worker at their door. What were they doing here? Surely they don't think that Kurt had anything to do with what's going on outside.

Then she paused in sheer fright.

She screamed so loud that one of the police officers pulled his service weapon thinking something is happening to her.

She ran off to the stairway door before the police could approach her.

Faster and faster, she ran down the flights of stairs until she reached the lobby. She ran clear through the lobby without stopping and outside. She pushed through the crowd so fast that she knocked some of them to the ground. Once she pushed through them, the police officer nearest to her reached out before she got to the car and stopped her. However, she got close enough to see what she needed to see.

"Kurt!" she screamed so loud and intense that she fainted in the police's arm.

# CHAPTER
## TWELVE

They were getting ready to broadcast on air in the next half hour and no one on the radio platform is going to be there live. All of it is going to be a previously recorded show. It seemed like; the calm before the storm and Sebastian is the one waging the war. Veronica Lane has decided that not only is she going to do Sebastian physical harm; but also now, she is threatening his way of life.

This is the oldest trick in the book to accuse a man of Sexual Harassment when it's sexual consent. She came on to him wearing those revealing tight outfits to work and then trying to say that he is disrespecting her on the radio. Veronica has surely played her game right. That's why he treats these women like the sluts they are; for this very reason. Now he has his career on the line for this idiotic mess. No doubt it will be leaked to the press and all of Chicago is going to have a field day with it. He is sure Veronica will see to that.

Sebastian knows he is alone. It's bad enough that his morning crew is acting funny because Lenny Martin's not saying anything. He is being silent to the whole thing. Sebastian tried to talk to him about it but he wouldn't. He is the one who got Lenny this job on his show and this is the thanks he gets.

Even Raina has said she is going to distance herself from him while the station does its investigation. She said some bullshit about not wanting to show favoritism on either side. However, she says that she is on his side. He thought that they were a team. No, he isn't going to take this sitting down. Veronica is going to pay for this.

****

This is the big day and Dr. Christopher Bower anticipates a big, swift win. Bradley Warfield is not competition just a nuisance. The word has made its way down that the Board has made their decision last evening. They wanted to make the announcement in the early morning. To avoid the hoopla that goes along with promotions these days the Board wanted to make sure everything is, done with decorum. This is after all still a hospital and not the local circus.

He sat in the office smiling in victory to himself because his politics and hard work is about to pay off. The Chief of Staff position is his.

The phone on his desk rang and he looked at it a bit before he answered it. This is it, he thought. It feels like something is about to happen.

"Dr. Bower," he answered slowly.

"Dr. Bower the review board called. They want you to meet them in the Main Board room in fifteen minutes." The female voice said.

"Thank you Julie," he wanted to laugh aloud.

****

Turning the corner down the hallway, Christopher couldn't help but think about his nemesis, Bradley

Warfield. The two of them have been cordial to each other by not allowing their differences to interfere with the daily operation of the hospital. It would only disrupt the normal flow of the hospital and cause the staff to take sides. With that, War would find out that he is not very, well liked personally and professionally.

It would be by all, means the right thing because for all sense and purposes he is more experienced than War. When he arrived here, it was on the heels of his last assignment at Chicago Hospital. Whatever medicine he was practicing at that psycho hellhole is beyond him; but it doesn't compare to his own glorious past accomplishment.

What kind of practice is dispensing mind controlling medications and shock therapy? Where is the experiences regarding surgeries, creating new medical procedures and consulting? He hasn't seen an evidence of it and therefore Bradley Warfield is no Dr. War. That loser is no competition for him. The war is over.

Dr. War is going to find that working for him will be a great experience but as soon as he opposes him one time, he will be out the door. Christopher will not accept any opposition from anyone, not even Natalie especially Natalie, who he will deal with later. He plans to do away with her practice just as soon as he is named COS and then for spite he will take the kids. No career, no money and he will be in control. She wants to know how it is to be on the opposite ends of his reach; she will find it out the hard way. Her so-called evidence will only be available to scrap in the most nearest shedder.

Christopher arrived at the outer area of the boardroom and he could see through the glass that surrounded it. Everyone is here already as if they're waiting on him to arrive, even Warfield.

The two of them eyed each other through the glass and Warfield has the nerve to smirk in his direction, he noticed. However, Christopher kept his face cool. This is exactly what he is going to do when he walks in there; keep it cool. Even when they all stand up to applaud him, he will remain cool. That is the only dignified way to accept such an honor.

As he walked to the glass door of the conference room and opened it, he thought to himself this is really it, I did it. I am the leader of my destiny. This position was mine when I applied for it.

"Dr. Bower," the Chairman of the Board, Mr. Morris Markell spoke to him as he came in. "Please have a seat." He said motioning to the chair at the opposite end of the table from the chairman. He sat down proudly.

Christopher noticed that there's no fanfare. The members and other staff remained cold to him just simply staring at him.

"Dr. Bower I called you here today to first commend you on your being selected as Chief of Staff by the board members. It is an honor..."

"I am honored Mr. Markell," Christopher said boastfully cutting the Chairman off from finishing his sentence and shooting Dr. Warfield a look. "As COS my goal is to ensure that Chicago Memorial's integrity is represented in the best light..."

"Ah...," Mr. Markell interrupted him with his left hand. "That is exactly my point Dr. Bower. This hospital's integrity cannot be compromised or tarnished."

"I agree Sir..." Christopher interrupted again.

"Dr. Bower please let me finish."

Around the room, the faces grew unfamiliar to Christopher. He could feel their negativity as he finally begin to pay attention. No doubt, they were envying his great success. He is about to be the face of this hospital.

"The members of the Board have been instructed to rescind their decision to make you the new COS. We feel that our position is that of the well-being of this hospital and its members. This decision is not up for debate."

"I don't understand. You selected me."

"We did. However, in light of the new circumstances regarding your activities, it has forced us to reevaluate that selection. We have no choice but to move on and select the other candidate, Dr. Warfield."

Inside he wanted to explode as he looked over at Warfield. He has that stupid grin on his face mocking him. He couldn't believe what he's hearing. What is happening?

"What activities are you speaking of?" Christopher said almost choking the words out. He isn't going down without a fight.

Mr. Markell rose from his chair to address Christopher.

"I really hoped to avoid this disclosure but since you are insistent, I will oblige you. Certain of us are aware of this but all should know, very well. You Sir have violated your Hippocratic Oath and your own personal integrity. In addition, you have involved this hospital in what could possibly be the most costly lawsuit in its history. This is all because you and Dr. Austin aborted your wife's baby. This hospital will not be, used as a personal tool to enact revenge on an unfaithful wife. You are ruined here as a doctor sir. I, we expect you to remove your personal things within the next thirty minutes, and then depart this hospital. Do not return. Someone from the legal department will be in contact with you in fifteen days. Of course, you will receive a minute financial separation package that I insist you sign. If you do not depart these premises in the allotted timeframe, I will have the authorities remove you, forcefully. Good day Sir."

Christopher bolted out of his chair.

"I will not be treated in this way. I will sue this hospital. No, I will tell the news media all that I've done. I will have this hospital closed down and disgraced from the backlash."

"And you will spend the next thirty years plus in jail. Would you like that? I guarantee you that this Board and its

CEO will weather this storm but you will not. This hospital must remain pristine at all cost. Decorum prevents me from outlining the steps that we will take to dispense with you. Take my advice Christopher, take the package and go quietly; time is ticking."

They appear like vultures to him sitting on buildings high above the city, waiting for the kill. They were too ruthless taking him through this sham and then snatching it away. This is the Board's way. He has seen them do it before. They are all some sort of sadistic cult. All of them watching him waiting to, see what he's going to do next. To them he's a murderer, he knows that now and they will destroy him. Not one of them will speak for him; too busy trying to save their own hide. He will not have any choice but to surrender to them this and do as they want.

How Natalie could do this to him, he thought. She's a cold bitch.

Then he looked over at Warfield again. Now he is sitting back in his chair nodding his head.

It's him, not Natalie. If it were Natalie, she would have told him to rub it in.

Somehow, he disclosed all of this to the Board. Gellar must have gotten to him before he died. He should have never trusted that Gellar would hold his tongue. He should have cut it out. Warfield, the bastard sent him to the wolves so he could steal the COS position. It is his dammit.

As he turned from the conference table, he held in his frustration as he slowly pushed open the door. He heard Mr. Markell address Warfield.

"Tell us what you have planned Bradley as Chief of Staff."

\*\*\*\*

It isn't the weather that is chilly it is still hot out; it is what Sebastian felt walking into Sonja's craft shop. It is no secret that he didn't like Sonja. She didn't like him either. Their many battles over the years have kept Michael on edge so much that he always tries to keep them apart. Sebastian felt that Sonja's difficulty with him is a choice that she purposely made to; further assert her control over Michael. That he didn't like. He also didn't like the fact that Abigail decided to work here at this ridiculous store. She only did it months ago to piss him off.

It was Abigail's idea to meet here because she wanted to talk to him. She knows very well that he never comes here. However right now he needs her as well, because of Veronica Lane's accusation.

"Abigail is in the back, you can wait over there." She said to him dryly. She tipped her head in the direction of the corner of the store.

Sonja stood behind the main cashier stand glaring him.

She never misses a beat to be nasty does she, Sebastian thought. She has her nerve wanting him to go over and stand in a corner of the store when she has a small coffee lounge area for customers to sit. The area is a newly built section to add a new twist to her business, Abigail's idea.

"I'm glad to see that your courtesy isn't wasted on me, Sonja. I'd been disappointed if you done anything else." He said walking over to the coffee lounge area and picking up a cup to pour some coffee.

"That area is for customers not rapist." Sonja said in disgust.

"Ooh now that was low even for you bitch." Sebastian said as he put the coffee cup to his mouth and drank a little then dropped the cup contents and all to the floor. "I think you're a little bit disappointed that I never had an interest in you. I'm right aren't I?"

"You're out of your mind. You know I'm going to tell Michael this."

"Maybe it will wake him up."

"Why would I be interested in you? You know that you couldn't manhandle me like you do every other woman you violated. I find you incredibly insecure and boring. I can't see why Abigail is wasting her time with you."

"Yeah well maybe or maybe she finds me as incredibly exciting as Michael finds Natalie."

"Sebastian!" Abigail yelled out to him.

She was standing in the alcove that led to the back storeroom.

"Get the hell out of my store you bastard! Abigail, get him out of here, now!" Sonja screamed.

Abigail went to protest Sonja's order but she saw a customer about to walk in the front entrance.

"Sebastian, walk with me." Abigail said calmly.

She walked towards the entrance pass the patron that just walked in. Sebastian followed her after he took time to give Sonja the middle finger.

Once outside the store Abigail spun around to face Sebastian.

"Why do you always pick a fight with Sonja? Just once I would like for you to show her some respect."

"I didn't pick a fight with her, she called me a rapist. No one every makes that woman responsible for her actions huh, no. They make sure I do though."

"This isn't about punishing you Sebastian. This is about you and me getting back on the right track. I want you to come to see Dr. Tanner with me."

"That quack, I'm not going to talk to her. She can't tell me anything that we can't work out ourselves."

"You don't even know her and besides it's more to it than that."

"No it's not. You want me to respect you and not sleep with other women, done. You want me to feel bad about my past, done. Everything is back to normal."

"Really Sebastian?" Abigail said losing her patience with him.

"I suggest that you end your sessions with her before she stirs up trouble and our marriage goes right back to where it was before." He said as he abruptly walked off leaving Abigail in front of the store.

****

The next day, Chicago Memorial Hospital was all a buzz about the new Chief of Staff selection. The rumor mill flooded the hallways and corridors. There were many mixed feelings.

Mona sat with Natalie in her office. They were also discussing the latest gossip topic, Bradley Warfield selection as COS.

"I'm telling you Natalie; according to my sources Christopher had that position hands down. Something happened to change their minds." She looked at Natalie knowingly.

"Before you ask me," Natalie said waving her hands in protest. "I had nothing to do with it. I chose not to approach the Board. Christopher gave me everything I wanted when he signed the custody papers I sent him recently. I'm done with him. He's moved out of my house and as far as the girls are concern to them he'll be traveling until I figure out how to break the truth to them."

"What about Michael?"

"What about Michael, Mona? I don't know what's going to happen there because I don't know where he is? He could be...no, I'm not going to talk like that. I'll cross that bridge when we get there," she paused to breathe. "What about Bradley Warfield, you know him well right?" she said changing the subject back to the previous conversation.

"No I wouldn't say that," Mona said nervously and defensively.

Natalie noted Mona's odd response to what she asked. She knows when Mona didn't feel comfortable about something. She didn't know what it could be about.

"You guys were an item?"

"Hell no, no way. We traveled in the same circles years ago, while I was in Detroit those years. The company I was working for used to do business with the hospital that he practiced out, of. I always thought he was bit of an asshole then and now, so no."

Mona didn't want to give Natalie any more information than she needed to know. As she has felt before and told the others, it isn't necessary to relive those years. Everything is different now. She has to keep telling herself that.

Months ago the past was not even close to being on her mind and now she finds she dwells on it every day. She has allowed herself to become weak and distracted. Maybe it's the ties to Chicago. Maybe it's the fact that she truly feels she is finally in love and that has opened her up to thoughts of regret. Regret can be an overwhelming thing.

"You know Natalie I'm beginning to think that Warfield is responsible for killing Gellar."

It is no need to bring up Paul because Natalie didn't know him. To Natalie his murder isn't connected to Gellar's but Mona knew it is.

"What would make you say that?"

Again, Mona didn't want to say too much.

"It's just a feeling. When he spoke to me a few days ago I just felt like he was threatening me and I don't know why. Maybe Gellar had something on him."

"You don't think that Warfield is involved with what Christopher and Gellar did to me, do you?"

"I'm not sure. This hospital is becoming saturated with corruption and I wouldn't be too surprised."

"I know it is. That's why I've been watching Janice." Natalie said. "She is about to make a move or something because she's been cleaning out her office. I think she's leaving the hospital for good."

"It could be the fact that Kimberly was murdered. Maybe she feels responsible for putting her there at Chicago Mental."

"I can't believe that you are actually giving her the benefit of the doubt."

"No it's not that. We blame her for what Kimberly did but for all we know, she was trying to do everything to help her. I'm saying this because I used to come and talk to Janice years ago about things that were on my mind. I had some heavy things going on then and she really, really helped me."

"Oh yeah, I didn't know that. When was that?"

"Just before you and I reconnected and just before her husband died. But after that she acted like she never knew me."

Natalie didn't say anything. She just took in what Mona just said. This is always the case, always the constant. After Janice's husband died and she took that time off, she came back to work different. So different that she seems like a different person, that could...

"Dr. Bower, excuse me," Kelly said as she walked into Natalie's office severing her from her thoughts. "This envelope package came to you marked urgent. It looks like it was delivered interoffice because there's no postage stamp."

"Thank you Kelly."

Natalie took the small package from her. She felt herself hesitate just a little. The last time a strange package came to her office it was a box full of Kimberly's latest threats full of dead roses. She took a deep breath and opened it as Mona looked on. At first, it didn't look as though there was anything in it until she turned it right side up. Then a thumb drive fell out along with a small piece of paper.

"A thumb drive, Natalie?"

"And a note," she picked it up and read it aloud. "-This is the final piece of the puzzle, sorry to get it to you so late.-"

Without delay Natalie plugged the drive into her computer and activated it. She navigated her way around her system until the only file on the drive popped up, labeled *Dr. Christopher Bower*.

Opening the file folder Natalie saw many medical documents of lab results, with Christopher's name on it. She recognized the formats. She instantly realized that this is his medical records she's looking at. Then she saw the one item that is, highlighted in yellow; a simple entry with a date.

She started to cry.

"Natalie what's wrong?" Mona said getting up and going to her.

"Christopher had a vasectomy when I was three months pregnant with Merry," she said barely able to contain her emotions. "He knew Mona. He already knew the baby wasn't his. That's why he murdered my child. That's why he murdered my child."

\*\*\*\*

They are all going to pay; he is going to make sure of it. They want a wolf at their door then he is going to be that bloodthirsty wolf. They have stripped him of everything he was and left him with nothing, professionally. He has nothing to lose. She screwed him too, personally for her lustful acts with another man. She is going to get hers as well.

Christopher Bower sat in his car on the street. He sat in front of Chicago Memorial, with thoughts of Natalie and his peers. He was debating on whether he should go in and retrieve his other belongings. Moreover, he wanted to see the Board one more time and let them know how the real Christopher Bower is. He wants to taste Morris Markell's cold blood for humiliating him in front of Bradley Warfield and the Board. The two of them were in this conspiracy to frame him from the start. More than likely Natalie is involved to destroy him as well.

Before he got out of the car, he thought against going. They would only have him jailed.

There's no need of going inside that hospital to be arrested and then humiliated again. That would surely happen if he did that. Revenge is a delicate road to travel if it is to be effective. It takes planning and patience to pull off a successful undertaking as to what he needs to do. He has to leave this city and get himself reinstated.

There's a place he knows that the undesirables in the medical world go to disappear. Bradley Warfield knows it well, Lennox Laboratories in Detroit.

It's a drug dispensing pharmaceutical plant that has a hospital on the same property. The place is under so many investigations from drug dealing to allowing doctors to operate and practice without a medical license. The funny thing is that no one ever gets caught there. Lennox's money must be deep in the pockets of Detroit's City Hall.

He will go to Detroit and start over. When he gets to Lennox, he is going to take it over and move up on its board. He will build a following that will do anything he asks to work for him. It'll take a few years but he will be back on top. When he returns to Chicago, he will return to greatness and a vengeance.

Those who stole his legacy will regret the day they took from him the Chief of Staff position.

# CHAPTER
## THIRTEEN

"So what makes you think that he's afraid to talk to me, Abigail?" Dr. Olivia Tanner asked boastfully to Abigail.

The two of them were sitting in her office talking. Abigail called her an hour earlier sounding desperate about Sebastian.

"It's obvious Dr. Tanner because every time I talk about making an appointment with you he flies off the handle. I think he thinks I'm trying to control him."

"And we know how he likes to be in control." Dr. Tanner said plainly.

Then she noticed the peculiar way that Abigail looked at her.

"Well according to you." She corrected herself quickly.

"Yes I did say that. It's true."

"Well let's get back to the part about him being afraid of me. In another scenario that would be hilarious. He hasn't met me before and we haven't talked. If I were to analyze this without seeing him, I believe his fear is that of not wanting to face an intelligent woman figure. Do you follow me, Abigail?"

"Yes I understand."

"You say that he's had affairs, many, right?"

"Yes."

"And you said that he has abused women as well."

"Yes."

"What makes you want to be with him so much if he is as one would say scum?"

"I love him. I know this sounds stupid but for some reason I want to protect Sebastian."

"Why would you want to protect a lecherous man like that?" the doctor blurted out with great urgency and without thinking. "He will hurt you in the long run and destroy your life. No one could exist in that man's world. You will only be his plaything and once he is done with you, he will go on to the next one. He's a dirty lair and his kind of filth doesn't deserve to live. He has to be, stopped here cold in his track so that he can never hurt women again...," the doctor said pausing and taking a deep breath.

"No!" Abigail interjected angrily as she looked on at her in disbelief.

She didn't believe what she is hearing the doctor say. Has the whole world gone mad? Who is this woman to say these things, she thought?

"Dr. Tanner, do you know my husband?" she asked her cautiously.

"No of course not Abigail, this was only an exercise. I do this sometimes. I was just seeing how you would react to someone verbally attacking your husband. I wanted to see just how much you love him." She said as she smiled to her.

The only thing that Abigail could do is cry. It's true that she loves Sebastian with so much of her heart that it hurts when he mistreats her. She is weak. The doctor is dead-on with her assessment of her.

"Okay Abigail, let's talk about those feelings of love you have. Let's just take it slow. When you leave here you'll know exactly what you'll need to do."

****

"Well look at this. The cat surely had a fight on its paws to drag this in." Mona said as she opened her condo door. "The great Radio Personality, Sebastian Black has graced us with his presence; imagine that."

"That's really funny Mona. Can't you be serious sometimes? I came here to apologize and be the bigger person." He responded as he walked in.

"Well this *is* something then, a first."

As he walked in, he saw Natalie sitting on the sofa and went to sit beside her. He felt awkward in the silence as he thought that he hasn't really been a good friend to Michael or her. He didn't contact either of them when they lost their baby. Hell he's going through his stuff too. He nodded to her and Natalie just eyed him as she smiled politely.

"Hey Natalie how are you? It's been a while." He said to her uncomfortably.

"Hello Sebastian." Natalie said evenly.

It isn't as if she has a solid reason, but she thought about how self-serving Sebastian has been; especially since the Kimberly thing. In some way now, she blamed Sebastian for the bad things that were going on. It's as if he's the catalyst. Everything started to be, exposed when Kimberly sought revenge on him. Maybe he's been this way all along. He has a problem and no one is willing to address it to him. Kimberly wasn't hallucinating about the assault.

"Have you heard from Michael?"

Natalie stared at him and Mona a made a sound in her throat.

"Michael is missing. Didn't Mona tell you that?"

"Yeah she did but seriously do you think that? I mean come on, the man left a note. Surely you know where…"

Natalie just bolted straight up from the sofa and walked out onto the terrace of Mona's condo. Sebastian and Mona looked on. Once she shut the sliding glass door, Mona addressed Sebastian, angrily.

"Do you ever think about anyone else but yourself, you lunch head?"

"What's wrong with her?" he said innocently.

"Michael is missing asshole. What has happened to you, did you take a fall or something?

"No. There's nothing wrong with me." He said proudly.

"Oh yes there is. Can't you see that Natalie is worried? You don't have any concern about that.

"For you information I've had things on my own plate too. I've been beaten almost senseless, almost ran over with a car, suspended from my job and possibly sued, what's your problem?"

"Sebastian, Michael is missing?" Mona reiterated the point.

"That's not true. My buddy just took time away to sort things out. Natalie knows where he is, she's just trying to cool down their involvement. Everybody already knows about their affair even Sonja. I don't see the point."

Mona gave up. She got up and walked over to the balcony door. She tried in vain to convince Sebastian that something strange is going on with Michael. It just didn't make sense. Why in the world would Michael just up and leave town, leaving his friends, leaving Natalie and especially leaving his daughter Tiffany? It's just not like him just to give up.

She could see why people would think that he would do that when after Natalie lost the baby; however, nobody really knows. The pregnancy destroyed his already shaky marriage with Sonja when she found out. She instantly asked him to leave and he did leave the house. She knew he didn't want to leave Tiffany there but he had to right now. Sebastian wants her to believe that right after that, he left Chicago. She wouldn't be surprised, she thought if Michael is tied-up in the basement of the Montgomery's home.

He left a flimsy note addressed to Sonja outlining his so-called need to leave town. However, he wouldn't leave his job without notice that's the funny part Mona thought. He never told his new job that he was leaving. Even though his letter stated he did take a leave of absence, Shanna says she hasn't spoken to him. They've been covering for him, because everyone damn it thinks he's freaked out over the loss.

She looked over to where Natalie sat out on the balcony. She wondered what is going on in her mind. She came over to Mona's place about an hour ago, but she hasn't said much since she's been there. Mona opened the balcony door and walked out. She sat down next Natalie and said nothing.

I know something is wrong Michael, Natalie thought hoping that he hears her thoughts somehow. She looked at Mona desperately and she spoke to her.

"I'm scared Mona. I need him. Where is Michael?"

**** 

Natalie awoke from her already restless sleep with a shudder. Michael, she thought. Where are you? She thought she heard his voice. She felt his presence but she must have been dreaming. It is getting close to midnight as she tried to find solace in sleep. Michael has been gone too long now. It's been fourteen days exactly and she knows that he is not gone on business as Detective Stephen suggested.

He actually believes that flimsy letter that Sonja presented.

Something awful has happened and she fears for him. She is beginning to think Sonja may be involved and that she may have done something to him.

It's just another tragic thing on the horizon of this reunion with Michael. Since the two of them have been together, whatever force that has been keeping them apart all these years; is still around. The more that they try to be together the more fate keeps them apart; or maybe it's God. Maybe He wants the two of them apart.

Maybe he's not her soul mate.

Then why is she so helplessly in love with him? She realized that she has always been. A void was missing in her life. That void was her heart missing him. It is so confusing. What is she going to do without Michael?

She lay in the bed alone at home. Christopher has moved somewhere, she didn't know and she didn't really care. He is out of her life for good and she didn't want any contact from him. She didn't know why she is even thinking of him; probably habit when something bad happens. She diverted her thoughts back to Michael.

It's bad enough that she lost the baby that they had together, now she's lost Michael.

No, they were both, taken from her.

No, she won't give up. She will search every inch of Chicago before she gives up on him.

The search begins tomorrow.

****

It is late she noticed and she couldn't believe that Mona text her to meet at her condo. Diana was almost skeptical as she neared the block where Mona lives. Just a few days ago, she had, been thrown out of her condominium. Now she wants to meet. Something smells fishy.

Just as Kurt predicted Mona could never resist the idea of making a little cash on the side. He was right when he said she would be eager to resume their activities in spite of what she claimed she wouldn't do.

Against her better judgment, Diana remained in Chicago. She was supposed to leave on the bus to Detroit thirty minutes ago but she received the text from Mona. In the text, it was specific that Mona wanted to discuss plans that the two of them could accomplish together. Finally, she's coming around to her old self; too late for Kurt.

Now with Kurt dead there is no need to hurry back to Detroit and since there is something more profitable to keep her here. She definitely needed the money. Kurt had all the money they had on them in the hotel they were staying. At least that's what he said about the money. It disappeared from the room unless he spent it on something before he was murdered. All she has is a few dollars in her purse.

That isn't going to be much of anything. She only had enough to buy herself a ticket back to Detroit. Once she got back to Detroit, she can bury Kurt. She can use the rest of their money they put away, to rebuild her life. If she's going to go broke she'll do it on own her home turf instead of this murder ridden city.

It has to be after twelve midnight. She is surprised that she has the nerve to walk the streets alone rather than spend money for a cab. She couldn't afford the luxury right now. She walked down the street from the bus stop. She remembered it from the few times that Kurt brought her here. He was always the leader of the two of them and she sure as hell is going to miss him. It doesn't make sense. Why was, he killed? Why were the others killed and who's doing it?

No one has any more to lose than the other did so it couldn't be any of them or could it be. Bradley seemed too evasive the last time she talked to him. He seemed preoccupied and that he would kill to be the COS of that hospital. He refused to help them.

All Kurt and her ever wanted from these traitors is a chance to start-over. Just a chance like the one they did.

It isn't until she walked on the street behind Mona's condo that she realized that she missed her destination by one block. The last few times Kirk and she came here, this is the route they took. Each time they joked about not getting the location right.

Immediately she saw that it is void of movement on this backstreet. The traffic noise she heard flowed from the other street in front of Mona's building. She stopped to peer down the dark, lengthy, alleyway that separated Mona's building from one next to it. She could see the traffic moving heavily between the buildings through the alley.

"You got a cigarette, Miss?" A man said stepping out in front of her from the shadows of the building. He appeared on the side of her.

"No," she replied startled.

She couldn't seem to find any words as her fear made her turned from his direction. She quickly began walking into the lengthy alley that was off to her side. She didn't intend to go through there because it wasn't safe; but the man caught her off guard. The moment she turned and headed in there, she knew it was a mistake. How many times has she heard of people making mistakes just like this one by taking shortcuts?

She turned to look back and found the man was following her into the alley. He walked slowly after her. Her heart dropped in a panic and she started to walk more briskly.

"Hey lady, stop," the man said aloud to her.

Diana didn't know why she stopped but she did. She turned once more to face him as he slowly walked towards her. Maybe it's the fear of what she knows is now becoming a reality. Maybe it's because she felt defeated and tired that she didn't have her wits about her tonight. Maybe that's what prey do, they go into shock and she felt like prey out here alone in the night.

Once he got within a few feet of her, he spoke.

"Run." He simply said.

The one word pierced her mind hard as it assaulted her ears and she followed the instruction. She turned and ran further into the, darken lengthy alleyway. Now it looked longer than before.

She didn't think that he was chasing her that close until she felt the painful pressure on the middle of her back. It felt like what she thought a knife would feel like. It just kept causing her more pain as it moved through her body.

She fell to the ground from the push of his hand and she tried to scream but she didn't. How she could be so stupid, she thought as she saw him towering over her.

"Hello Diana, you don't seem to recognize me," the man said to her cheerfully, purposely stepping into the light so she could see his face. "Now isn't that better?"

"You," she gasped as she recognized him. "Please what do you want?"

She tried to scream but still couldn't. It seemed as if her lungs were bursting to get air, but she knew they were filling with blood.

"I have what I want; you on the ground wriggling in pain. You really should change your traveling routine. Anyone knowing you could easily anticipate where you go," he laughed. "I didn't get a chance to talk to you alone when I last saw you. Now well it's too late. I really would have enjoyed it, because soon you will be dead. You know you're about to die right. Rhetorical..."

"Please...why are you..."

"Shhh, don't say a word, just listen. You remember years ago...well maybe I should just tell you in your ear, just in case there's someone listening. You always have to be on guard, you know. I'm not ready to be caught yet."

He got down on the pavement beside her and snuggled up close to her. Diana knew she was dying and she listened patiently; partly because she didn't have a choice as he talked.

After he fell silent, she looked at him and wondered how funny that her life would end like this. None that Kurt and she have done prepared her for this kind of personnel retaliation. They were only doing what they did best. Only doing what drives this country, supply and demand. Isn't what happened going to happen anyway? Why blame them?

As she embraced the end, she noticed that she stopped fading away. She thought quickly that maybe she should fake that she died by holding her breath.

Hopefully, he would leave her alone lying on the ground.

That's when she felt the repeated strikes against her stomach as the knife plunged deep each time into her gut.

"Well I had to kill you didn't I?" he said with a chuckle.

It is the last thing she heard him say as she passed out. He pulled a black marker out of his back pocket and began writing.

****

The next day even though Natalie didn't get any sleep the night before; she is bright and early at Chicago Memorial. She stood in the main security office of the hospital talking to the on duty supervisor.

She decided that she is going to take matters into her own hands because the police seem to be dragging their feet on finding Michael. She was tempted to call the police to talk to the captain but she didn't want to get Stephen in any trouble. She didn't want to do it especially if Michael's indeed out of town on his own accord. There's always the possibility of that being true. She has a light schedule today. She insured herself of that. It's been that way since she got back to work after her ordeal.

"Do you have a specific time frame of that day you want to research Dr. Bower?" asked Tate, the supervisor of Natalie.

"No, um Dr. Warfield wasn't specific about the time. He just wants to be sure that all of the digital footage pertaining to Dr. Austin's murder was giving to the police. I'm here to insure that."

As much as she didn't want to admit it, Bradley Warfield is one that does get things moving around here. It's only because the staff secretly feared him. They fear him even more now that he's the new Chief of Staff. They don't want to be on the other end of the spectrum if that happened. Warfield is, known to be very intense in his pursuit of vengeance when he finds out that there's someone against him. Although she never worried about him before it's different now.

"Dr. Bower, the police received a copy of all the footage from that day. I put the package together myself."

"Well Tate, you know Dr. Warfield, how insistent he can be. He likes to be sure. Now if I could see the surrounding footage of the other corridors and the garage even; that should be good." She persisted so that Tate wouldn't continue resist her. She knows that if he wanted to take it further and ask for authorization she would have to give up this pursuit.

"Okay let's start in the garage."

"No how, about the camera footage from this corridor; can we pull that up?" Natalie directed as she pointed to the third monitor and the fourth camera of the eight displayed.

"That hallway is nowhere near Dr. Austin's office. It's not accessible to the non-staff members," Tate said plainly.

"Who said I was looking for a non-staff member?"

Tate looked at Natalie with bewilderment and Natalie knew she hit his right button. The whole time of Gellar's death, she can imagine that Tate never considered that the killer could be a hospital employee. That worked in her favor because she could see the delight in Tate's eyes as he walked his mind through the concept. Instantly the security supervisor dialed up the correct camera number on the board for replay.

The selected camera number began its semi speeded playback.

Natalie saw Michael on the monitor screen and smiled. It wasn't him in the flesh but seeing him brought her hope. She steadied herself as she began to watch the footage. She saw Michael as he walked steadily towards Janice Edwards' office door and paused a little then he went inside. Over thirty minutes elapsed. Then she saw both Michael and Janice Edwards emerged from Janice's office.

"Tate could you stop it right there and back it up to the point when the two of them come out of the office?" Natalie asked too politely trying not to seem too desperately anxious.

The supervisor did as he was asked then he gave Natalie a strange look. He didn't understand why she wanted him to stop the footage at Dr. Edward's office.

Once again, the footage began to playback the same scene and again she saw Michael and Janice together. As the footage played on, she watched Michael barely moving down the hall with Janice's arm intertwined in his. He staggered a little and it seemed as if she pulled him against his will. They disappeared as they turned a corner.

"Wow Dr. Edwards's friend seemed a little tipsy. They must have been drinking something strong that evening for it to have that quick effect on that guy. He didn't seem that way before he got there."

"Yes he was tipsy," Natalie forced her own self to agree, even though she knew Michael was not. Natalie knew full well that Michael was, drugged; which is Kimberly's way. "Tate, can we follow them to see where they went?"

"Yes, Dr. Bower. Most likely they took the stairs that's around that hall."

"Okay do we have a camera on the stairway they took?" she said anxiously.

Quickly he switched over to the camera that focused on the stairway. There Michael and Janice were again in the stairway going down and they watched them. Each time they were out of view of one camera they would be noticed the next one. This went on until at the very last staircase Michael fell down a few steps and hit the exit door. Janice appeared angry with him and she kicked him before she aided him to his feet. Natalie flinched with anger and she dared not respond.

"Wow, Dr. Bower did you see that, she kicked the hell out of him? Wonder why she did that?" Tate blurted out.

Natalie didn't answer and her silence told him that he should continue.

Once Michael was to his feet, he was, escorted through the doors into the garage. The two of them, Janice and he walked to his car. Once there she pushed him into the passenger side of his vehicle and she then got behind the steering wheel. The last of the footage that was relevant showed Michael's car driving away.

"That was strange." He said.

"Yes. Well we know now that the man with Janice didn't circle back as suspected and commit the murder. He was too drunk to do that. Tate, make me a copy of the footage we just saw and thank you so much."

The young man complied as Natalie sat there wanting to take off running for the police. It was Janice, who took Michael. She saw it with her own eyes. Why did she do it?

What is she going to do with the footage? She couldn't really go to the police, not right now because she didn't trust them. She didn't trust anyone, not even Tate, but she's going to need more help from him. The police would take too much time trying first to believe her, then watching the footage and be too late attempting to do something. It would only result in getting Michael hurt if he hasn't been already. She even surprised herself how calm she is but she knows she has to be or this thing could go south.

She has a plan.

She is going to go it alone.

****

It is like a nightmare only in the daytime. Mona felt like all of Chicago PD was swarming all over her condo building. She is visibly scared and she wished Stephen were there to comfort her. There has been a murder behind her building in the alley. That is too close for comfort.

She didn't know whether it was an occupant from her building or not. The police were going door to door to ask if anyone heard anything. One of the neighbors from the lower floors called her to give her the heads up. Really, she felt the woman just wanted to know if it was her or not. Thank God, she answered the phone or she would have been, rumored as dead until someone had the nerve to approach her door. The tenants in this building are so nosey. Mona is like there resident celebrity since the Cultrax and Kimberly thing. Everything that goes on at this condominium is, shoved in her direction.

There would be no way that Mona could have been lying in that alley because she isn't stupid enough to travel through it. No dark place is the rule of thumb, no matter how much of a short cut it may be. She would rather live to see another day than take her chances on a short cut.

Unfortunately, the woman that traveled through there last night was stupid; she thought and did not deserved Mona sympathy. Maybe she was dragged in there or dumped from another place after she was killed.

Where are you Stephen? She wondered.

When the police gets to her door she will merely tell them the truth. She was lost in a deep sleep and didn't hear a thing. She didn't even realize that Stephen left the bed to go home until she woke this morning. He is supposed to be here this morning but he is not. After the lovemaking, they had another drink together and she went off fast to sleep. If she didn't know any, better she would've thought she passed out but she hadn't drank that much alcohol. She is still tired from the night before.

Stephen is her perfect lover.

Eventually she will ask him to move in with her because she really didn't want to be alone anymore. It will definitely be sooner more than later. She is ready. He is everything that she looks for in a man and that excited her. She is ready to move on with their life together.

The knock on the door jarred her from her muse and she went quickly to the door to answer it.

Pleasantly surprised she saw Stephen standing there.

"Stephen, oh my gosh I'm so glad you're here." She said hugging him.

However, the man did not return the embrace. Instead, he looked at her in a gaze and said nothing.

"Stephen what's wrong," she asked intently.

He paused before he spoke, taking in a deep breath.

"I have bad news about your friend."

She didn't hesitate for the information to sink into her mind. It is how he said it and that made her believe the worst.

"What happened to Natalie? Is that her body in the alley? Oh, my God she's dead. How can that be? Why is the killer toying with me?"

Mona fell back into her home fortunately falling back into the wing chair nearest the door.

Stephen walked towards her.

"No Mona, not Natalie. I know that would really hurt you, no I didn't say her. It's Diana."

"What? Diana? What would she be doing in an alley? What was she doing here?" Mona said completely relieved it wasn't Natalie.

He is right she wouldn't be able to take that. Why would Stephen lead her on like that, saying it was her friend? Diana was not a friend. She could care less about her really.

"I don't know. There are no answers. Once again, I'm not privy to the investigation information because I'm not a police in this district. From what I could gather, she was, found with the words '**I Am Here**' on her forehead and '**Time's Up**' on a piece of paper next to her. It was just like the others."

She knows that he didn't mean to sound as eerie as he sounded. She couldn't help but make note of it. Another murder of someone in Mona's past and this is close to her home. Was Diana on her way here for some reason? That could be the only explanation. Was she coming to tell her something? Once again, she is, left in the dark and Stephen is no help at all.

"I have to go down and speak to the police." She said moving towards the door.

"No you can't," he said to her excitedly, grabbing her arm.

"Why? I know her Stephen. She was, killed near my home. I have to find out why. Supposed the killer wasn't just after her and is after me?"

"I'm with you Mona. You don't have worry about anything, I have you."

He saw her take comfort in his words and relieved that she did. However, he knew he had to tell her more to halt her from talking to the police.

"You have to be careful Mona. This is beginning to involve you and not in the way you think."

"What do you mean?"

"I mean that you are slowly becoming a suspect."

"How can you say that, I've done nothing?"

"That I know for sure, but you do have motive. You are also, connected with each of the murder victims. I also took time to find out without your knowledge a bit more information. The first is that by your own admittance you don't have an alibi for any of the times that the murders occurred. You were, overheard having heated argument with at least three of the murder victims. These alone put you at the top of the suspect list. If I were investigating this case, you would be on my list and you are. Consider all of that."

It's incredible but she started to see the clear picture he painted. It did all point to her. She thought that if it were anyone that they knew it, would be Kurt or Warfield. Those two were the grittier ones out of their bunch and couldn't be trusted. Hell their own personal rival with each other over Diana was enough to suspect either one of them.

That's it; it's either Kurt or Warfield. One of them killed Diana and used the others to cover up his prime target. She was target all along. One of them killed her for being with the other as simple as that. When they came back to Chicago, it made it easy for Bradley to get to her and for Kurt as well. Who knows how long those two were in Chicago before they made their presence known. It a far stretch but a crime of passion has always proven to be a powerful motive for murder; anybody knows that. Because of that fickle trash, Kurt or Warfield killed Paul and that worthless Gellar Austin. Maybe it is over something else.

Stephen seemed like he is ready to feed her to the wolves. Well he is a police detective after all, she guess she can't blame him. She needs somebody to help her before she ends up in jail again for something else she hasn't done. Of the people to help her now, it would be Michael. He would know what to do now.

Where are you Michael?

# CHAPTER
## FOURTEEN

In the late hours of the night, in a dimly lit room, he awoken exhausted. It smelled of floral. As he eyes begin to adjust to the lighting that filtered into the room, he realized that it's a bedroom. He also discovered as he tried to move that he is tied down by, some sort of restraints. It felt like plastic of some sort.

When he looked down at his wrists, he saw plastic strip restraints; like those that the police uses. He sat upright in a hard, wooden, chair with his wrist firmly, bond to each armrest. His legs were, bound as well in the same fashion.

The last thing that Michael remembered was that he went to see Janice Edwards. He went to her office to ask her about the two pieces of documents that he got through the mail. After everything calmed down from the ordeal with Kimberly, he remembered about the envelope.

He wanted to find out more about it and what it, meant.

They never really got to that part of the meeting.

He only remembered being in darkness.

Instantly Michael thoughts were, interrupted. There is someone else in the room with him, possibly standing behind him. No, they were over to the left of him in the corner of the bedroom. He saw the figure and it's a female.

"What is this? Why am, I tied up? How did I get here and where is Dr. Edwards?"

"Oh, Michael still so, many questions and so little time to really get to know you again. You are safe as long as you are with me. You see I'm in charge here."

"Who are you? Where am I?"

"You mean you don't know by now? I'm always around when you least expected. Guess."

He didn't know.

However, it's something in her voice that sounded very familiar, like when he was in Janice's office. It was like a distance memory on the wisp of the wind. He knew it barely, but he knew the voice.

"Kimberly, impossible it can't be you. Kimberly's at Chicago Mental Hospital right now."

He didn't want to let her know that he's been to the mental hospital himself.

"You see why you can believe the media when they report things they can't possibly know for sure. People see what I want them to see. I'm glad that little rumor is not true or I'd be in such a state; you agree?"

"Where is Janice? What did you do to her and how did I get here? Did you kidnap me? I was in her office."

"Janice is dead, killed by your friend weeks ago. On how you got here, well let's just say it was by magic and I assure you that you came on your own accord."

He didn't want to believe what this woman told him about her being Kimberly, but he did believe it. Strange things have been going on since Kimberly's first attack and other little minor things that have her written all over it.

Frustrated, Michael tried relentlessly to break free of the restraints but to no avail. As he knew, it would be but he had to try. He had to show Kimberly that he's not going to be her prisoner for long. What did she mean by saying Janice has been, killed by his friend? Sebastian.

She was alive when Mona and he left the other night. Why is this woman saying that she was, killed weeks ago? Unless it means that, he has been here wherever this is for that long. Wait where did the missing time, go?

She is trying to play games with him he thought. He is not going to roll over and submit to anything that she demands. She will have to kill him first.

The thought made Michael feel a little eerie; because he knows, she is capable of doing just that. He has to be smart when dealing with Kimberly, this he knew.

"Why are we sitting here in the dark? I know you, you know me what's the big deal? Can't I at least look the woman that I once loved in her eyes, like I did at the Cable station, that night?" He said trying to appeal to her humanity.

"I don't think you want to go there Michael, I warn you. I don't have fond memories of those times." She said nervously.

"It's what you said. You remember, you said we would be together. I thought it was something else, I didn't know that I would be here with you. Show me your face, please."

"Calm down," she said to him pathetically. "Oh yes you don't know the truth yet, that's right. Oh well it's time you do."

He hadn't tried to sound alarmed but it actually came out that way without much effort.

Michael is beginning to form ideas in his head as to what's happened. It's a farfetched theory but it's beginning to be more possible then not. After his trip to the mental hospital another possible scenario began to come forth, one he thought is so surreal. One he has never considered. One, no one has considered. It was something Janice said when…

Kimberly moved across the room towards the door and that interrupted his thoughts again. She stood there in front of the closed door for a long time. It's as if she's wrestling with some decisions. Michael could see the frame of her body in the dark, vibrating from the trauma of making it. Then without hesitation, she reached out and then flipped the light switch.

Instantly, the lights came on.

Slowly Michael's eyes began to adjust to the new level of illumination. Once his eyes were clear, he instantly looked toward Kimberly and into her face. However, the face before him is not of the Kimberly he just saw at the mental hospital. This woman is Janice Edwards.

"Well Michael how do I look?" She said as she spun around in circles for him to get a better view. "Almost like a whole new look huh?"

"I don't know what the game is Janice, but you are not Kimberly. There's a similarity, but I hope you know this is not working. I'm not fooled."

"Now Michael you know that I'm always and have always been a few steps ahead of you. Think about it awhile and I will be back to see how smart you are." She said as she walked out.

He did as she asked, he thought about it. However, there's nothing he could think of. He is thrown and didn't get what's going on.

Dr. Janice Edwards is telling him that she is Kimberly and that Janice is dead. How could she be Kimberly?

Sure, they all knew by now that the two of them are, related somehow.

There is the question of what is the purpose of the other names, Kimberly Prentiss and then the marriage license with the name Kimberly Edwards? Are those aliases?

Clearly, Kimberly was married to someone related to Janice Edwards.

So, all along Janice knew that Kimberly has been disturbed and threatening to kill people. However, that night Kimberly said 'she's making me do this'.

Natalie is right it's not so farfetched to think that Janice sent her to the cable station that night on purpose. She must have thought that Natalie would discover their dead bodies for whatever purpose. Somehow, Jackson fitted into the plan as well and it was a deep plan. According to the police, he wasn't supposed to be killed so the plan was altered somehow. He stole company secrets from Mona and was supposed to flee the country. Still there is something more to all this. What could it be? He's dead now and can't tell it. Someone wanted him silent.

Kimberly shot Sebastian because what she said about Sebastian is true. However, what was the full plan? There is something else more to it.

It went slowly in circles around in Michael's head. Nothing made any sense.

Janice wanted Michael to see her new look and she claims to be Kimberly; but so did the first Kimberly, at the station. She said a whole new look.

It's been years since he last seen Kimberly before that night. Now that he thinks about it, this Janice/Kimberly really looks a lot like the first.

Ugh, Michael thought in his head. This is crazy.

The Kimberly that is at the mental hospital mumbled something about a 'switch' and that 'she will kill again'. It is one husband, two Kimberly's and one is posing as the other, think.

Oh damn, that's it. It's simple they switched places.

It's just as she said. The Kimberly at the hospital is really Janice and she's now dead. That could be a lie. This is the real Kimberly. The one he knew in college.

However, if that's it then what the hell is going on? Why did they do that? So which one of them committed the murders? Why would Janice Edwards participate in this?

"Time's up lover." Kimberly said appearing almost out of nowhere.

Michael watched her carefully as she came over to him and stood behind. She encircled him from behind his neck and Michael felt her squeeze a little. Then she let him go but remained behind him.

What happened to her? This Kimberly seems more determined, more sure of herself. She is more ruthless than, Janice, posing as Kimberly was before when she held them, at gunpoint. He could feel it. Michael felt that she would probably carry out anything that she said she would do. He decided that he would play stupid and maybe Kimberly will tell the whole story.

"I give up. I have no clue to what's going on. I guess I'm not that smart."

"No Michael you aren't too swift these days. I guess it happened once you married Sonja. What did you see in that woman? She is evil and selfish. She made sure that you and Natalie didn't make it. I saw it all. I was there. She used to watch the two of you in bed. Well so did, I. I saw how she manipulated Natalie to ensure that the college pressures wore her down. In some way, she's sort of like me except I'm smarter. How she deleted term papers from the computers Natalie worked on. I was even there when she turned her mother against you. She took away your pep. Everybody knows it's stupid to carry on relationships in college; they only hurt you and destroy you…"

Her voice trailed off into thoughts as Michael watched her. She wasn't always like this. He knew once another Kimberly, a normal Kimberly or at least he thought. Although she was a little standoffish and selfish, she was still seemingly stable.

The hurt resonate in her voice.

Of all people, Michael could understand the way she felt. He looked at her with empathy.

"I know that look and I know what you're thinking Michael. You think that you will get an opportunity to sweet-talk me back into your arms. Then you will try to escape. Forget it that will not work. I've been over you since you were willing to take a bullet for Natalie Vincent Bower, so I'm told. There's nothing you can do for me now but die. However, that won't happen for a while to you and then again, I'm not sure what I want to do with you. You are merely innocent. But I will tell you that you will have a ringside seat to the excruciating pain that I will cause your friends; for the pain they have caused me." She said as she stepped closer to him.

Michael couldn't say anything. He's afraid that if he did it would only enrage her further. So he kept quiet thinking of a way that he may get out of this alive and stop her from killing his friends.

"What's the matter Michael, cat's got your tongue? We're very old friends. We should have lots to talk, about. Don't you want to hear what I've been up to since I left school and you left me?"

"I think you've told us all that we really needed to know; or rather Janice did. Sebastian did this bad thing to you and now you want to do a bad thing."

"Yes I do. I don't think that Janice was able to capture the true essence of my pain in this matter," she said sharply. "Obviously she didn't because you are too causal with your response to all of this. You friend is the devil and he is surely going to die."

"Stop this circle of evil now Kimberly, please."

"No Michael I don't want to stop it. This is exactly what I need to do. Don't get yourself caught up in this. Anyway, I'm going off track. Let me tell you this. Yes, I've had extensive plastic surgery so that I can look like my cousin, Janice. I drugged her and used hypnosis to get her to get the plastic surgery that made her look like me. I needed her to do that because I am so tired of living…life as poor, abused Kimberly; so she took my place. Janice's life is so much better than mine is. She has the riches and she is well, liked. I've been cut off from my mother's money. Her family loves her and she has this fantastic career. Only my stepfather cared about me. So, I wanted that. I wanted to feel good about myself again and live how she is living. I will have it dammit, I already have it."

This was the full plan that Michael didn't know; the missing piece. She is unhappy with her life. She's really Kimberly and her cousin, Janice, is dead. The police need to know this.

"I killed my husband, Everett which was really Janice's husband first. It was a scandalous little affair and it wasn't supposed to get them divorced. But the little goody two shoes caught us in Everett's office together having sex. So it became a battle of who could get the man. I only wanted him for one thing. I had to marry the incompetent idiot to continue to get close to him. I had a bit of revenge to carry out on him. He had to die because he botched my abortion and of course, he had a life insurance policy worth five hundred thousand. It was good but not enough. Jackson was a stupid fool that I unwisely allied myself without knowing his full agenda. He insisted on complicating things by trying to frame Mona. He became a loose end when Janice failed to kill all of you at the cable station. He had to die. So, you see that I've been getting away with murder for very long time and it's beginning to get easier with each body." She paused to breathe in deep. "Whew it feels so good to get this off my chest. Sometimes you know you just need to purge and relish in the confession. It'll make you feel so much better about things. Do you have something you would like to say? Do you want to talk about Natalie, now?"

"You know people are going to noticed that I'm gone."

"Oh, I've taken care of that. Well okay, you've twisted my arm. I'll just confess to you. It's so wonderful to spend this time with you Michael, really. You are still so easy to talk to," she said cheerfully. "I've been in your home Michael. I was the one who called your show from your home."

"What did you hope to accomplish?" He said angrily to her.

All along, he thought it was Sonja but it was Kimberly.

"Like everything I do it was a distraction from my real reason for being there. You see I've been planning to take you for some time now and I left a note so your wife could find it. She thinks you have abandoned her and probably for Natalie. She won't be looking for you. Yes Michael I think of everything don't I?"

Michael started to tune her out. He didn't want her taunting him anymore because he knows now for sure that Kimberly is insane.

His mind started to reflect on their first meeting when they met twelve years ago, his first year in college. There off and on again relationship was draining and he was glad to be, rid of her then.

Then he found Natalie two year later and that was like hitting a lottery jackpot. He thought about how easy it was to fall in love with Natalie and their love together. He thought to himself that there is no other woman he could love this much.

Then, it hit the memory of meeting Sonja. Now that he knows that she purposely set out to destroy his relationship with Natalie, some things started to make sense.

She was there all the time, always around them. Then when Natalie broke up with him, she was there all the time around him; and he fell into what he knows now was her trap.

The pain of when he lost Natalie that day long ago hit him and it was so intense that he closed his eyes. That was a darkest period in his life. He was about to go wild with hurt. He didn't believe that there was one person on this Earth that really knew how much his breakup with Natalie changed him. It was as if he became a person that he really didn't know and he couldn't do anything to prevent the change. He felt like he wasn't worthy anymore and that crushed him; that everything he did was for nothing.

Overall, it was an undeniable ache; in his heart that never went away. It was almost like depression.

Deep in his heart, he was angry. He never understood how Natalie could just leave him like that; just abandon him and he felt abandoned.

He was young like her; just becoming an adult with the same kinds of hang-ups. She left him alone and empty is what he had become. He was an empty man with the hope of falling in love again with the one woman who held his heart in hers.

It happened as if he wanted. She was back to him now. She was near to him but still so far.

Now, all that he wants is the warm touch of Natalie's hand in his to let him know that he is all right.

Then he felt a pinched on his neck…

\*\*\*\*

…Michael jarred from his sleep. He had fallen asleep or could it have, been something that Kimberly did.

It seemed late but he didn't know for sure.

He couldn't believe that he was so caught in his small issues back then that he didn't notice she was lurking around. It didn't seem right what's happening to him. All he could think about right now is that he missed his daughter and Natalie.

How did he end up here?

Natalie, I love you, he thought to himself. I need you, his groggy, thoughts managed to express.

# CHAPTER
## FIFTEEN

It is the end of the workday. Natalie couldn't believe that she did not implode from the sheer pressures of waiting on Janice to make a move. She had cut her workday in half to get all of her plans ironed out correctly. She needed helped, so she took a chance on tempting Tate's appetite for all things law enforcement. By focusing on Janice as a suspect, she amped up the charade some more. Of course, he didn't believe her but he was more than happy to enlist himself as her sidekick. Probably just for the pure excitement of it that Natalie would be suspicious of someone so visible. His sole job was to watch Janice's every move. He is to report to Natalie via her cellphone if Janice even gave the slightest hint that she's leaving the hospital.

Natalie would in turn be waiting in the garage, in the car that she rented so that Janice wouldn't recognize her. She decided that she was going to follow her and see if she was going to lead her to Michael.

Like clockwork, Natalie received her call.

"Dr. Bower, the psych is on the move," Tate said seriously, as he whispered through the phone.

"Okay thanks Tate. You are on your job."

Natalie really wanted to laugh because he is being really, silly calling Janice the psych. Almost as if they were in a spy movie. As serious, as this whole thing is she welcomed a humorous break from her mission.

A few minutes later Janice came through the stairway exit door as she did when she was with Michael. Preoccupied with her smartphone she didn't look up to scan the parking garage like they warned woman to do when they are alone.

She strolled over to her car actually passing by the rental car that Natalie sat in but didn't notice her. Even if she did look up, Natalie took care of that by purchasing a wig and pair of glasses that changed her look slightly. She decided that Kimberly isn't going to be the only one who is a master of disguises.

Janice drove her car out of the parking space it was parked in. She then drove through the area to exit the underground. Natalie followed safely seconds later. She didn't want to lose Janice, but she didn't want to alert her that she is following her either.

When they got to the exit gate Natalie pulled up to the other exit gate just slightly later than Janice did. She kept her head turned away from Janice's direction slightly pretending to look through her purse. Janice's gate arm went up first and she exited. Natalie then followed.

It was dark outside which is the perfect cover for Natalie. She proceeded in the direction that Janice went.

****

Natalie could barely keep up with Janice's car anymore because the other woman is speeding. She's going so fast as if she's driving an ambulance. It seemed almost as if Janice knows she's being, followed. There are so many cars on the streets tonight that it made it somewhat easy to be, camouflaged. It seemed like hours they drove. Natalie didn't know the area because she hasn't been on this side of town before. It's unnerving the tension involved in following someone secretly. For all she knows Janice could be leading her into a deathtrap and that meant that she has to keep her eyes wide open.

Janice's car drove off the main street onto a side street. Natalie slowed down and pulled over to the curb. Janice's car drove on straight ahead. As Natalie's eyes followed the car, she saw the huge building in the distance. She recognized the facility as Chicago Mental Hospital from the pictures in the doctor's lounge.

What is Janice doing here she thought? Kimberly is dead. There is no further need to travel here personally; at least to her there isn't any reason. Janice must surely have a reason. Natalie drove her car back on the street towards the facility. She has to find out what.

Once Natalie arrived at the facility, she parked her car. Janice was nowhere to be, found but her car sat in the parking lot empty. She was only a couple of minutes behind Janice so she couldn't figure out where she went that fast. Natalie decided that she would wait patiently in the car until she spotted her again.

****

Kimberly speed walked through the security checkpoints and keycard accesses of the hospital. She's on a mission. She can't be, stopped. She held a large envelope clutched near her breast as she boarded the elevator.

Soon the elevator rested to the lower level floor and Kimberly exited through the doors, as they opened. She continued hesitantly down the corridors until she came to an office door. She entered the door without knocking. Dr. Murphy turned from a high counter he was standing at to address her.

"Hey Janice, what brings you here?" he said cheerfully.

"I came to see you." She said coyly.

"Oh. Well I won't get off until three hours from now but you can keep me company so I don't die from boredom. I got the duty of wrapping up the patients' lab results for this month. It's a pain because I got a little behind."

"I know I heard. Well do you need any help?" She said to him moving closer into his personal space.

Dr. Murphy isn't sure but Janice seemed a little flirtatious to him. She surely has changed from the way she's been lately. It had to be the stress of her patient Kimberly Stanford. Now that she's dead, she can rest more easily. The inquiry about her lapse into the coma hadn't been finished before her murder occurred. Somehow, the blood lab samples were, sent from the hospital to the city morgue for a few months. Now after the samples retrieval test were ran and now all he has to do is place them in her file. He didn't even have a chance to get Kimberly's autopsy lab work done yet.

"If you want to," he said to her. "I'm just about to finish up so there's not much to do; just this batch. What is that you have in that envelope?"

"Well I wasn't really being honest with you," she said putting her purse down on the counter. "I had some things I had to clear up regarding Kimberly. Whew, I never knew how much work was involved in a patient that was out of control. She was a lot of work. I'm glad that it's all over but not how it happened."

He noticed the sincerity in her voice. That made her more appealing to him. Maybe it was just the stress of it all that; made her turn cold from time to time.

The two of them started sifting through the files that were, spread out over the counter. They were on opposite sides of the high counter top to cover both ends of the paperwork. Kimberly moved around a few files inserting some of the lab results and other adjoining documents that went with each file. She came across the lab results with Kimberly's name on it in the stack she had in her hand. She placed them in her hands. She then searched the counter for the file with her name on it and found it.

She looked at Dr. Murphy first before she attempted to retrieve it just to see if he's watching her. She saw that he wasn't. Instead, she reached into her own envelope and pulled out the documents that were in it. Then she grabbed the folder and smiled seductively to Dr. Murphy.

She caught his eye and he began to watch her. He became suspicious of her mainly because she is being too friendly. It's something in the way that she smiled at him that made him think that she's up to something. Her efforts seemed, forced.

"Can I see that file, Janice?" he said pointing to the file in her hand.

"It's Kimberly's file."

"Okay, I just want to see it for a minute."

"Is there something wrong, Murphy?"

She called him by his last name to distract him. It's well, known by those who dealt with him personally that he likes to be, called by his last name. He loathed his first name, Morris and favored his last name as identification. Sometimes the little idiosyncrasies in a person's life can distract them and trap them.

"No Janice, I thought that I had already put paperwork in Kimberly's file and I wanted to check."

He of course was lying.

Picking up the file, she began walking around the counter. She still had in her hand also, the documents that she retrieved out of the envelope she brought with her. Suddenly she tripped and fell into the counter pushing some of the documents and files off the counter top. Dr.

Murphy scampered to catch some before they fell, unsuccessfully. The contents of many files sprawled all over the floor.

That was on purpose, Murphy thought. She didn't want him to see what she was doing, that he knew for sure. Kimberly bent down behind the counter out of the view of Dr. Murphy. She quickly slipped the new documents that she held into her own file. She took the other papers and inserted them into her purse; mission accomplished.

Between the two of them, they gathered the papers from the floor and returned them to the surface of the counter. Kimberly returned to the upright position before Dr. Murphy. Again, she reached into her purse and pulled out a small type, hypodermic needle. It was small enough to fit in the palm of her hand. The safety cap was on the tip to prevent it from stabbing into her, own hand.

When Dr. Murphy rose from the floor, he stared at her. The tension in the air became thick enough to cut with a knife.

"What are you doing here, Janice?"

"Huh, I don't understand." She said very doe-eye like.

"You're acting strange and I want to know what you're doing here." He said to her agitated.

This is perfect she thought as she moved towards him. She knew he had seen her movements and for that, the back-up plan has to be that she kills him. She can't allow him to link Janice's death to her at all. That's why she had to substitute a false lab result for the real one. The real one will show that Janice had a small amount of barbiturate, potassium solution and paralytic in her system.

It was supposed to be lethal but it wasn't. That was her own fault, Kimberly thought. She should have measured it more thoroughly. There's a certain art to all of this and small mistakes will certainly botch a plan.

Though she's sorry that Janice is gone now she knows that it had to be, done. Still after she thought about it, she could have handled her as she did all these years. She wasn't given the choice because that pathetic Sebastian Black killed her. She is going to make his death so painful; he'll wish he had angel wings.

She stood in front of Dr. Murphy staring up into his eyes as she pushed her breast out to entertain him. He is such an idiot to fall for the oldest trick in the book but she has learned that she could do this to men. Her horrible experiences have not left her helpless.

"You know you confused me Murphy." She said encircling her arms around his neck and pressing herself tightly against him. "First I put up my guard so you will chase me and you shy away. Then I let my guard down so you can catch me and you get mad at me. I'm not sure what you want, don't you like me?" she finished.

"I um, I didn't know. I thought..." he stuttered.

He is, prepped for the kill, she thought. The mere thought of it made her anxious for thrill. She wiggled against him and then she kissed him. The hand with, the needle reposition itself in order for the other hand to remove the cap; it is time. Once the cap is, removed, she is going to plunge it so hard in his neck for touching her with his disgusting hands.

Instantly the door to the office swung opened and a woman stepped into the office. Dr. Murphy and Kimberly quickly broke their embrace. Kimberly quickly hid the needle back into the palm of her hand.

"I'm sorry Murphy. I thought you were by yourself," the woman said apologetically.

"Hello Alexandria, this is Dr. Edwards." He said awkwardly. "She..."

"She is just leaving. It's been a pleasure to meet you Alexandria." Kimberly said grabbing her purse quickly while walking to the door, exiting it and then closing it behind her.

Dr. Murphy didn't say anything. As much as he wanted to protest, he couldn't. Although Alexandria is just a friend it is for the best that Janice left, so he could retrace her moves. He really didn't see anything that she did but it's just a feeling that he should check things out.

****

Outside the office, Kimberly leaned against the wall. That was too close, she thought. She almost had him. He should be grateful to Alexandria for saving his life. It was unnecessary anyway; Murphy isn't a threat to her. She switched the documents and that's all that mattered. Now is the time for other things she thought, as she walked down the hall towards the elevator. She has to get back on the road.

****

As the car in front of her turned the corner so did she. Then Natalie stopped at the curb. Janice stopped her car halfway down the block and parked her car in front of a condominium building. Natalie cautioned herself not to get too close as before, while she followed her. Natalie has never been to this section of Chicago before. It is a most prominent area of the city with rows of townhouses, duplexes and condos throughout the blocks she passed. It's common knowledge that Janice financially is very well off due to her family. Her career as a psychiatrist is pretty much her passion. She can afford these places without working.

When they first met, it was clear that Janice came from a wealthy family. It was, also known that her husband, Everett had been this prominent surgeon. With all this, she never displayed snobbery to Natalie. She would be so gracious and she cared about people. That was all before Everett died and after that she took that year off from practicing to mourn his death.

What happened during that time off, Natalie wondered? When she came back to work, Janice changed. She became colder and more flamboyant in her looks. Her work began to show more and more each day her lackluster attention to her patients' needs. The good friendship that Natalie and she shared before seemed forced and rehearsed. However out of respect for her lost, Natalie stuck by her side. They resumed being close. There was no indication then of the things that would eventually become the mystery that is now unfolding today.

Watching, Natalie waited patiently to see if Janice would get out of her car or pull out from the space, she parked her car in. She received her answer when Janice quickly emerged from her car. She ran around to the back of the car and opened the trunk. She retrieved a small box and closed the trunk. She proceeded to the building and went directly in. However, Natalie didn't know due to the high hedges blocking her sight.

Natalie got out of her car and walked towards the building slowly. Once she got to the entrance, she found that she needed a key to get in through the entrance. It is just as well because she didn't know where Janice went. She saw the entry box on the wall and decided against using it.

There is no other recourse but to do what she thought is the only thing left to do so that the night wouldn't be, left wasted. She whipped out her IPhone.

"Hello," Natalie said when the phone call connected. "Janice thank goodness I caught up with you. Are you still at the hospital?"

"No Natalie I'm not. I left earlier. I'm on my way out of town. I have something to take care of at Everett's summer property in Madison." Kimberly answered.

"Madison, Wisconsin?"

"Yes while I'm there I'll visit my parents and drop by to see Kimberly's grave as well. I didn't make it back for the funeral so it'll be good to do that." Kimberly said trying to sound convincing.

"I didn't know that you were from there. How long were you…?"

"Natalie, I'm sort of busy, you were calling for something?"

"Oh yes, Janice my mind wandered," Natalie said quickly realizing that Janice is aware that she is stalling her. "I have this issue with Christopher. I don't know what to do."

In her mind, Kimberly didn't have time for this conversation with Natalie. It sounded funny to her that Natalie is coming to her after months ago telling her that she didn't want to discuss Christopher. It is especially funny since the last time that they talked; they didn't leave the conversation in the best light. Natalie walked out of the office leaving Kimberly wishing she had bashed her in her skull. Then the adulterer slut almost died losing what had to be Michael's baby. That alone should make Kimberly hang up the phone. She should lure her here and kill her for getting pregnant. She felt her own stomach. Somehow, she felt a little a little remorse for Natalie.

"About what Natalie?" Kimberly said dryly.

It is clear to Natalie that Janice was a bit, disturbed by this call. What is she up to?

"I'm sorry about the last we talked."

"Oh Natalie, you're being silly. We're friends sometimes friends fight. I say we put it all behind us, how about you?"

"I would love that. I need your help."

"Well I'm sort of busy I…"

"Please Janice."

"Okay, so what's going on?"

"I would prefer to talk to you face to face. Can I come by your place?"

"Natalie I said that I am about to leave town, so I won't have the time for all that. On Monday when I get back in town we can get together and have coffee at Moonbie's okay."

"I need help now Janice please. Let's meet somewhere and I can really talk to you, I'm desperate."

Damn it, Kimberly thought. If she don't do this, the harlot may become suspicious of her and start some buzz about it. She still has to go to work next week before she disappears for good and hide in plain sight again.

She has decided that she would keep Michael for herself as she glanced over at him sleeping on the bed she has him strapped down, on. She will take him to Everett's summerhouse in Madison. He may resist for a while but with the proper medication incentive, he will come to adjust. He will even come to love Kimberly again. They will be together as she has always planned.

"I guess I could meet you," Kimberly said grudgingly. "Where?"

"I want to make it convenient for you. Somewhere near you. Where do you live?"

She is clever, Kimberly thought. For some reason she thought, Natalie wants to know where she lives when; she has never been interested before. The game she's playing is so obvious. She must be suspicious of her. Well she is going to lead her far away from here by meeting her somewhere far from this place.

"Do you know the Starbuck's on First Street?"

"Yes that's near the hospital. You live near the hospital?"

"Yes about thirty minutes," she was of course lying.

"Okay I'll be there in thirty minutes as well. See you soon Janice and thank you." Natalie said as she hung up.

Of course, she will be late, Natalie thought. That Starbucks' is on, the other side of town more than an hour or so away. Janice lied to her. That is what she is going to base her decision on whether to precede with her investigation or not. What is she hiding that she couldn't admit that she is on this side of town?

Natalie stepped back towards the street and looked up at the tall seven-story building. It's a wild guess but she has an idea how she could determine which condo is Janice. She determined by the look of the building that these were condominium homes. This meant that every unit in the building only has two condos per floor. So all of the condos face the street. She just simply stood by.

Instantly and simultaneously in two condominiums, lights are turned off. One is on what Natalie could determine by count the seventh floor and the other one is right in front of her in a basement dwelling. She quickly realized that the basement condominiums have their own entrances. The front door to the basement condo opened. She quickly ran down to the sidewalk and began walking up the street. She turn slightly to see Janice emerge from the below stairway and hesitantly moved to her car.

****

As soon as Janice got in her car, she drove off. Natalie ran back down to the building and quickly ran down the three short steps to Janice home. She tried the doorknob and found it locked. There would be no way of getting in and now Natalie desperately wanted to get into that condo. She didn't know what she would find but it could be something that could shed on Michael's disappearance. She has to get inside.

Desperation began to take control of Natalie as she ran up the stairs back out to the street. She then ran between the two buildings, into the alley. Once she reached the back of the building, she ran up to one of the windows that she knew belonged to Janice's condo. She reached down and tried the window to see if it would open. When it did not open, she gave the window a quick kick with her foot and the glass shattered it into pieces.

I've really done it now, Natalie thought to herself. Chastising herself she realized that if there's an alarm the police is about to be notified and are on their way. She didn't have that much time. However she decided that if she is going to be, arrested she's going to be, arrested alone. So is Janice.

She is almost sure she will find Michael here or at least some trace of him. Putting on leather gloves she had handy, Natalie bent down and cleared more of the glass away. Then she slipped her way in through the window.

What am I doing she, thought again?

This is bad this is really, really, bad.

Once inside of the condo she started looking around. It's a duplex all right because she saw the stairs that led up.

Janice's home looked very generic from what Natalie could see in the dark. There were some basic things here and there with no pictures hanging anywhere. It's strange to her.

Wasting no time Natalie started boldly up the stairs; not really knowing what she would find. In her, mind a community conversation started. One of the thoughts is how she didn't even wait to see if there is not a boyfriend or someone else in the home. It is her own arrogance to believe that Janice would automatically tell her she is seeing someone.

It is a beautiful, spacious duplex that easily can be, thought of as a townhouse. What the place lacked Natalie thought made up in rooms. She walked around to each room she came to, opening doors and peeking in.

It reminded her of the night Mona and she illegally entered Sebastian's home. He took it well when he found out and mentioned it to Mona. Mona thought Michael told him by returning the key to him but he didn't. Of course, Michael wouldn't tell on Natalie. It's just Sebastian being the sneaky, untrusting man that he, is. He also had a hidden video camera watching the house. For sure, Abigail didn't know about that.

She felt déjà vu when she got to the room at the end of the hall. In every horror movie this would be the time that the audience would yell out not to go into the room. She shuddered slightly as the eerie thought passed her mind.

It is now or never because Janice is not going to be gone all night. She still has to get to the other side of town in order not to be a suspect in this unauthorized entry. However, she felt she's not going to need an alibi.

She grabbed the doorknob. She forcefully opened the door all the way, until she heard it hit the doorjamb behind it. She could barely see anything in the room because it is so dark in the room.

"Is someone in this room?"

Good one Natalie, she thought. If someone were waiting in there for her, they wouldn't simply announce their presence. They would wait to ambush her. It's now or never, she thought.

She entered the room bravely. She castigated herself that she should have at least got some mace from the local police store near her home. She thought about getting mace now anyway since she has separated from Christopher and for what she is about to do. She decided that she is going to have him arrested for the death of her unborn baby. She didn't trust that he would be jailed for his offense against her. His shyster lawyer will probably see to that. The lawyer will more than likely try to determine if there was life in her unborn child to; stop Christopher from going to prison. There was life. Michael and she gave their child life.

"Mmm."

She heard a muffled voice lying on the bed away from the door.

"Are you hurt? Do you need help?"

"Mmm," the voice sounded again.

Natalie walked into the room slowly. She took out her cellphone and instinctively she turned on the flashlight. She pointed it to the direction of the bed.

"Michael!" she said excitedly. "Michael. Oh my God Michael," she found herself unable to stop saying.

She went back over to the door and felt the wall for the light switch. She found it and turned it on then she returned to Michael's side at the bed.

"Michael what happened to you? What has she done to you?"

Michael didn't responding to her question. She saw him strapped down with; leather restraints to the bed with a gag in his mouth. He looked semi-unconscious to her. She removed the gag.

"Michael do you hear me?"

"Kimberly let me go, please." Michael said groggily not opening his eyes.

"No Michael not Kimberly, I'm Natalie. What has Janice given you?" she said busily releasing him from the restraints.

"Kimberly, please," he said again and then he paused. "Natalie is that really you…" He perked up with a burst of energy as he opened his eyes.

Michael's been in the dark or dim light so long that he gave up opening his eyes. It's only because he didn't want to see Kimberly's face anymore.

"Yes Michael it's really me. Are you…"

"Kimberly, where is she?" He asked trying to gather his thoughts out of the fog of the drugs Kimberly shot in his system.

"Michael, why do you keep saying, Kimberly? It's Janice, who brought you here. Get up we need to get out of here and get help so…"

"No not Janice, Kimberly. Janice is Kimberly." He said panicky.

"What did you say?"

"He said that I'm Kimberly. Don't you ever listen, Natalie?" Kimberly said as she stood in the doorway.

Natalie spun around to face the direction of the voice, expecting to find Kimberly standing there but Janice stood there. She stood in the doorway with both arms folded behind her back.

What is going on, Natalie wondered?

"Janice."

"No Natalie, Kimberly. Janice is dead. Kimberly's been free all along; that's Kimberly." Michael yelled out.

"Michael don't strain your brain, obviously Natalie is not as smart as we all thought." Kimberly said mockingly. "You thought you were very clever trying to lure me on the other side of town. I almost fell for it. However, as I was going along I started to wonder why my BFF; wanted me to meet her in the still of the night. I was curious and that made me vulnerable. Then I started to wonder what if the little mistress had been following me from the start. Could she be that smart? So I decided to double back here and protect my property from a burglar."

"I was smart enough to find this place Janice."

"You know the last person to tell me how smart they were is dead. I wouldn't be so arrogant home wrecking harlot. By the time that they find your body here it won't make a difference how smart you are," Kimberly said as she moved her arms from around her back and brought her hands forward. In one hand, she held a Taser and in the other what is, known in the police department as an ASP expandable baton. Right on cue, she swung the baton forward causing it to extend to its full length. "And by the way I'm not Janice. Oh forget it."

"Whoever you are, I'm not going to let you hit me with that baton."

"Oh Natalie don't be silly, I'm going Taser you first and then I'm going to hit you with the baton. Why should I work that hard?"

"Kimberly don't do that." Michael said trying to lift off the bed.

"I can't let her interfere with you and I, Michael, it wouldn't make any sense after coming so far. We belong together not the two of you."

Kimberly launched her attack on Natalie. She swung the baton at her as she lunged forward almost jumping at her. She missed Natalie by a half inch as the baton swung passed her. However, Janice recovered enough to; slightly graze her with the Taser. Natalie staggered to the floor but didn't pass out.

"You are so weak Natalie; always the goody two shoes. I don't even know why I became your friend." Kimberly said standing over top of her.

Natalie realized that Kimberly is right she is weak but not in the way that will make her surrender. Her weakness is that she never fights fully for what is rightfully hers; she just accepts defeat. Tonight however she is going to change all that. Tonight she is going to fight because Kimberly means to do as she says.

She can't let her kill her in this place and no one would find her for days, maybe weeks. If that happens what would happen to Michael? He will become a prisoner to her forever and no one will even know that Kimberly did it. Nobody will know that she is Kimberly Stanford instead of Dr. Janice Edwards who is dead.

She rose up to strike back at her.

Standing to her feet, she grabbed at the baton, taking it from Kimberly and they began to fight as the baton hit the floor. The Taser was, knocked away from them.

"You are not my friend." Natalie said forcing Kimberly to the floor.

The two of them fought profusely around on the floor below Michael and he tried to recover from the drugs in his system to help Natalie. He could see what is happening but he couldn't really move.

Kimberly got on top of Natalie and began banging her head to the floor. It's just as she envisioned doing to Natalie in her hallucination weeks ago. Now she is savoring the release of all her repressed frustration and Natalie's death will ease her lust for the kill.

Feeling herself getting woozily Natalie began to panic. She thought she'd better do something quick. She felt around for the baton but didn't feel it. However, her hand brushed against something on the floor. She felt on it a little more and realized it is the Taser. She grabbed it quickly and jabbed it hard into the side of Kimberly. She turned it on and Kimberly responded to it by gyrating, then falling off to the side of Natalie.

Getting up off the floor Natalie ran quickly to Michael while Kimberly lay motionless on the floor.

"Michael, are you okay? We have to get out of here." She said to him urgently. "Can you travel?"

Michael tried to speak as he looked pass her. Natalie turned to see what he saw behind her. Kimberly regained consciousness or from faking, being unconscious. At the same time, the sound of a police siren could be, heard outside. She stood near Natalie with the baton in her hand. She heard the police sirens as well. She instantly dropped the baton and ran out of the bedroom.

Natalie embraced Michael and held him tight. This is the man, she loves and she knew no matter what he loves her. They have been through a lot these past months that goes with being, said. There is always something standing in between them and she is losing hope that they will ever be together.

"You are always saving my life. You are an angel." Michael said to her and gave her a kiss.

"I need the two of you not to move." The police officer with his fellow officer said with his weapon drawn along.

****

It took a moment for the police officers to wrap their minds around Natalie's story. Their arrival was due to an anonymous tip. They didn't believe that Kimberly was at the condo because it was no way she could have gotten away. The police had the entire building surrounded. After Michael was, treated by the ambulance attendants that were, called to the scene the hunt for Kimberly was, on.

They searched the entire condominium and didn't find any signs of her. The officers that entered the building through the lobby knocked on what the officers inside of the basement condo thought to be a wall. A privacy screen sat up against the area of the door apparently for decoration. Kimberly must have placed it there as camouflage. It stood on the landing that led to the bedrooms right at the top of the stairs. Natalie didn't pay too much attention to it before. When the officer moved the screen from the wall, the door was exposed. They used some sort of metal flat, thin bar and stuck it through the lock of the doorknob.

When the door opened, they all walked out into the lobby of the building.

"We are going to have to go door to door. She couldn't have gone out of the rear of the building because we have the building surrounded." The lead officer said.

"That could take all night." The other of responded.

The lead officer shot the other a look.

"Men move out. Get the word around that we are going to canvas this entire building, door to door." He yelled into the police radio.

****

For hours, the police searched the condominium going door to door asking the whereabouts of Kimberly Stanford or Janice Edwards. Some of the occupants remembered the name from the recent news months ago. They couldn't say they seen her. Panic began to set in and the people started to exit their homes. The police couldn't contain the onlookers. Some of the officers tried to stop the occupants. Michael and Natalie watched as the police conducted police business. They refused to leave not until they caught Kimberly.

"Miss, you have to return to your home." The officer said to a woman walking through the lobby to exit.

"Officer its okay, I do live here. I'm only going to visit my mother around the corner. She's worried about me." The woman said pleasantly.

"Okay I guess that would be alright. What's your name and what unit are you in?"

"I'm Olivia Tanner and I'm in 7o7."

"Do you have any ID, Miss?"

"Certainly officer, right here."

# CHAPTER
## SIXTEEN

The next evening, Mona sat in her usual spot, parked in her car across the street from the police station waiting for Stephen. He is supposed to be waiting she thought out front. She's early as he asked her to be, because they were going to dinner. Then the knock at her passenger door window cause Mona to jump. It is Stephen and he laughed. She didn't know why he would do something as cruel as to intentionally scare her. Maybe she's jumping to conclusions. He has been everything he could be for her these days considering how she has become so needy. What would anyone expect with a murderer running around?

Another knock on the window and she unlocked the car door.

"Mona before you say anything let me say I'm sorry. I wasn't thinking." Stephen said as he got into the car. "You know I told you nothing is going to happen to you as long as we're together. Your mine, every criminal knows that and knows to steer clear. So what, your friends were roughed up a little by some crazed woman, not Kimberly; she's dead."

"It is Kimberly, Stephen. You're just mad because the police department has once again botched their investigations. You guys have, been played. The real Kimberly kidnapped Michael. She held him in a condo that was registered to Jackson and Leanne Crane."

"Damn it, Mona!" Stephen said hitting his fist repeatedly on the dashboard console, hard. "That's not Kimberly Stanford. She's dead I know it. She's dead."

Mona stared at Stephen in shock. She knew that he is under a lot of pressure about this case. Many nights he would sleep in her bed restless talking and mumbling in his sleep. She shouldn't have pushed him with this latest information. Information she got through Natalie and Michael. Information, they got from one of the responding police officers. This is more information than what Stephen's precinct has uncovered.

"I'm sorry, I don't know why I did that," he said to her. "I'm, I've been exhausted lately and I let the tension get to me."

"It's okay baby. I think that you know now that it's a possibility that it was Kimberly all along."

"Come on Mona give the credit to the men right now. Each crime scene has a man written all over it."

"This is so funny because before you were the one that insisted that it could be a woman. Why the sudden change?"

"Kimberly Stanford is dead now Mona. She died at Chicago Mental hospital; strangled to death by a male killer. There can't be two of them. Don't confuse your friends' amateur theory as fact. It's no way she could be alive. Let the dead rest."

"She's alive. Her cousin was the one that was killed at that the mental hospital."

"Who told you that?" He said urgently.

"Michael told me. What difference does it make?"

"Too much privileged information is getting out there. This case is in shambles. I don't believe it."

"I think we should go back to my apartment and I will cook you a nice meal. You need to relax."

****

Later Mona and Stephen arrived at her condo. They had stopped by the grocers and were carrying a few grocery bags. Mona whipped out her keys to unlock the door. Once she unlocked the door and opened it, she felt a push on her back. She was, shoved into her condo to the floor and the grocery bags spilled its contents everywhere.

She braced herself because she didn't know what happened to Stephen. He didn't make a sound. He was probably dead by now or unconscious. She didn't want to turn around because she feared who could be standing behind her. The killer it has to be the killer. She has to fight though. She has to fight to stay alive. That is who she is a fighter.

Mona turned before she got off the floor to look behind her. She realized there is no one behind her not even Stephen. She got up quickly off the floor and ran to the door. She slammed it shut and locked it. She peeped through the peephole and didn't see anything. Then she thought that she should call the 911.

As she ran to the phone, she heard a loud thump at the door. She stopped midway and ran back to the door. She looked in the peephole again but didn't see anything this time either. She heard a low pound on the bottom of the door and she started to panic. The killer is toying with her. He won't get her because she will not open this door. She pressed her ear against the door and she thought she heard a voice.

"Mona let me in…" She heard Stephen say.

Mona quickly opened the door and when she did, Stephen fell backwards into the condo. She pulled him in and with all her might; he assisted her a little. She immediately slammed and locked the door and ran to the phone.

"Hello…I need an ambulance."

"No Mona. I'm alright." Stephen said to her getting up off the floor and holding his right side of his stomach.

"Um never mind, I was mistaken." She said to the dispatcher and hung from them.

She noticed that he has a little blood on his left hand that he used to hold his side. She went to him as he sat down on the sofa.

"What happened? You need to go to the hospital." She asked clearly shaken.

"I'm fine. It's just a superficial cut."

"You were stabbed?"

"I don't want you to be upset, okay?"

"What is going on Stephen you're scaring me?"

"I need you to be calm okay?"

"Stephen!"

"I noticed when we were driving to the grocer that this car was following us," He paused as she looked at him in shock. "Then when we got back here the same car was parked out front, but no driver."

"Why didn't you say anything? We could have gone to the police," she said to him trying to remain clear-headed. Then she realized as he stared at her simply it indicated to her that she is with the police. "Yeah sorry."

"Then we got to your door. I just happened to look down the hall. The guy came out of nowhere. He charged at us so fast that I only had time to shove you in here, so you would be safe. He sliced me with the knife that he charged with, when I tried to stop him. He caught me off guard. We struggled a bit in the hallway and he sucker punched me. Then he ran off. That's when you found me. I must have been dazed from the punch but I'm good now."

Mona jumped up from the sofa and went to the phone again. She picked it up.

"Mona what are you doing?"

"I'm calling the police. I'm not going down because your ego is bruised."

He got up from the sofa and walked over to her. He took the phone from her hand and set it back down on the base.

"Okay, but we do it my way. The first thing we have to do is get in front of this thing. We have to get away from this guy. We have to leave town."

****

A few days later Michael, Natalie and Sebastian came to Mona's condo. They were getting together because Mona told them that she is going to be out of town for a while.

"So where are you going?" Michael asked her in disbelief.

"I'm not sure yet. Stephen said that he at least wanted to make the location romantic and wanted to surprise me."

"I get it that he thinks that your life may be in danger…"

"Is in danger Michael, we were attacked here remember?"

"Okay, your life is in danger. Can't the police do something for you here?"

"Like Stephen says you guys are also in danger as well as long as I'm around you."

"I'm not in danger. I just have female issues." Sebastian mockingly said chiming in.

Michael just looked at him and didn't make a comment.

"Mona what I don't understand is why are you even in danger?" Natalie asked her. "I know Kimberly is still out there but she's probably in Madison by now. Besides Stephen told you that it was a man that attacked the two of you, right."

"Right."

"No, my question is why this guy is after you? Is something going on with you? Are you in some kind of trouble?"

Watching the conversation, it finally hit Michael as he noticed how Mona flinched when Natalie asked her that question. She is hiding something from them and it is really, serious. What in the hell is up with Mona and Sebastian? Why are their lives so riddled with, secrets? He thought he knew them both but they seemed to; always unfold into something new as time goes on. In the past twelve years since they all met freshman year at college what have they been doing? He thought he knew it all but there seems to be more, lots more.

"Nothing that I can think of Natalie," she paused to think. She wasn't expecting any of them to be so blunt and direct least of all Natalie. "Except that I think someone is still after my project."

"You mean at Cultrax?"

"Yes doesn't it make sense? Nothing that Kimberly left in her plans, in that book the police found mentioned anything about framing me."

"I'm not following you. Sounds like some crazy crap to me." Sebastian chimed in again.

"Well focus because I feel like I'm being interrogated; I won't be repeating myself. Jackson must have had an accomplice someone that is now picking up where he left off. I think that it's Bradley Warfield."

"Warfield? Why would he be involved in company espionage? It doesn't make any sense." Natalie asked suspiciously.

"And yet it makes sense that he would become the Chief of Staff at the hospital?"

No one said anything, which is just how Mona wanted it. She couldn't see telling them about her connection to Warfield and the others that were murdered. She knows that there is a crazed killer running around murdering her former partners. Just recently, she found out that Kurt has been, killed as well. That is enough reason why she would be in danger, to her. She just can't tell them the whole truth.

She got up from the wing chair she sat in and walked out onto the balcony; Natalie followed her.

Sebastian and Michael sat there for a brief minute not saying anything to each other. Sebastian noticed the awkwardness in the air and decided he should say something to break the ice.

"So Mic what's been up? I'm glad that you're okay. That Kimberly is a crazy bitch isn't she?" he said with a chuckle.

"Man Sebastian you sure are a piece of work."

"Huh? What's wrong with you?

"You *do* only think about yourself. You are really selfish."

"Now come on. I know you've been under a lot of stress being kidnap and all but, you don't have to go at me like this. What have I done?"

"That, right there, that. Every time something goes on with you, it becomes denial on your end. You attacked Kimberly and that sets her off. You sold drugs to JC and now he's dead. Now you're being, investigated for sexual misconduct on your job. What else is going on with you? When are you going to wake up and admit that everything that you're doing is your fault? When are you going to take responsibility for it? We could all be dead now because of you."

"Hey, hey, hey ease up." Sebastian said holding up his hands in surrender." I don't need you to judge me. How can you even attempt to judge me when you're sleeping around on your wife with Natalie?"

"Yes we all have our lies and I accept mine. I made a mistake marrying Sonja and I'm going to correct it. I'm going to be with Natalie, yes I am. Why don't, you be honest with yourself and stepped into the light."

"I have nothing to say."

It was no way that he is going to say anything to anyone about anything. Yes, he sold drugs while he was in college but so did many other people. He didn't have the money to, even be at that college. He had a specific lifestyle to live on campus that he was, known for living. When he hit that college, he had to convince people that he had the income to be there. There was no other way he could have lived.

He also had those gambling debts that only JC knew about. The two of them struck a deal because it was the only way to remain under the radar with their friends and the college. Sebastian would be his direct supplier and JC would be his finance. Only JC became an addict. Mic didn't need to know all this because he is just too naive to face reality. Everything with him has to be above board. That's why Mona insisted that they keep their little romp in the sack a secret. Nobody wants to disappoint the great, mighty, moral Michael Montgomery.

He is nothing but a hypocrite.

"Go to hell, Michael." Sebastian snorted.

He got up off the sofa. As he walked towards the front door, he glanced at the girls on the balcony. He gave them a sniff and walked out of the front door. Good ridden, he thought this crowd was getting a little stuffy anyway.

****

It is another late night for the new Chief of Staff, Dr. Bradley Warfield. Sabrina just left to go home after the two of them spent another long, grueling day together. It seems as if she is going to stick close to him from now on. They are a good pair the two of them and he feels he can trust her, unlike Diana. She betrayed him when she chose Kurt and so she got what she deserved following behind him.

They were penniless together so it isn't a total lost. Kurt has no real way to make a buck only doing those criminal activities. The both of them were bound to, be, locked up one day anyway or worst. He is glad that they were both gone and out of his hair. They should have left town when he told them to. Things wouldn't have gotten out of hand.

Sabrina just told him today that Diana came to see him and left a note. What did she come here to talk, about? The two of them have nothing else to say to each other; and he didn't want anything more to do with her or Kurt.

He lifted up the folded note to read it. He knows that Sabrina probably has already. She has taking upon herself to be his sidekick among other things and he thinks he can trust her. Besides, if he knows Diana like he knows her very well; she has written this letter in a way that only he would be able to read.

He began to read the letter, lying comfortably back in his chair with his feet on his desk. No, doubt some last ditched effort to appeal to his heart. Well someone should tell her that it's too late.

Then he sat up in his chair taking his feet off the desk. The letter is more than he expected and has some interesting angles in it relating to what's going on.

A few minutes later, he opened his desk drawer and pulled out an IPad. He turned it on and began scrolling down a list that is on the device. He picked up his phone and dialed a number he retrieved from the list.

"Good you're available." He said through the phone.

"What do you want Bradley?" Mona said to him.

"I called because I need to meet with you. I need to talk to you about something, something important."

"I thought I told you to stay away from me? That means calling as well. You may have everyone else fooled but I know you killed Paul, Gellar and the others; but you won't get me."

"What are you talking about what others?" he asked curiously.

"It is incredible how you can sound so convincing after murdering four people in cold blood."

"Four people."

"Okay if you like I will say their names. I will play your game and afterwards I'm calling the police; Paul, Gellar, Diana and Kurt."

"Diana and Kurt are dead?"

He had to lie to her, just in case they were overheard. She has to trust him and he knows that is going to be hard.

"This is too funny. If I cared anything about Diana and Kurt, I would be angry that you are trying act as if you didn't know that they were dead; but I don't. Paul was my friend and Gellar well, was just like you. I see you're at the hospital. I hope you get a good start because the police will be coming for you. I won't be your next victim."

"Look Mona I don't know what you're talking about. I called so that we can talk about what just came across my desk. Something that Diana wrote in a letter to me."

"So what is it?"

"I don't want to talk about it on the hospital phone you never know these days. I am after all the COS. I'm not trying to take risk. I like you but not that much."

"I don't care. Goodbye."

"You are in danger Mona. You are only safe if you come meet me and we can talk. You have to know this but I'm not talking over the phone."

"Like I said Bradley, I'm not going to become your next victim. I have a police detective standing by to put a bullet in your head if you ever try to attack us again. Keep away, jerk."

She hung up the phone.

Well it was worth a try. Mona Daniels is the stubbornness woman he has ever met. So be it. If she wants to be on the chopping, block than let her.

However, no one hangs up on the COS of Chicago Memorial Hospital. He will have the last word.

\*\*\*\*

When she hung up the phone, she was infuriated. Does he think that she's that stupid to trust him and lead herself to death? Diana was stupid but she is far from it. She is going to disappear with her boyfriend and stay away until Bradley can be, caught.

She decided against calling the police because she didn't want any more ties to Bradley Warfield than she needed. It could lead to many questions that she isn't ready to answer to Stephen. He isn't slow. She can already feel that he suspects her of something. However, he decided for some reason not to pursue asking her about it. He said he didn't want to bring up the past and he has stuck by his word; and so will she.

\*\*\*\*

Early the next day Michael sat at home speaking to Mona over the phone. He tried to convince her from leaving town.

"I don't think that you should it, Mona." Michael said to her.

Michael talked to Mona while Natalie and he were at La Maria's for lunch.

"It's the only way I'm going to feel safe Michael."

"That's not my point. You can be safe here. At least you know your surroundings and the police can protect you."

"Heck no, there's already been an attempt on my life. Now you want me to sit idle by and let the killer succeed. I have a Stephen to protect me, so I'm good."

"Some police detective. The way Natalie tells me if it wasn't for her I'd be in Madison, Wisconsin right now. No offense Mona but your detective friend is, not very swift."

"Michael I love you, but your little Mona has everything under control. I'll keep in touch. See ya around."

She hung up the phone and continued to pack her suitcase.

**** 

The line went dead and Michael hung up the phone. Then the phone instantly rang.

"Hello."

"Hello Detective Montgomery, this is Dr. Murphy from Chicago Mental. I was trying to reach Detective Dunn but she wasn't answering her phone."

"Yes Dr. Murphy what can I do for you." Michael asked him reluctantly.

If it wasn't for the fact that Mona and he could get into serious trouble for impersonating a police detective; he would tell the doctor the truth.

"We sent this information to the police department already. It's about Ms. Stanford the autopsy report came back. As we suspected she was strangled and obviously by a male."

"Well that's good news that the autopsy report revealed that. Was there anything else?"

"There was something strange that the coroner discovered on the body near the neck area. There is a large patching of bruising in one portion of the neck. It left a mark. As far as the coroner could tell, the killer had something in his hand or had something between his fingers, something small. I hope that information can help the two of you. I hope you can find out who did this."

That is a true statement Michael felt need saying as he hung up with the doctor. He thought against telling the doctor that; it was Janice Edwards that has been lying in his hospital; not Kimberly Stanford. It would only raise more questions and Dr. Murphy would eventually found out that he wasn't talking to a real police detective. That is something for the police to tell him.

Forensic and coroner reports are not Michael's forte so what the doctor told him meant nothing to him. He should call Mona back to speak to Stephen. Maybe he would have better luck with the doctor's news.

He'll wait until they get to where they're going and when Mona gives him a call. Maybe that will bring them back to the city and put an end to this hiding out. If he tells them now they will still be desperate to leave town and go anyway.

Besides, later on at noon, he has something that he has to do with Natalie that is too important to resist. It's time to get their life back together.

****

It felt like a real date. This is the first time that they've had a chance to be together in a long time and it is great. Michael and Natalie relished in their alone time together. It is also the first time they've allowed their children to meet. They were at one of the local kids' oriented restaurants that incorporate rides, video games and junk food to keep the kids occupied. It is a place called the Kids' Mart. This gave Michael and Natalie time to talk and be together. Like a happy ending to what was once a tragic love story, the two of them watched as the initial bond between their children started off without a hitch. Michael is especially happy because this is how he always wanted it to be.

They were careful not to expose the depth of their relationship to each other, to the girls. This is going to be a process that the two of them are going to allow to go slow. It seems they now have all the time in the world.

Michael's cellphone rang. He looked at the screen and saw Sebastian's number pop up. He let it ring. The last time they saw each other Michael believes he said more than he intended to. Furthermore, Sebastian's response wasn't too cool either. What he told Sebastian about himself is correct and long overdue. His violation of the women he encountered all these years was very reckless.

No way would Michael judge anyone because of his current mess with his life. He's not saying that he's better than anyone is. Nevertheless, there are limits and boundaries. At no time in his life did he ever think that he would be on his way to divorce court on a speeding train. It was cards dealt to him and this hand is still the worst. He honestly can't say at this moment if he's winning or not but at least he's still in the game.

He couldn't imagine what Sebastian wanted other than the fact that he wants to continue to pretend. That is his biggest thing in life pretending that nothing ever happens but the good stuff. Sebastian's life is just like his radio show one big game to play and be something that he's not. It was okay he guess at some point in his life; but Michael has seen the real Sabastian and frankly, he doesn't like him.

He will probably never forgive him for making JC a drug addict or at least supplying him with meth. He didn't deny it or offer any explanation. So is it true? Just like everything else, that he does is, left in the air and goes quietly down the river.

"The girls are really getting along Michael." Natalie said breaking his thoughts.

"I told you that they would." He said proudly.

"I hate to interrupt them since they are having fun, but we've been here for nearly four hours."

"That is so funny. The last time we were somewhere for four hours it was La Maria's, on our first date."

"I didn't want to leave then either."

"Well if it's any consolation, I fell in love with you that night."

"So I guess we're off to a good start." He said and then he kissed her.

Michael cellphone rang again this time a text came across the screen. He looked at it. Sebastian again and this time what he read gave him urgency.

"Natalie I think we better go."

# CHAPTER

## SEVENTEEN

While Stephen went in the Quickie Mart to pay for the gas Mona got out of the car. She leaned against rental car, closing her eyes as she breathed in the mildly, warm, nightly air. The warm air brushed across her face, lightly. They were out in the sticks. She could tell that because the gas station didn't have pay-at-the-pump. She still didn't let that little detail deter her from feeling good about being away from Chicago and all of its problems right now. Even though it is fast becoming the murder city of the country she is glad she didn't move when she thought about it.

From a near death experience with Kimberly, to the murders of the others, she was sure she was going to snap.

It isn't Kimberly this time it is someone else she knows that. She fled the city once her Dr. Janice Edwards disguise was, discovered.

How did they did not see through her guise? Mona really felt that Natalie had put her own life on the line dealing with that lunatic. To believe that Natalie use to sit and have coffee with that nut.

She has even run into Kimberly posing as Janice at the hospital. It was probably the real Janice that day in the elevator, months ago having a complete melt down under all that hypnosis and drugs. If she had recognized her then she could have possible saved JC. It has been years since she last seen the real Janice. Kimberly looked so much as the real Janice that she didn't questioned it.

It's good that she literally escaped from Chicago. Her former associates were involved heavily in some illegal stuff and gotten themselves in something deadly serious. What did they do?

Now that she thinks about it, Paul was acting different toward her at times. She noticed especially when she was, accused of selling company secrets. That means that he had taken up with the others and got into something that cost them their lives. It was probably more swindles and cons.

It's no coincidence.

She is definitely watching out. She doesn't want to end up like them.

Dr. Warfield and she are the only ones left. Maybe he is the ringleader. If he is, he seemed to escape being, killed or is it as she suspected all along; that he killed them. He of course had access to everyone and she wish she knew the motive. Except she did overhear Austin Gellar's physician assistant, Sabrina tell Natalie's assistant Kelly, that Dr. Warfield planned to get revenge on some former colleagues of his. Which colleagues is he speaking, about? Now he's the COS at the Chicago Memorial. A position that was, guaranteed to be that asshole's Christopher Bower. She couldn't explain that one. One thing she does know for sure is that whatever happened, it happened after Gellar's murder and right into the others. What did they have on Warfield, because she knows nothing?

She pondered further over the fact that she is now one of the sole survivors of the Lennox group. In a way, she's happy because she doesn't have to worry about anybody else reminding her of those dark days. Still she is scared. However, she at least has a police officer to stand guard over her day and night.

She never trusted Bradley Warfield even in those days and she will be watching him very carefully now; once she returns to the city.

He won't catch her off guard; she's not how she was back then.

She was naïve then and was looking for a quick buck to pay off her student loans and her heavy careless spending habits. They were plaguing her something terrible. She got financial relief from her involvement with them. However, she left a little of her soul there.

The more she falls in love the more she realizes the things she did then were wrong. It's all that she could think about silently these days is her horrible past choices.

They were things that she wanted to bury under the dirt in a hole and cement it over. There were things that she did to people, doing cons and giving false hope. She used people's tragic situations to exhort money from them, her and the group.

Being with Stephen changes things.

Stephen startled her as he stood beside her; breaking her deep ruminates. He stood there not saying a word, just looking at her expressionless for a bit. Maybe he's thinking the same thing she is, how being with her now changes things. She only thought that because sometimes he seems very sad; when he didn't think she was looking.

"Hey. You look like you are a million miles away. Everything's okay, you have that look of recollection on your face?" He asked simply and smiled breaking his stare.

"Yes everything's okay."

"I thought you might have seen that car."

"What car?" she said concerned.

"There was car, a blue Volvo that was trailing us for a bit. It stopped up the road. I guess I was a little jumping myself with all that's been going on that I thought that it might have upset you, if I told you."

"Where is the car? Did it leave?"

"Yeah it pulled off a while ago, we're good."

"That's good."

"Well what were you thinking of?" he persisted.

"Oh nothing really, I'm just reminding myself how life really changes and how sometimes your wrongs can be righted somehow; and you get a second chance."

"That's really deep. I agree, sometimes you do get a second chance to set right things again. That makes all the more reason to live to get that second chance. Now lighten up and drink up. I brought us some water. We don't want to get dehydrated while we're on vacation, so far out."

He passed Mona the opened bottom of water and she thought how sweet he is to have opened it for her. It is a small gesture, but those little things are what mean the most to the new Mona these days. It is those little tokens of love, she thought as she gulped down the contents of the bottle.

**** 

Later back in the city, Michael, Natalie and Sebastian rode the elevator silently on their way to the twentieth floor. Sebastian received some disturbing news and wanted them to come with him. Dr. Olivia Tanner called frantically trying to reach Sebastian to tell him that Abigail was in trouble. Something about a nervous breakdown and that, he should come quickly to her office, because she was trying to hurt herself. Each of them was thinking the worst.

Sebastian wasn't sure at first that Michael would show up after their blow up. It is good to know that he will stand beside him no matter what.

This is just one more of Abigail's outrageous outbursts. She had better be in a damn coma when he sees her. If she is just sitting in an office just crying hysterically he's going to give her something to cry about. She knows how he feels about seeing this psych. This may be her way of forcing him to see Dr. Tanner.

This thing with her has gone too far and he just really doesn't feel like dealing with it anymore. He could easily get any woman; after all, he's Mr. Sebastian the Morning Lover.

Michael watched Sebastian with curiosity. He wondered what's going on in his buddy's head. He's hoping that he has finally come to his senses and decided to make things right with Abigail; because Michael knows he loved her. Those two have been through so many trials over the years and been together so long it is impossible to think of them apart. Abigail stands by Sebastian even though she knows of the heinous things that he has done. Her loyalty is incredible.

He wished he had fought to stay with Natalie long ago. Their love, a love like theirs should not be, stifled or controlled. It isn't fair to be married to other people and those people, resist loving them the way they needed to be, loved. He reached out and held Natalie close to him.

Natalie relaxed in the embrace Michael gave her. They just reunited together after he was missing for a while. She thought she'd lost him to Kimberly. It almost drove her crazy to find him and then suddenly lose him again.

"You know Mic; this thing with Abigail is just too much." Sebastian said.

Michael didn't say a word, he just thought. It's just so funny that everyone else is rooting for Abigail and Sebastian's marriage everyone except Sebastian. He didn't understand him and he felt he never will. He only cares about himself.

"I know Mic, I'm speechless too. It's bullshit. It's bullshit that I have to, keep dealing with this. Abigail has blown a gasket and I'm just going to check to see if she's okay. Then I'm leaving, the hell with it. You guys can stay if you want to but I'm out of here."

Michael still didn't say anything. He just listened to Sebastian and thought what an ass. One of these days, he's not going to be able to think of only himself. One of these days, something is going to get through to that thick skull and maybe, just maybe, he'll change his wicked ways.

"Has anyone heard from Mona?" He asked simply to the other two. "At least she has common sense not to deal with this crap. I might call her and go out for a drink; so we can catch up." Sebastian continued.

"Mona has left town Sebastian, remember?" Michael said shaking his head.

Self-involved, he thought.

"Oh yeah..."

To Natalie, Michael look as if he is exploding inside his head, she could tell. He isn't trying to say too much so he won't get into another fight with Sebastian. The last one was subtle but it's just a matter of time before they go fist to cuffs. She knows now that the gates were open and another one is just around the corner.

As much as she loved Michael, he will have to face the fact that he can't write out what his friends must do. They have their own lives and no matter how hard he tries to gloss them over; they are going to get a little dirty.

That's the reason why she hasn't told him about what she found out about Mona. She thought that it was too strange her behavior lately. So once again she started her investigations and called in a favor. Sabrina turned out to be very knowledgeable Mona and Warfield's interactions with each other. Interactions that included Gellar and three more people while they were at Lennox Laboratories. After she got over the initial shock of it all she decided that she wouldn't mention it to him because it would devastate him. It would only get back to her and right now; no one else in this group needs their life tarnished further.

Not that it's anyone's business but Mona's.

Natalie is positive that if given the chance to reveal this to her friends Mona would not. The past is the past and it should remain such. Besides that's her secret to tell one day if she feels she wants to. No matter what Mona has been in the past, she has been a best friend to Natalie.

Once they reached the 20th floor, they stepped off the elevator half expecting to hear Abigail wailing uncontrollably. There were no sounds. Dr. Tanner's office was all the way down the hallway and they took their slow time getting there.

Sebastian got to the door first and knocked. He tried the doorknob and found it unlocked.

They all walked inside the office and found the lobby empty. Sebastian called out and no one answered. A few doors led to the other rooms. They chose the first one they were closet. Opening it, they all single-file walked through the door and it became a hallway. The hallway led to an office door. Sebastian opened the door and they walked into the large fancy office. They saw no one as they piled into the office until they spotted movement off to the side of them.

Kimberly stood off to the side holding a gun on them, instead of Dr. Olivia Tanner and Abigail.

At first sight, they each saw a different version of Kimberly. Michael saw Kimberly as Kimberly. Natalie saw Janice Edwards even though she knows she is Kimberly. Sebastian seemed confused.

"Kimberly," Michael said mechanically.

"Well thank you for coming so quickly." She said "And to think I thought I would have to hunt you down to kill you Sebastian. Natalie I wasn't expecting you and Michael. This is an extra bonus treat. Now I have you all rounded up like little rabbits. Some of you are missing, like my girl, Mona. I wonder what she's doing. No matter, I'll catch up with that criminal some other time. Please come in. You two over there and Sebastian, you can sit at my desk, so we can talk."

"Where's my wife, Kimberly?" Sebastian demanded as he did what she commanded.

"Humph. Sebastian, who do you think you're fooling? You could give a frog's fat ass about poor Abby. You are so pathetic. Haven't you taken off that suit of innocence you like to wear, yet? Well I see that you all are still dumb as hell. You fell for another psychiatrist guise of mine. Didn't see that coming did you?"

Out of the three Michael must have been the most horrified and shocked. After all, he just escaped Kimberly and here she is again. No one but him has known her as the real Kimberly, lately.

It is easy for her to pose as this fictional, Olivia Tanner and fooled Abigail. Abigail never saw Kimberly as Janice before. There were no ends to the lengths to where this woman would go to achieve her revenge.

Did she kill the real Olivia Tanner or took her place? On the other hand, did she simply invent her? She is capable of doing that. What about the other murders that revolved around Mona, recently? What did those people do to Kimberly? Were they just bodies to make her murder of them look like someone else?

Regardless of what happened, they were once again hers to do with what she wants. At least, Sonja, Abigail and especially Mona were safe.

\*\*\*\*

Driving on the highway in the nightly hours, Detective Dunn and Mona were traveling north. They were on the road to their planned getaway. He told Mona that he wanted to make it the best surprise he could, so he isn't telling her where they are going.

She has to admit that she is curious and feels out of control. Control is something that she didn't quite relinquish so easily. However, she trusted that Stephen would deliver the most exciting of all getaways. This will be their first. She hopes many more because she's really in love with him and she knows that he feels the same.

Even though it isn't late, Mona started to feel sleepy from the ride, she assumed. They had been driving what seemed like hours and long since driven off the main interstate. They were now driving on a single lane road and the streetlights became few and far between. Mona looked out the window feeling a little disappointed. She really thought the trip would be a fun cruise or at least the beach. Instead, she thinks it's going to be camping or a cabin. Either one is not her taste at all. However, she is with the man she wants to be with, so anywhere he wanted to take her is fine. She needed to get away from reality. Too much was going on.

It is bizarre that Kurt and Diana returned to her life be it all briefly due to their death. She didn't need them messing up her character now that she is who she is. It was easy with Paul. He cared too much about his status ever to upset their secret. Even doctor Austin remained quiet. Dr. Warfield, well he remains to be, seen.

So far, she has never had to let her friends know what she had to do in her past. However, she is something fantastic now. She is greatness.

Although she likes to think that, she has changed her heart was still cold to the gruesome deaths Kurt and Diana endured. The killer really did a number on them. It isn't that they didn't deserve it, because they did; and Dr. Austin too. They were all greedy scum. What was he doing working with Christopher to actually kill Natalie and Michael's baby? He didn't have to do that.

Just not knowing when to, give up and be done with it. Mona is glad however, she is free to love and live her life with her new man.

She laid her head back on the seat rest. She still couldn't figure out why she felt so tired. She had a full night's sleep. However, she did go out for drinks with Stephen the night before. Maybe it's catching up with her.

"What's wrong baby? You look a little out of it." Stephen asked thoughtfully.

"I'm just a little tired that's all. Are we almost there to this place?"

"Yes, we're almost there, but you have time to take a nap before we get there. It will probably do you some good to take one, because we have a lot to do once we get there."

"Whew, so mysterious this place of yours. I'm all yours."

"You certainly are…would you like it if I told you a story?"

"Like a bedtime story?" She chuckled. "No, not really, I'm not going to sleep forever; just taking a nap. I would be bored." She said groggily.

"No I think you would like this one." He said insistently and paused for a moment before he spoke again. "I have to tell you. I have really started to love you again and under any other circumstances; I think you and I would have been great." He said bluntly.

"Again? What do you mean any other circumstances? We are together. Are you trying to break up with me on our vacation?" She said becoming more alert with an instant flow of adrenaline.

"Mona Daniels, trust me. I know what's best."

What is he saying? It confused her. How is she to trust someone who is now telling her that they might not work out?

Damn, why is she so damn sleepy? She needs to have a clear head for this. What does he mean by again?

"Stephen, what's going on...?

"I know I can see in your eyes, the confusion." He said and his voice changed, shifted to a slight, haunting, whisper. "I'll clear it up for you. First, let me tell you my story. I want to tell you so badly I could burst. It's about this wonderful family that had all the love in the world. It was a man, his wife and their little girl. They lived a very quiet life. One day the little girl fell ill and the parents didn't know what to do. She had developed a blood disorder that was affecting her main body organs. She needed something to stabilize her because her systems were shutting down at a fast rate. The parents couldn't afford tens of thousands in treatments. The father who was a pharmacist didn't have healthcare; some clerical error, go figure. Just one wrong misplacement of a document and zap you're helpless. A real tragic story, huh?"

He stopped to let her register what he just said.

Mona didn't say anything. Her head became groggier and what more she started to think that she heard this before, somehow. She lived it. It was one of those darkest moments in her life when she was all about money and the heartless way she went about getting it.

Those were times she's been trying hard to forget.

"So they found this woman who was interning in a lab as a sales rep," Stephen continued "But really the woman found them. She offered them a prototype medication for their daughter that she insisted would work. Of course, the parents were skeptical but the woman was a real charmer and she was a real seller. The man especially because he has a med school background. She convinced them to let her company do free drug testing on the little girl and she appeared to get well the first weeks. For four weeks, she returned to normal and they were all happy again. The woman didn't tell them that this was not legal, what she was doing and that she was in some sort of ring that sold stolen pharmaceutical medication. Medication that had not yet, been cleared from testing. She worked with four others and she was the last of them, the face of their frauds. Then out of, the blue the woman told them that she couldn't give them anymore free medication. The trial was over. The couple was, told that they had to pay five thousand dollars every two months to keep receiving meds. So, the first thing to go was the home that the parents built together; but it didn't matter because it would save their child. Everything seemed back on track. One day out of sheer weakness, the man kissed the woman because she led him on. The wife caught them. She thought they were having an affair, but didn't leave him. The other woman continued to make herself available. This made the man more curious and attracted the woman. He became obsessed with her; though she didn't know it then. Then the woman disappeared, but sent information on how and where to send the money. Of course, the couple did as they were, instructed. Suddenly exactly six months later the child began to go in and out of consciousness and rushed to the hospital; excessive bleeding. After the test are ran, it's discovered that the child's body is full of toxins. Toxins that were destroying her body from the inside out. Toxins, that came from untested medication. Poison medication sold by you. You Mona."

"You're Duncan Stevens aren't you?" She said barely able to keep her eyes open. She had to hear him say it, even though she knew the answer already. "Your hair it's not the same color. Your eyes and your voice; you've changed. The mental hospital that was your wife? The woman she was your wife?"

He didn't respond he just looked at her as much as he could divert his eyes from the road. She looked at him. He is someone she definitely did not know anymore. He is turning into a monster right before her eyes with his evil grin.

She remembered that time at Lennox Laboratories.

She remembered when Paul, Diana, Kurt, Gellar Austin and Bradley Warfield were partners with her. They were in a laboratory drug conning scheme that brought them each, thousands of dollars, weekly.

When they first started, they would approach families with sick love ones, mainly sick children and the elderly. It worked out for Lennox also. They were able to test their drugs on humans and not be responsible for the fallout when their meds killed anyone. Because no one could tie the six of them to Lennox.

If an individual involved was caught they would be sacrificed for the good of the Corporation. That's their name. The individual would take the fall no questions asked. They would do the jail time that resulted from stealing drugs from a pharmaceutical company and selling them illegally in an attempt to gain profit personally.

The Corporation is ran by organized crime groups. Groups that were ruthless enough to make good on their promise of death if say a salesperson talked. However if you were good to them, they would watch out for you to insure that you aren't caught in a police sting operation. Lennox Laboratories has a one hundred percent success rate. Mainly because their money is so far down the pockets of the officials at the Detroit City Hall that they ran the city.

Many people are involved. They have doctors, nurses, dentist, lab technicians; anyone with a medical background making this process flow easily. The Corporation existed because they can always find people covetous enough to perform these unscrupulous tasks.

The whole thing worked by a salesperson, as they were, called, who would convince families to buy their experimental drugs on the side. It was easier for a family to pay one thousand or two rather than tens of thousands.

Most of the time the drugs were not FDA approved. The pills would work for a time but then would eventually make the person sicker than they were before. That was the main reason they couldn't be approved. They were literally toxic. Most of the pills were in the early testing stage. Companies paid big money for unofficial testing and it saves them time.

You don't see people you see dollars.

Mona did this for years.

Then the last big score came that made her quit it all because of the death of that little girl. She mentally blocked it out. No wonder she didn't remember Stephen Dunn as Duncan Stevens.

It was a cruel thing to do but most of the people were terminally ill anyway including Duncan's little girl. That's how the others convinced her to go through with it, but this was a child. Damn it this was a little girl.

He wasn't an easy mark either, because he was a pharmacist himself. He knew the medical community. She didn't know that when they selected him. That was Diana's fault. Her job was to do the background on the mark before the initial encounter. She was to make sure they weren't being set-up by the feds. She dropped the damn ball. It took that extra coaxing that Mona knew how to do so well. The kind that the others felt left them valuable by getting in too personal with the customers. She remembered she rather liked him. She wanted to play with him a bit before she con him out of his money. She had to make that score. They had put too much time in prepping him to let him off the hook, so she poured on her charm. It worked and he gave her what she wanted, his money.

She was desperate then and in a lot of debt. She would have sold street drugs to get out of that debt. That was a long time ago and she has tried hard to forget about all that she has done.

However, it always stayed in the back of her mind.

Mona attempted to get out of the car even though they were traveling a speed well over fifty miles per hour. He reached out and grabbed her arm as she struggled with the door handle. Something was wrong with it. She was also too weak now to resist him.

"Please…Stephen, Duncan. I thought you and me were…" She begged.

"No, you used me to take my money, stringing me along. Now I know why you never wanted to see me on a regular basis. I must have been one of many men you seduced. Like the thief you are you used me and tested your drugs on my daughter; that's what you did," he said trying not to explode in his anger. "So, I suggest you just sit back and enjoy the ride. Be calm, because with what I'm going to do to you next, you're going to need your strength. You will feel every bit of pain my little girl felt before she died in agony as I heard her screams. And once you do, you'll wish that I had killed you as quickly as I did the others. I told you I was coming." He said with a snarl.

Unbelievable, he was the one that killed Paul and the others. He sent the messages on the dead corpses. All along, she thought it was Bradley Warfield, to protect his involvement with them so he could be the COS at Chicago Memorial. How stupid has she been to believe it was?

How did she miss this?

Everything that happen Stephen has been setting up to include the attack at her condo. He probably stabbed his own stomach to scare her into leaving the city with him. Michael tried to warn her but she didn't listen. She never listens.

She became frantic and she couldn't think.

Why didn't she recognize him?

He looked the same, she thought now that she's remembered him. Except he seemed more rugged than before and less the professional. More of her memory of him started to resurface. She remembered he was a pharmacist. He worked at Chicago Mental Hospital as the manager of the dispensary there.

He did seemed familiar to her when they first met but she just thought they matched, not that they'd been acquainted with each other already. Could she really be that jaded that she didn't remember a man she met just seven years ago? How many men have gone through her life? How many scores of this kind has she done?

She tried the door handle again. She couldn't get out of the car because the door handle wasn't working. He must have rigged the door somehow. She looked out of the window trying to get a gage on where she was located, but she was so tired.

He had this plan all this time. He must have drugged her. The water! When he stopped to get gas, he had already opened it, before he handed it to her. She thought he was just being sweet, damn.

"And my beloved, yes that was Erin that lashed out at you at the mental hospital. That's where you put her. She went insane from the loss of our little girl, that she now spends her time staring out a window of her room there. You met her but you were, so immersed in your world that she wasn't important to you at the time. She remembered you killed our daughter. She blamed me for letting you and your kind in our lives. She never forgave me. She will be out soon and I don't want you around to hurt her again. If Erin saw you, again it might also be possible that she would remember that night when she saw you and me. I need her to forget. I owe you especially for that. The opportunity to, track you down and hunt you like the she-devil that you are. I wanted to play your game. You are so very corrupt; I know that for sure, now. I have been watching you for a long time but you never saw me. You and your counterfeit corporate lady behavior; you never paid any attention to a custodian worker at Cultrax; you or Dr. Monarch. That's the reason why I took that job there. I was there to frame you. It was me who organized that little espionage job with Jackson. Quite a big deal wasn't it. I almost had you. I remembered being there when you were arrested; and thought that it was finally over; that I could finally rest and not have to do all this. Then you were, freed and I decided that you had to die. Even before that when you were supposed to be, killed in some crazy plot by that psycho Kimberly Stanford according to Jackson. She was in my way with her idiotic thoughts of revenge. I had to get to you before she did. That's why I killed that psycho for interfering with my plans. She had to die. There's only going to be one monster in this story and it's me." He said as he grinned at her.

"But she's not...," she attempted to say.

"Shhh let me finish my story," he said to her not really hearing her. "After that I knew I had to continue my job to afford to convince you that I was a police detective. I knew you wouldn't see anyone out of the ordinary. That's always a thing with you, the only constant; is your greed for money and your lust for men that don't belong to you. Just like me, you dispose of them like trash. Your absence in this world will definitely do it some good."

"Please, Duncan, no...I...listen..." Mona passed out before she completed her sentence.

# EPILOGUE

At the high-rise office suite of the fictitious Olivia Tanner. Kimberly had the three of them blocked from exiting the office door entrance. Michael and Natalie stood side by side off to the left.

Sebastian now standing had backed himself into the center of the window actually touching it. He hoped he could attract somebody's attention who's working late in their office in any of the adjacent buildings. They could see what's happening and call the police. They were pretty, high up; twenty stories high.

Kimberly has won the final hand so it seems.

Now this is the final time. The final time when all good things must come to an end.

With Janice's money that she has been syphoning off over the years into a secret account; she can start over and be whomever she'd like. This revenge will be a clear getaway.

The anticipation of their deaths will energize her and she will be at peace.

First, to suffer is Sebastian for his brutal violation of her. Next Natalie for exposing her Janice Edwards disguise. Then finally, Michael will be hers. She didn't want to do it but couldn't resist. This is the final plan.

Oh, she felt the euphoria of what she imagined would be the results. She may go after Mona, Abigail and Sonja next to make it a set of six.

"Kimberly, this can't keep going on. You need help. Murdering innocent people will never take your pain away. Only putting love in your heart and moving on will help you. I will help you." Michael said.

"Don't you tell me about love, you self-righteous bastard. It's because of my love for you that I ended up in the hands of that monster. He murdered Janice." She said wildly as she steadily aimed the gun at Sebastian.

"I did not, you're crazy." Sebastian said.

"I should've bashed your head in when I hit you with that bat or at least killed you with that car."

"You're crazy. That was you. You are sick." Sebastian hissed at her.

She steadied herself before she spoke again.

"It's a necessary means to an end Michael," she said ignoring Sebastian. "The only logical conclusion to my story is my happy ending."

Then she felt something tug at her that she isn't quite sure what it is.

"Except maybe...maybe if Sebastian would do the right thing..." she finished surprising even herself that she is even suggesting what she said.

Sebastian rolled his eyes to the ceiling when she wasn't looking, what now? What is it that this crazy, psycho want from him now? He is getting tired of her and if she didn't have that gun he would go over there to smack her senseless. It has been exhausting over these years with her taunting and baby crying crap.

He knew she was crazy when he met her and told Michael not to date her but no, noble Michael wouldn't listen. What a dumb ass. Now he has to stand here and what fear for his life from this psychotic loony?

It is beginning to get annoying and he has had enough of it, he thought. So what he had sex with her? She needs to get over it. She should have cooperated and it would have been fun for her too. What sane person cries all their life about being a victim and holds innocent people hostage; bullshit, bullshit.

"What right thing Kimberly?" Sebastian said so boldly that it caused Kimberly's skin to crawl when he spoke her name.

She instantly flashed back on that night when he disgustingly attacked her with no remorse in his eyes whatsoever of what he had done.

"You can at least say you're sorry..." She said meekly.

Michael felt that this is the way to get to her, by Sebastian admitting to her that he was wrong. That might snap her out of this blind rage long enough for them to get out of this bind.

"Look, I said I was sorry. I said it to Janice when I thought she was you. I said I thought you wanted it." He said so vehemently.

Michael couldn't believe his ears. How could Sebastian be so callous and just plain dumb; is his arrogance actually that high? They just recently argued about his crazy, reckless behavior and now this. The idiot could ruin everything.

When they get out of this, he is going to have another serious talk with his friend about how out of control he's been lately. It isn't just the thing with Kimberly; it's how he's dealing with Abigail and all women.

She at least is trying to salvage what little relationship they had. She didn't know that Olivia Tanner is really Kimberly. She didn't know she was being, manipulated by her.

Sebastian is being unreasonable.

"Yes Kimberly, we all heard him say that he was sorry; but he can say it again, right Se?"

They all looked at Sebastian. Then Kimberly started to move towards him slowly, waiting almost appearing to hunger for him to say his apology.

"Well Sebastian, do you repent seriously? Are you sorry for what you did to me; for killing Janice?"

Sebastian eyed Kimberly suspiciously. He felt that she toyed with them because she has the threat of the gun in her hand. He is tired of these women and their whiny little fragile feelings. Veronica Lane has screwed his career for good and he's not going to lose his balls to this bitch, not tonight. He just can't take the strain anymore, so he cut loose, Sebastian style.

"Hell no, I'm not sorry. I'm tired of fearing your attacks. I'm tired of you sicko females always crying rape. It had to be the best night of your life. It's not every day that a woman gets to sleep with Mr. Sebastian, the Morning Lover. You should be grateful, you stupid-crazy-bitch."

Time seemed to stop for Michael. Natalie gasped almost choking on her own breath. They were both thinking the same thing. Why would he say that to her, not knowing what she might do? She has a gun. Is that really all that Sebastian thought of his self; that he is some radio personality god?

Simultaneously, the harsh words registered to Kimberly's mind and then touched that area where her reasoning is, shut off.

She shot almost a full clip of rounds at Sebastian. All of them miraculously missed him except one. It hit his right shoulder and he grabbed at it, clutching it; wincing from the pain.

He leaned back against the window as he did it. Kimberly instantly turned the gun on Michael and Natalie and they froze in their places.

The other bullets had cleanly went through the window in an inch or two, wide, cluster pattern off his right shoulder. The window itself started to crack. The crack eventually stretched across the span of the gigantic window quickly in response.

That at least is a good thing, Natalie thought because now security should see the window break alarm in camera room. That was something that she learned from Tate.

Sebastian threw his hands up in surrender. He could feel the nightly air sipping through the gaping hole, behind him.

She is a terrible shot she thought as she looked at him and realized; that she needed to calm down to make the shots accurate. Is he surrendering she thought?

Well she isn't falling for it.

While she prepared to take the next shot by quickly discarding the empty clip for another full one, she stared at him and then she saw it. She saw that grin, that devilish, arrogant, grin. He always seemed to wear it as if it was a piece of clothing he couldn't take off.

He wore it that night years ago.

It seemed to fit him so nicely, sinister. It is even more sinister now, as if it is trying to take strength away from her, again. All that she has done and all that, she has planned is now being mocked by him. He is causing her plans to go haywire.

It is him.

That night he took something away from her, her last chance to be happy. Just like her father. Just like all those men. Just like her first husband, the second husband. They all grinned at her as he is grinning right now as if they knew the dirty secret of how to steal her power. She would never escape them, never. She knew that she would never be able to be truly happy even as Janice Edwards. Sebastian took that away from her. She has lost. She has lost the battle.

Well, never no longer.

She breathed heavily as she thought about it and then she decided to do it. He has to be, stopped. Stop him from taking away strength from many other women.

No one expected what Kimberly did next.

Instead of shooting Sebastian, she dropped the gun and she charged at him with all her might, screaming.

It was so fast; no one had time to react. She caught Sebastian off guard in seconds.

It was too late for Michael to respond as well.

She charged with so much speed and so much hate that, she crashed into Sebastian hard. He in turn is pushed back against the window with so much force that it broke; weakened no doubt from the bullets that had been fired through it. The glass fell outward into the night.

It seemed as though Kimberly just kept on charging and the two of them went out of the window, together. She embraced Sebastian tightly and he continued to fall backwards.

Out of fear and the realization that he is falling, he began pushing on Kimberly to get her off him. She held on tight not letting go. He was able to get an arm freed. However, as he grasped at the air he realized he was falling too fast to do anything about it. Sebastian began shrieking with the most blood curdling sound. It was the worst shriek that Michael has ever heard as the two of them steadfastly plummeted to their death.

Natalie let out a scream as well from the shock of seeing Sebastian and Kimberly go out the window knowing the gruesome outcome. The combination of the scream and rush of the late night air that poured in was enough to jar Michael from his shock.

They ran over and looked out of the broken window together. Michael looked at the window and its leftover broken shards of glass. It was a freakish thing that as thick as the window glass is the bullets shattered it. Sebastian and Kimberly had already fallen to their deaths; lying together on the streets below. They could just barely see their forms from the city lights below. The city traffic screeched loudly to a halt from the sudden surprise of the fallen bodies.

Natalie quickly turned her head away from Michael as they stood side by side.

Again, it's happening again. This year she thought has been the most troublesome of her life. As much as she loves Michael, it seems as if fate enjoyed surrounding them in chaos.

She thought that it is going to be impossible for them to be together in peace. This must be the punishment that, they have to endure but could she really. It's hard trying to be together when the whole world seems like it's against you. You would think it would make you stronger but she didn't. However, she surely loves Michael Montgomery and she knows that he loves her too. Even though they loss their baby, there has to be a happy conclusion for them because their love is too strong.

Michael's thoughts were running everywhere. He tried to grip the facts of his own sins; and how he thought he could have done more maybe done something differently. He refused to believe that somehow all this turmoil is because of his selfishness. Did his need to be, with, Natalie damaged the balance or scale of life? It couldn't be, but sometimes one act be it good or bad sometimes changes a lot of lives either way. Their baby together proved that because they survived its loss.

One selfish act has changed the game at the fork in the road.

Maybe it's what Sebastian did way, back then. He never really took responsibility for the things he was, brought up on and possible for the things that weren't seen. Things seem to, always be free to Sebastian. However, tonight he paid the most, ultimate price for his kind of freedom.

Kimberly literally begged Sebastian for his repentance. She gave him a chance to redeem with her and he didn't take it.

Was it fair to, just ask him point blank like that, with a gun in his face; with all this tautness in the room?

She probably didn't think he would be that stubborn and neither did Michael.

Did Sebastian just snap or was he always as he just last saw him?

He guess it was his way that, he lived.

He guess she chose the only way to ease her pain. Sebastian never really felt he had done anything that was not, meant for him to do. It looked like Kimberly decided that this is the only way to get her revenge, by taking Sebastian to hell with her. He briefly saw the smile of satisfaction Kimberly had on her face as; Sebastian screamed uncontrollably. Especially when it, was clear that the two of them were going out of the window together. She seemed to ride it out the window.

"Oh my God, Michael why did she, do that?" Natalie said crying in his arms. "Didn't she know that wasn't the way?"

Natalie thought about the woman who she had called friend for years. After all, she thought she was Janice Edwards. They had shared a lot of laughs and good times together but Natalie wasn't the wiser. She saw a side of her that nobody saw her social side, her need to be normal. It wasn't an act; she really felt that Kimberly was her friend. She has to feel some type of way about this tragedy; it is troubling.

"She was in pain and I think Sebastian was too; in his own way. It made them both selfish and they couldn't see pass their own goals; no matter how it hurt others. I can't believe this happened."

He wanted to say more to her but thought against it. He went over to the phone on the desk, picked it up to dial 911. As much as he didn't want to admit it he didn't know what became of his friend or this woman that he once knew.

He didn't know anything of what was going on with any of the people around Natalie and him; just like Kimberly had once said. She was right.

All he could think about is that he has lost another friend.

How could he let them slip away like this?

What other blows are in store for Natalie and him?

He didn't know but he knows one thing; that there is always hope.

**** 

She screamed piercing screams as he held her chin roughly in his hand looking deep in her eyes. What he is doing to her is unimaginable; the cuts he is making all over her body. It looked like symbols he is designing on her skin, like tattoos. Her body semi-nude and exposed. Her body ached from the assault of the blade he held tightly in his hand. Her screams could be, heard for miles, but no one is listening. He made sure this cabin was, built on his family's land in a very remote section of the property.

He wants her to fear him, to look him in the eyes as he slowly ended her life. He wants her to die slowly as his daughter did in intense pain.

She is strong but she won't last too much longer. With each cut and the way Mona shrieked, he relished in it like a warm blanket that he could wrap himself up in tight.

As he did with the others, he bathed the ring that has occupied his mind for so long in her warm blood. It flowed slowly from one of the cuts. He was, told that the symbolism of the ring was his insurance that he would live again. He would live again, with whomever he chooses to live again with him. Her sacrifice will be the ultimate.

She is the last one of five wicked people that got away with murder; the murder of his daughter, he thought. This is what I become because of the selfishness of other people.

They thought they were free to continue preying on the weak and the good. Well no matter, this is what my mission is now to punish all the wicked.

He is feeling content; the rage has finally cooled in his head just so. It has been a long journey hunting down these people. Killing them in the cold blood that they deserve because of their unforgivable lies. But he managed to do it quickly and easily. No longer, did he think about right or wrong; revenge has taken over. He felt he had to do this for his wife and his daughter.

He knows that one day his time will come for punishment, for these deeds that he has done; or it may not. In this world, people don't always punish the wicked; but sometimes the wicked get what they deserve.

Suddenly, Mona began to laugh almost insanely and hysterically. Then she spoke through the pain.

"What…you think this is over don't you?" she asked directly.

It is all she could do to stop Stephen from ending her life. The pain he is inflicting on her is almost unbearable.

"It is over. Tonight you die." He responded mildly with a sinister whisper.

"No it's not," she said exhausted but with confidence.

She knows she has to tell him something that might save her life and she knows that he would want to hear this…

"There were six of us."

# THE END

## Novels in This Series:
## Lies Hidden in Darkness

*MORE NOVELS TO COME*

For Further Information and Purchases
Go To:

## www.dharveyrawlings.com

REVIEW NOVELS ON WEBSITE
REVIEW
Amazon.com

## LIKE ME on Facebook
## D. Harvey Rawlings Page

## TWITTER

41619627R00155

Made in the USA
Charleston, SC
03 May 2015